to lovely —

with great affection

Falling Apart

Rod Hacking

ISBN: 9798859225606
Imprint: Independently published

To Lucy

the one who understands

Author's Note:

This story was written in 2002 and only now, twenty-one years later, seeing the light of day. It is a work of fiction, but also a true story, in that what happens to Edwin, and the work done between Edwin and Libby took place thirteen years earlier in 1990, much as described, but not verbatim. It is a true account of depression, not as something that comes and goes when we are feeling low, but as a sustained darkness, frightening in its intensity.

All names and immediate contexts have been changed but I have kept it in Salisbury where it all took place more than a decade before it was first written. The only person who has read it did so at the time it was written and makes a tiny but vital appearance in the story, and happy that it is so.

I want people to know that tablets cannot cure depression and, though I understand and do not condemn any who choose to end their lives, working with a highly skilled therapist as described in the story can enable small pockets of light to appear. Survival (even if only just) is greatly under-rated. We must live with what we have and not engage in the fantasies of salvation.

RH

How terrible – to see the truth when the truth
is only pain to him who sees!

(*Oedipus the King – Sophocles*)

1

The waiting room was warm and uncluttered. It overlooked a grassy bank and a neatly pruned rose bed. He was embarrassed to be there and had been at pains to inform the receptionist that he wasn't a patient, just a colleague of Dr Gordon's husband, and that she was expecting him. But he had still been ushered into the waiting room where patients gathered before their appointments. Mercifully the room was empty. Why, he wondered, should he be embarrassed just because he was in the waiting room of a psychiatrist? He had consulted psychiatrists in the course of his work and never felt anything. But perhaps that was the point. This was different. Because, as he knew only too well, he was here not on behalf of others but because of his own needs.

He had sometimes wondered what it must feel like to be one of his own clients, to be held against one's will, to enter the degrading process of arrest and interrogation, to stand trial and be imprisoned. Some simply gave up, others struggled to maintain a sort of dignity. How would he manage? Probably not too well if his reactions to being here were anything to go by.

Grace arrived late and flustered.

'I'm so sorry Edwin,' came the gentle Scottish voice, 'I've a CPN off with flu and we had to sort out some priorities. Have you got a drink? Come on in.'

She was loaded up with briefcases and files and wearing a full-length coat which seemed to dwarf her. She didn't look like a psychiatrist but then what did a psychiatrist look like? Edwin wondered whether he looked like a solicitor and feared that he might.

Her office was large. She dumped her papers and bags on the desk and showed him over to a more relaxed area with a couple of arm chairs indicating one for him.

'Do you mind if I eat my lunch?' She had pulled out a bag from one of the briefcases and was already extracting from it a roll of indeterminate content. One bite and she was ready. 'So what can I do for you?'

It had taken Edwin a considerable degree of courage to ring Grace and, as it turned out, a considerable degree of good fortune actually to get through to her in working hours. He had said he needed to see her as soon as possible about something important. She had suggested her lunch break and on the same day, here he was. Would he have the courage to tell her?

'Grace, I think I'm in some kind of trouble'. There seemed no point in not being direct. After all he knew he was in trouble though he had no idea of what kind.

He waited for a reply, but she continued eating and looking towards him.

'There's something going wrong inside me. I don't know what it is or why, but I know something's not right.'

'Not right?'

It was a simple technique that doctors and lawyers and, for all he knew, every counsellor under the sun, used to encourage a client or patient, to play back their last words with a question mark. Edwin had used it himself often enough and it worked now.

'I expect Hugh mentioned that Sylvia, Megan and I went to France at Christmas to visit my mother. You know she lives there?

2

Well we did, and it was disaster. I couldn't bear it. I felt sick the whole time and at times could barely speak. I simply withdrew into myself. I found myself so full of feelings that I couldn't handle, and since we returned they have been constantly there. I'm not sleeping very well and I don't understand it'.

Grace rose and walked to the door as he finished. Before opening it she asked 'Tea or coffee?' Instructions were accordingly given to a hidden somebody (who turned out to be the receptionist when she arrived moments later with the cups).

In a way Edwin was glad that Grace seemed to be taking this so normally. By just getting on with her lunch and the practicalities of her day she wonderfully defused some of his anxieties. She began eating again as if prompting him to continue.

'To be honest Grace, I'm at a loss to understand what's happening. I know that Sylvia's noticed something. At the time she was very concerned about what was happening, kept asking whether my mother and I had rowed about something, but there was nothing. It was just inside me. When I left I could barely bear to be near my mother, let alone give her a farewell peck on the cheek. It was horrible.'

Edwin waited whilst the tea arrived.

'I've been aware of it all getting worse and I just don't know what to make of it, so I thought I'd just give you a quick ring and see what you thought.'

He picked up his tea and however hot it was determined that the cup would adhere long enough to his lips to make it clear that he wanted to hear from her.

The pause was long. She continued to eat and then, all of a sudden, shot out of her chair and returned to her desk where she opened another case and extracted from it a diary or organiser. She looked through it, checking it contained what she wanted before returning to her seat.

'Have you ever come across Elizabeth Francis, Edwin, – well,

3

she usually calls herself Libby?

'Does her name ring a bell? Not in the course of work?'

Edwin paused before replying but he was certain it did not.

'Well,' continued Grace, 'she's a psychotherapist here in town. Quite good. I send her people from time to time and the feedback tends to be very positive. She's not cheap and she's often booked up so you might have to wait but I think she's your best bet. Indeed what you're telling me sounds right up her street. She's what's called an analytical psychotherapist which means she specialises in relationships with parents. And I think you'd like her too. I have her 'phone number if you want to call her. Just tell her I suggested you rang'.

'And that's what you think I need?' Edwin mumbled somewhat dumbly given that she had just suggested it.

'It's quite normal, you know. Even solicitors need to sort out bits of their past. Even psychiatrists'.

She bit into her roll again.

Edwin felt at a loss for words. He didn't even know why he might have wanted them. The tea cup again came in useful to cover up his hesitation. A thought occurred to him.

'Does Hugh need to know I've been to see you?'

Grace and Hugh had not been married long. Originally she had come to the city as Hugh's lodger whilst she sought a place of her own. She had recently been appointed a Consultant Community Psychiatrist and a mutual friend had put them in touch with one another. Much to everyone's delight and surprise, not least their own, it soon became apparent that the couple had fallen hopelessly in love with each other and quickly married.

'Edwin', responded Grace with conviction in her eyes, 'with the sort of afternoon I'm about to have, it's highly unlikely that *I* shall remember that you've been let alone pass it on to Hugh. In any case, all of Hugh's partners have consulted me at various times, unofficially of course, on matters relating to clients. Even if Hugh

4

found out you'd been, and I don't see how he would because I shan't tell him, he would probably assume it was work-related, which is what I thought it was.'

Edwin could see she was needing to get going again, and indeed so did he. He stood up and took out a pen and some paper.

'Ok, give me that number and I'll do it'.

As he wrote it down, she said 'Give it a try. You've nothing to lose, you know.'

Edwin's own afternoon was spent out at the small office they had opened in Dunton, a large village some five or six miles from the city. In some ways this was the work he most enjoyed, giving time to a small country practice. Appointments normally lasted longer than in the city and he felt as if he really got to know his clients. There wasn't always a great deal of work but he discovered that local people really appreciated the office being there and he enjoyed the range of work. He had always felt specialisation a dangerous thing and whilst he realised that it was unquestionably the way of the future he was determined to remain a Luddite, even if only in Dunton, for as long as he could manage it.

However, even there his time there was infringed upon. A call came through mid-afternoon for him to go to the police station. He was on-call as a duty solicitor for matters to do with juvenile crime and Social Services wanted him to join them as soon as possible. Fortunately, he was able to do so without inconveniencing anyone but himself.

Sylvia Lyons was, by a remarkable coincidence, exactly the same age as her husband. She had discovered this when as a legal secretary she was looking through the papers of the new junior. Within a year they married and neither ever forgot the other's birthday. They had toyed with the possibility of marrying on their birthday so that they would not forget their wedding anniversary either but thought better of it. Now they had been married fourteen years and had a twelve year old daughter. Sylvia had ceased work when Edwin had left that practice to go to Edinburgh. She had loved it there. Edwin was teaching at the University and the college had rented them a wonderful house in Morningside. Megan was born there and Sylvia had delighted in the opportunities of the beautiful city. It was there, some five years ago, that she had become a Christian, had enjoyed the sort of conversion experience of which she had hitherto only read. It had changed her life totally, giving her a completely different set of perspectives. University life meant that Edwin had more time than he might otherwise to look after Megan, and Sylvia took advantage of the opportunity to throw herself into the life of the local "community church". She studied and prayed and eventually began to lead groups and began to consider whether or not she should herself become a pastor. Then came the thunderbolt. Edwin wanted to leave and had seen a partnership advertised in Wiltshire that he was interested in.

Sylvia had been devastated. She couldn't understand how Edwin could do it to her and she couldn't understand why God could let it happen. She cried and cried and cried. At the end of the day of course she knew she was under obedience to her husband, though she did wonder whether this really applied if he was not himself a Christian, which she was sure he was not. She talked this over and over with friends and the pastor, but in the end they decided that if God wanted this then He would make everything fine. And so it came to pass.

They were invited by the senior partner Paul Raven and his wife to a dinner party to meet the other partners prior to the formal interview. In the course of the evening Sylvia "witnessed" to her faith and her church involvement (perhaps hoping thereby to put them off) and found to her amazement that Paul and Betty were leading members of the local evangelical church themselves. Paul was an elder, no less. Sylvia knew that Edwin would get the job when, in the kitchen, Betty whispered to her 'We're so thrilled. We've been praying for Christians to come for this job'. She hadn't felt able to mention Edwin's religious shortcomings, nor when the time came did she refer to this conversation when Edwin was invited to join the firm. He may well have thought that he had got the job by his own merits; some might have thought she got him the job by her merits; but she knew that it was the Lord himself who had done it all.

Now she was well-established in the life of the Church and employed part-time as "Women's Pastor". She was not allowed to preach or teach in public worship but she had a considerable ministry among the many women who flocked to their church. And being married to a solicitor helped even if he didn't come to Church.

As for Paul Raven, his own reading of the appointment process of Edwin Lyons would have been equally theological, but with different emphases. Certainly it was a delight to have a Christian such as Sylvia on-side, but he had already decided on Edwin before the dinner party. His academic experience lent the practice a certain *gravitas* it otherwise lacked, and he encouraged Edwin to maintain his academic work for the sake of the practice if not himself. In this way Paul felt sure that the Lord had indeed completed his work and seen that 'it was very good'. He was even patient with Edwin's strange obsession with the office at Dunton and his good works for the police and social services. They were an excellent foil for the academic side of the man and won the practice even more friends. Yes, all in all a good appointment; a sound man, and a good Christian wife. How could he but doubt that the Lord had blessed them all.

Edwin only managed to telephone Libby Francis on the following morning. He had been detained until quite late at the

7

police station and he did not want to 'phone from home. He wasn't sure what Sylvia would make of it. He remembered only too well the difficulty surrounding their move and the fuss made by Sylvia. The last thing he wanted to do was to give grounds for new anxieties. Eventually she would have to know something if he went ahead with therapy but there seemed no need to say anything just now. Sylvia knew that all was not well between her husband and his mother; how could she not? Christmas had been terrible. But saying no more about it just for the present seemed sensible.

Frustratingly, but perhaps unsurprisingly if she was as busy as Grace had suggested, his call was received by an answering machine. Unusually, however, the message was singularly helpful. It confirmed the day and date and informed callers of exact times later in the day when she would be free to receive calls. Edwin warmed to her voice. Eventually the departure of a client coincided with one of the times indicated for calls.

'Libby Francis'.

'Er, hello. I am so sorry to call you' (what an idiot, he wasn't at all sorry), 'but a friend of mine, Dr Gordon, er, Grace Gordon, suggested I do so. I am not one of her patients or anything' (oh no, definitely not!) 'but she and I had a conversation and she thought you might be the person, well you know, someone who might be able to help, well help me understand and make sense of something. But I know you're likely to be full up, so it was just on the off chance that I rang, really'.

Edwin was appalled; what a blithering idiot he had turned into and why did he feel ashamed about making the call anyway?

Whatever Libby Frances thought about this outpouring she was clearly not intent on saying.

She kept it simple.

'I shall be delighted to see you. When do you want to come?'

Edwin felt a great sense of ease with this approach. He had felt so uneasy about making the call and afterwards he realised that of course she would not want to go into any sort of detail on the telephone. Nevertheless, he felt a sense of peace that at least this stage had been accomplished so easily. They arranged for him to go and see her on the following day. Both had gaps in their late afternoon diaries, and they arranged to meet at her house at 3-30. 'You need to set aside about an hour and a half for a first meeting' she had said.

Libby Francis lived in the old part of the city, quite close to the bypass. A small park lay across the road and as he stood by the door he gazed at mums playing with children fresh from school. He was sure one of them was a former client and so by the time the door was answered he was facing resolutely towards it.

Mrs Francis was in her early 50s. She was very well-presented and the hall through which he followed her was very smart and boasted some lovely, original, works of art. Clearly therapy paid well! They went up some stairs and entered a room on the first landing. It was simply but tastefully decorated. There was a chaise longue and for one awful moment he thought he might be expected to lie on it, but he was guided to an arm chair beyond it and they sat facing one another.

Their initial meeting consisted mainly of him telling the story of how and why he had made his way to Grace Gordon's room, of the Christmas catastrophe and of his sense that something was wrong, something indefinable which shouldn't be there because everything in his life was exactly as it should be. It was odd because he became suddenly much more defensive than customary. He hastened to tell her just how good his life was, of all that he had achieved and all he was doing. At one point he almost thought of getting up and leaving and asking pardon for wasting her time (how often he had heard that from his own clients!).

Libby had made notes throughout his account but now asked him specific questions relating to his general health which somewhat unnerved him. He hadn't really expected to have to give a medical history although he could see it made sense. She was clearly a professional.

'I suspect that all you have described to me' she said, after laying down her note pad, all her questions seemingly completed, 'indicates something that will require careful and probably unhasty attention. Quite often when people reach the stage in life you have, you know: outward success, ambitions achieved, career flourishing, then that is precisely the time when something from the past, something largely forgotten, something hidden even from our own immediate awareness, but something with which we are not actually at peace, begins to make itself felt. It may be something apparently trivial which as a child assumed for you proportions so gargantuan that the only way in which you could cope with it was to suppress all memories of it. It may not be something trivial. But in either case all you describe suggests to me that we should explore that possibility and see where it takes us.'

'I see' said Edwin, but not doing so, or perhaps not wanting to. Libby Francis continued.

'We would need to see one another at least twice, and preferably three times a week, and I must warn you that it may take some time. We would need to make an agreement with one another – I would normally call it a contract but that seems a somewhat ominous word to use with a solicitor – that neither will break this agreement without discussing it fully with the other first. I say that because I know how clients sometimes get the panics or the doldrums and peremptorily stop coming. It can be unwise to do that. Endings have to be worked at so that difficult things can be lived with and survived. It is after all meant to be a healing, a therapeutic process. All I am saying is that as we agree with our doctor to complete a course of antibiotics even when we begin to feel better, in this work too so we conclude the work properly'.

'Yes, I understand that', observed Edwin, recalling only too well those of his own clients who had run away mid-course.

'Everything said in this room is confidential, though you will need to know that each month I go to London for supervision where I do have to give an account of my work and inevitably that involves discussing particularities. But I do so pseudonymously and I cannot think of any way in which those present, even if they wished to do so, could ever learn your identity. I mention this because I am sure you take confidentiality totally seriously in your work and I believe it is only right to let you know about my own.'

'Thank you'.

Libby Francis had obviously completed what she need to say and waited to hear from Edwin.

'Well, I guess I have no real choice and just as my clients have to trust me when they come to see me, I have to trust your judgement that this is the right way forward.'

'No, not necessarily' she responded, much to his surprise. 'You can always go and see someone else and seek a second opinion. I can, I will, happily supply you with names of colleagues whom you could, perhaps even should, consult to see if they agree with my assessment. I wouldn't regard that in any way as an insult. Some would even suggest it as the right way to begin.'

Edwin was impressed by her disclaimer and gently shook his head.

'No. I think we should start here. I think I know the truth of what you are saying. I don't necessarily like it and I can't say that I shan't want to run away. Indeed a huge part of me is frankly scared stiff by the whole process but I also feel somewhere inside myself that I have no choice or at least the choice is so stark, between light and darkness, that in effect I know what I must do'.

They agreed on three sessions a week beginning a fortnight later, each at 8-00am and lasting, what he would later discover, was the ubiquitous and magical 50 minutes, allowing him time to arrive in his office ten minutes later without anyone knowing where he had been or what he had been doing.

Or so he thought.

2

The law meant everything to Edwin Lyons, or as he might have preferred to express it himself, 'Law' with a capital meant everything to him. Whilst he felt unable to share his wife's new-found religious beliefs he did believe profoundly in the order of the universe. It was, so he believed, a meaningful world. There were laws of science and the natural world, and equally laws which human beings needed to accept as providing the foundations of living. He was always asking himself about the ends of things: that for which they were made, or towards which they were moving. In his teaching he urged his students to consider such things as they reflected upon the laws by which society sought to govern its life. Not all, indeed not many, students wanted to think. They

seemed more concerned with treating their profession simply as a means to wealth and in which they could read off a chart the various prescriptions accorded to particular circumstances. Edwin feared that many of his erstwhile academic colleagues thought likewise. Academic life had proved a disappointment to him.

He was never quite sure whether he could accept the existence of a Law-Giver, in the sense of a first cause 'whom all men call God' as the medieval philosopher Aquinas had expressed it, but he suspected that possibly he did, albeit a God singularly detached from the outworking of the created order. Occasionally he attended Choral Evensong on a weekday evening in the cathedral.

The perfection of the music, the order of the worship and the structure of the cathedral, mostly and fortunately devoid of congregation, appealed almost exactly to his sense of the place of Law in human existence and being. It was enough. On any official form he described himself as 'C of E', even though increasingly he viewed the antics of that denomination with amusement giving way to disdain.

He believed that only a balance between theory and practice could hold him together. Whilst delighting in an ordinary and varied practice he maintained a strict theoretical framework which he supplemented with a little teaching at Bristol University (mostly supervising theses) and a stream of writing for journals, almost all of a philosophical kind. He was now editor of a journal which probably went into the office of every solicitor in the country though was, sadly, read by very few. He used it as a means of encouraging his colleagues to think and reflect, and knew he was probably wasting his time.

In many ways at 37 he had already largely fulfilled all his ambitions. He was in print - one book already published to considerable acclaim, another on Natural Law he was working on (he knew it might have a rough critical reception but he was committed to it heart and soul) and day by day the post brought new books to his attention for review. He had taught in a university, and still did so. He had won the admiration of his peers and supplemented it with a commitment to legal aid work which was financially unproductive but left him with a sense of doing something worthwhile. It was a perfect balance, itself a law of human necessity, or so he thought. Or was it an obsession as sometimes he feared? After all why were others not driven thus? He knew for example that he did his legal aid work because of a deep seated anxiety that the police all too often exceeded the scope of the law in their work. He became profoundly disturbed when he heard of corrupt police officers, and even more of corrupt lawyers. The idea of the law as simply a profession and not a way of being appalled him however much he knew that most of his colleagues thought him odd for thinking thus. And he often wondered about the consequences when law collapsed and the base instincts of human animals took over, for he was sure that law was the defining quality of what made us human, when we act contrary to our own advantage simply because something is right.

He was, he supposed, happily married. It was true that he and Sylvia had drifted apart of late. Her church work took up more and more of her time, and as Megan grew she needed less of the shared attention they had earlier enjoyed. Perhaps it was just an adjustment to what might be called early middle-aged life. It was true that neither seemed to get the best of the other. Sylvia clearly gave of her best to her Church work and he poured himself into the various strands of his work. Their sexual relationship was certainly not what it had once been though in the light of some of the experiences various clients had recounted over the years perhaps it had never been all tremendous in the first place. He had been faithful to Sylvia throughout their marriage. There had been a woman on a conference to whom he had taken a shine and she had made it clear that had he chosen to he need not have spent the last night of the conference alone, but he was glad that he had resisted the temptation. He found marriage as a legal fiction most disturbing, and in any case there was an indissoluble relationship between law and truth that he knew he would find it difficult to contRavene in his own life however much others seemed to manage it with impunity. All the same he knew that he and Sylvia were functioning more in parallel than together and it concerned him, though it was not something he wished to discuss with Libby. There was a confidentiality of the marital chamber that he believed had to be respected. It had never occurred to him that she might ever have been unfaithful to him. From the beginning of their relationship he had felt certain that Miss Marsden, as she had been when they met, was a one-man woman. He rather assumed that her new found evangelicalism strengthened that, even if at other times he found aspects of it grating on his sensibilities and intelligence.

So it was with some concern that Edwin entered into therapy. Might it just be that cracks were appearing in the structure of his universe, or, was it, as he believed and hoped, that all that was happening was that he was experiencing was a painful example of they way in the which the laws of cause and effect emerge eventually? Were that so, however painful the effects he had to endure, he would at least be assured that the structure of his world remained in place.

'I had a word with Grace Gordon the other day about what happened at Christmas, you know how it was in France, with my mother and all that', said Edwin to Sylvia as they ate their toast on the following Saturday morning. Megan was still in bed and it seemed an opportune moment to introduce the news about Libby Francis.

Sylvia stopped in her tracks. 'Oh?'

Edwin decided to complete what he wanted to say.

'She thought it wouldn't do any harm to go and talk to someone who specialises in family relationships, you know, just to talk it over, and try and make sense of it.'

'What sort of someone?'

'Well I think she's a psychotherapist but this sort of thing is her speciality and Grace said she'd probably be able to help me understand what's going on.'

Silence.

'Why didn't you tell me before? And before you mentioned it to someone else?'

'Oh I haven't been concealing it; it was simply a chance to speak to Grace informally and I thought I'd just mention it. All the partners have dealings with her in an unofficial way and it just seemed the right time.'

'So why wait until now before telling me?'

'It was only this week, for heaven's sake Sylvia', continued Edwin becoming a little flustered primarily because of his economy with the truth. 'I didn't want to talk about it with Megan around and this is the first time we've had. Anyway it isn't a big deal. Lots of people have these sorts of things they need to sort out. I bet there's a fair few of your congregation who need counselling at various times. Even you needed support when we were leaving Edinburgh, remember?'

'I'm not likely to forget it, am I?'

'No, of course. All I'm saying is that I'm trying to get this all sorted. We were both concerned about it and I think this is being sensible.'

'You'd be better talking it through with Jeremy Bullen than some weirdo woman speaking psychobabble'.

Jeremy Bullen was the Pastor of Sylvia's church.

'And I don't want you talking about me and us to someone I don't know. You have an important place in this city and gossip could ruin our life here. Have you thought about that?'

The conversation continued, Edwin endeavouring without obvious success to reassure his wife that what he was doing was going to be ok and not threatening and just something simple that would probably be sorted before they knew where they were.

And he was also, simultaneously, unconvinced by own words. Sylvia disappeared into Church activities over the weekend and remained markedly quiet when she was at home.

He decided to say nothing about this new development to any of the partners. After all he felt no particular obligation to inform them of visits to the dentist! This would not interfere with his work any more than that did. In the week ahead this included the appointment of a new partner. He and his colleagues had just met and interviewed three prospective candidates for a vacancy they had created. Among them was an young American Jayne Callard whom Edwin thought most appropriate for their practice. She had been practising in her native New England before deciding to come to live and work in England and had now completed the formal process of registration and needed to practice. Her qualifications were impressive, and she was clearly ambitious and ready to work hard. Edwin also felt that they needed another woman partner. Not that Jayne was a particularly feminine woman, he thought. She was over-weight and a little graceless, but she was a woman, and the other two candidates were not. Women still had to work harder to win acceptance and a measure of positive discrimination was, thought Edwin, not contrary to law. His arguments won the day though he also thought that the victory, if victory it was, was due not least to Peter Raven's wish for a partner who could take some of his area of work from him, something Jayne professed herself anxious to do. Having pressed her cause so hard he was deputed to let her know. He rang her at home in Bristol.

'Jayne, this is Edwin Lyons,' he began in response to her telephone greeting. 'Well, it's good news. We'd like to invite you to join the practice'.

'Wow! I'm really surprised. I was sure one of the guys would get it'.

Edwin winced at the language but assumed it meant she was pleased, and they went on to discuss times and seasons. She then said to him that one of the reasons she hoped she might be appointed was that she wanted him to supervise a project she was doing for Bristol University. She knew that he did some part-time work there and people had spoken warmly of him.

'Well, let's discuss it when you get going but in theory it sounds something worth doing', he had said in response to her gushing tones. He should have said No. He should have said that it was not particularly wise for partners to have that kind of relationship. He should have said that he was already hopelessly over-committed. He should have said No! But it was a word that did not easily come to his lips, and it did not so do now.

Edwin knew that he was over-working. His colleagues certainly felt he was over-doing things but they had come to recognise that this was how he operated and it wasn't their place to interfere. On the other hand, Edwin also wondered just what he would do if he stopped working. What else might he do? There did not seem an easy answer to that. His daughter no longer needed him in the way she once had, and he missed the intimacy of involvement with her. His wife had her own world and intimacy in the bedroom seemed to have taken a long holiday. She had once told him that not wanting any more children meant not needing sex. Apart from the law what did he have? Well, perhaps it was a non-question, for after all the law was his life. Much ado about nothing.

His first session approached. He had no idea what was to come so it was hard to prepare for it. She had told him to come unprepared, but he did nothing unprepared. This was unsettling. He didn't sleep well the night before and was up early. In any case, this was useful as he had a busy day ahead and he could get a flying start. He was going to be leaving home earlier than usual but still had time to sit with Megan as she worked her way through Frosties and talked about her science teacher. Edwin was not really listening but seemed to get away with the occasional grunt. At least they were made sufficiently near to the right places for Megan not to notice how distracted her father was. In any case she didn't want conversation but an audience.

He drove into the office car park and then walked the half mile or so to Libby's house arriving just before the clock on the parish church on the corner struck the hour. She came promptly in response to the door bell, smiled a welcome and ushered him past her up the stairs to the first floor landing. She had warned him that there would be no small talk to get in the way of business so he was not surprised by the silence. Libby closed the door behind him and then, to his horror, indicated the couch.

'I think we will both find it easier and certainly more productive if you use the couch', she said.

'Oh', he mumbled, somewhat embarrassed and awkward, a feeling made worse when he sat on it before realising that he was meant to stretch out.

'Right', he said, somewhat bewildered, for she was now mostly hidden, sitting behind him to his right. All he could see was her feet.

'All you need to do now', she said, 'is say whatever you need to'.
Silence.

If ever there was a moment when Edwin wanted to run away it was now. If ever there was a moment when Edwin thought he had made an utter and complete fool of himself, this was it. And yet it was because he didn't want to make an even bigger fool of himself that he stayed. And he realised in a moment that perhaps the worst was over, that he had made a beginning and that perhaps the start was the most difficult part of the process. In fact, as he would discover only too well, it was not. The worst most definitely was to come, but it was true that one huge step had been taken that wouldn't need to be repeated. That step made others possible and, yes, it did include awkwardness and embarrassment but that did not matter. Indeed within seconds Edwin was in full flow, his anxieties and clumsiness forgotten and hardly ever to be recalled.

He began with Christmas and told again the story of what had happened. Interestingly, as he retold Libby all about it he remembered things somewhat differently, and he remembered different things. Occasionally she would ask a question but mostly let him continue, and the words poured out. He was amazed at how easy the process was. In part it was because being invisible to her he was addressing himself.

Before he knew it the time was up.

'We must stop now', she said, gently but firmly, even though he could have gone on and on. The clock on the small bookcase indeed indicated that fifty minutes had gone by. He pulled himself round and stood up and if he had been expecting small talk now he was wrong.

'Just let yourself out" she said. 'There is a loo on the left behind the front door if you need it. And I very much look forward to seeing you again on Friday'.

That was it.

He walked down the stairs somewhat light-headed by the experience, and let himself out of the door. Outside the city was in the rush hour and he was aware that for most of the last hour he hadn't been in the world as such, but somewhere else. It was most odd.

He made his way back to the office. He had a difficult client coming to see him at 9-30 and his mind needed re-aligning before he could begin work. But once he walked through the front door of the office half a dozen voices addressed him at once and he discovered that landing in the ordinary world was going to be easier than he had imagined. For now.

Sylvia was keen to hear about his experience. She had to wait until Megan had gone to bed and then Edwin was on the telephone for a very long time to one of his students in Bristol, but eventually she sat him down and interrogated him. Edwin could see that she was somewhat perplexed when he described the session and Libby's invisibility and the fact that she more or less had said nothing. In Sylvia's world the helpers do the talking and the idea of something as non-directive as he was recounting was wholly foreign to her way of thinking.

'Is that all?', she asked when he finished his account.

'It was only a beginning'.

'Didn't she have any ideas or anything? Did she make notes?'.

On the rare occasions when Edwin had, reluctantly, accompanied Sylvia to her church-in-a-former-carpet-warehouse he had noticed that just about everybody made notes during the pastor's talk (or sermon as he called it), though he was hopelessly at a loss to know why as it all seemed so eminently forgettable!

'Do you know I don't think she did. In fact I'm certain she didn't.'

'She just sat there for an hour and how much did you pay?'.

'Nothing, well nothing yet, not until the end of the month. Anyway, she's cheaper than me, a lot cheaper'.

It was clear that Sylvia was unimpressed, and Edwin felt uneasy telling her about any of it.

He needed her to know that what they talked about was for therapist and client only, not even for those nearest to him, not even for her. It wasn't that he was concealing anything, it was just that he needed to be free to say whatever he needed to without having to give an account to anyone. Well, that was she had told him at their first meeting, and already he could see how right she was.

3

'You often speak of your colleagues and peers, Edwin, but one word I cannot recall hearing in our meetings is 'friend'.'

Edwin enjoyed the precision with which Libby Francis spoke and the austerity of her language. She perhaps would have made an able angler. She cast the bait and had the necessary patience.

'Well', he replied, and then hesitated. 'Well, I don't think I have that many friends. I'm always hoping that colleagues and acquaintances will grow into friends but perhaps I'm not an easy person to have as a friend'.

Ahead of him was a built-in cupboard with a design upon its doors that already made him feel at ease whenever he gazed upon it. Indeed, he was already, just three or four weeks into therapy feeling safe and relaxed, perhaps more safe and relaxed than he had done for years, if ever. Even now, whilst he recognised her question as a little unsettling, he did not feel it to be a danger.

Libby, as was her wont, continued to allow the salmon to play.

'I mean I'm not always easily accessible – not just time-wise, but in terms of my interests.

'Many lawyers, sadly most lawyers, don't want to discuss the law when they leave work. They mostly do loads of other things and I want to get on with my writing, or reading. Of course I have friends, though I can't really say I have any in the city here, except Sylvia of course. I mean she's my best friend. Anyway, perhaps we all use the word far too lightly.'

He was feeling uncomfortable.

'Why? Is it a fault?', he suddenly said in a tone he had not used before, turning round to look at her.

True to form the angler kept her cool.

'I offer it as an observation. Nothing more'.

'I wasn't accusing you', be blurted out somewhat more defensively than he might, thereby managing to convey almost exactly the opposite of what he had said. He pressed on.

'Perhaps it's a touchy issue, I don't know. It's something to do with being an only child. You get used to, even become dependent upon, your own company. You own inner life matters because for most of the time it has to sustain you in the face of them – parents I mean. Managing by yourself becomes the way you handle things. Your inner life is a place of refuge. It becomes more real than anything outside you. It's often struck me that Hamlet could only have been an only child, and maybe Shakespeare too, because he understood the process of soliloquy. In a way you learn to become your own best friend'.

He paused and thought.

Finally, he said slowly, 'But what happens when you fall out with your best friend?'.

Edwin remembered this session long after he had forgotten others not simply because it was the first in which he had encountered something to make him feel uncomfortable, but because of the telephone call he received on arriving back at the office a soon as had returned there from Libby's house. It was from his father.

Frank Lyons lived in Maryport, on the Cumbrian coast, just south of Carlisle. He had been divorced from Edwin's mother for many years and was now happily married to Iris, a warm-hearted

Cumbrian widow who clearly thought the world of Frank. In recent years he had been somewhat less than wise in his business dealings (he had for many years been a furniture dealer) and, although only in his early 60s, had taken (been forced to take, would be more honest) an early retirement he obviously disliked. Edwin knew full well that circumstances had taken a heavy toll on his dad in recent years (though he was to soon to discover that they were far greater than he had known) and he was concerned to receive a call from him. They could go weeks on end without being in touch with one another though that seemed to make no difference to their relationship. He liked his dad, even if he wasn't altogether sure he knew who he was.

'Dad? What on earth are you doing ringing me at work? Is everything ok?'.

He noticed at once that his father avoided the questions and, as usual made light of everything.

'Very grand world you're in son. Mr Lyons used to be me. Very grand. Anyway, Mr Solicitor, how's tricks?'

Edwin knew something was wrong. 'What's up, dad?'.

'Oh well, probably nothing. Iris bullied me into ringing. You know what women are, they make a fuss about anything. It's just that I've got to go into hospital. I'm having problems with my breathing and they want to run some tests'.

'What sort of problems?'.

'Oh I keep getting out of breath when I go up the stairs and so on'.

It was Edwin's turn to lighten the conversation.

'When did you ever go up the stairs apart from to bed? I thought that's what Iris was for'.

'I'm sure it's nothing. Probably just tell me to cut down on the cigs. That's what the quack told me, and I know for a fact that he smokes just as many as me. Anyway, I'm going in tomorrow. Carlisle'.

25

'Tomorrow!', said Edwin in frustration. 'How long have you known about this? Why didn't you tell me before?'.

'Look it's probably nothing at all and I didn't want to bother you. You've got quite enough to be getting on with. Which reminds me, did I tell you that I met Arnold Westover at Rotary, he's a solicitor from Penrith and was doing the after-dinner talk, and he said he read the journal you edit and thought you were one of the best things around'.

A long coughing session followed, and then Edwin was certain he could hear the equally long draw of a cigarette. His father continued. 'I'll only be in for two nights. The doc said they might give me one of them puffer things to breathe with. But there's nowt to fret about, son'.

'When will you get the results?'.

'While I'm there I suppose, I don't know. You know what the medics are like, they never tell you anything and even when they do you can't understand a word. They're even worse than you lot. Do you know I once had to design a desk for a doctor... '

Edwin listened to a familiar story from his dad's early days, days when he did what he most loved, designed and made furniture with his own hands, days long gone.

After the call ended, he sat there wondering just what the matter was with his dad. It must be more important than he was saying otherwise he would never have called. Perhaps he ought to go up and see him; it was ages since he'd been, probably six months at least. No, even longer.

They'd called in on the way back from Scotland and that had been in August.

What Edwin had omitted telling his dad, had omitted telling Sylvia, and had omitted telling Libby (so far), was that he too had an appointment at the hospital. A couple of weeks earlier he had noticed blood in the toilet. He was not troubled at first and had assumed it must be something he had eaten that was too rich for him, or had it been beetroot which always caused a fluster the morning after. However, it continued, and in something of a panic he rang the surgery and made an appointment to he see his GP. Oddly the GP, whom he had never met before, seemed more concerned that his tetanus was not up to date than with the symptoms he was presenting.

Eventually, however, he felt Edwin's stomach and then did something horrible up his backside with an instrument that hurt like anything.

'Well, there's nothing I can see, Mr Lyons,' said the doctor as he washed his hands, 'but that's perhaps more perplexing than otherwise. I might have expected a haemorrhoid, but I can't see one. So it may be that you have a small ulcer or something further up. The good news is that you're not in pain so it probably isn't too serious, and we shall probably just be able to give you some medication for it. But we'll need to find out, so I want you to pop into out-patients and let them take a look. It only takes a couple of hours, and they'll write and let you know when. Mind you, that can take ages. But I don't think you need be too worried. We'll get to the bottom of it'.

If his joke had been deliberate, he showed no sign of it, but at least it kept Edwin chuckling all the way back to his office. An appointment card had arrived two days later (Edwin always got to the post before Sylvia and secreted the envelope into his briefcase before she could see it) inviting (!) him for a colonic investigation three weeks later. Edwin wondered whether he should consult his dictionary of etiquette and look up 'Colonic Investigations, Replies to Invitations Thereto'. Three weeks in which to mention it to Sylvia.

And two of these three weeks had passed and still nothing said. And now the news about his father.

Frank and (Edwin's mother) Bella Lyons had had a stormy marriage. At least Edwin later recalled that all he could recall was seemingly endless arguments and rows, constant shouting and then long silences with which his mother used to punish her husband, and later, her son. As a child he had often fallen asleep in tears because of the row going on downstairs. In his own mind he always blamed his mother for the arguments. After all who could ever argue with his dad? His dad was gentle and fun. Bella was a social climber, of that he was certain. That was why, despite their humble origins, he had been sent to Boarding School. She seemed determined to live out her own fantasies through his achievements. Not that Sedbergh School was in the top rank of Public Schools, though to hear her speak you would think that Eton looked up to it.

Edwin had hated school, the only redeeming feature of which had been the wonderful scenery surrounding it. He often escaped up Crook or Winder, the two fells immediately adjacent to the school, or along to hidden Dentdale or Garsdale. As a younger boy he shouldn't have done so but he always managed to find ways of keeping secrets. The only thing he enjoyed at school was cricket. He wasn't so good as a player though he did manage to bowl a good leg-break and had just about perfected the googly when that sort of bowling fell out of fashion in English cricket. But his love for cricket was as much a love of its complexity. He bought each new edition of Wisden as it was published and studied its laws and any changes thereto with great interest. At University he had decided to become an umpire; strictly speaking he was one still and better qualified than most, though he couldn't find the time for it and had not umpired a game in years.

Away from school, his parents moved house again and again, as his mother sought to ascend the social ladder and pushed his dad into jobs he didn't really want. Eventually she goaded him into starting his own business. In a way that was the beginning of their end. All their money had to go into the business, and this meant that they could no longer afford continually to move house. Now they had to face each other. It couldn't and didn't last. His mother had friends who lived in France and during a visit to see them she had met a widower who owned his own apartment near Avignon. Clearly that was preferable to life with an unambitious furniture maker in Garstang, just off the M6!

So, with Edwin at University, off went his mother, Bella to la Belle France – "Everything is just wonderful; Claude is just so successful".

Frank married Iris within a year. Edwin suspected that they had already been an "item" as they say, before Bella departed, but he could not find it in himself to blame his father for that.

Although he had begun his sessions with the subject of his Christmas experience in France and the feelings it engendered, he quickly discovered there was much else of which to speak.

Sometimes it didn't seem related to the matter in hand but Libby never interrupted him. Where he began, she followed. When he had been paying over £300 a month for a couple of months he did find himself wondering whether perhaps she oughtn't be doing a little more directing than she was, but then he felt guilty about the thoughts and dismissed them. In any case he did not begrudge the money. What was quite remarkable was the discovery of just how much he obviously needed to say. He was also discovering his feelings about his colleagues. Up till now he had largely not allowed himself any such expression, even to Sylvia. In any case he supposed he didn't have much in the way of feeling. Mostly he strove not to; about anyone. That detachment was absolutely necessary for his work, absolutely essential for his life. Feelings were ephemeral and in those he encountered day by day he saw the consequences of living off the force of their feelings, sometimes with disastrous consequences. Yet here he was, having to come to terms with the fact that he too had feelings, however odd it felt to admit the fact, and however ashamed he was of some of the negative feelings he expressed. When he mentioned this, Libby was helpful.

'Feelings just are', she had said, 'they are neither good nor bad. What you choose to do with them is up to you. But they are there and perhaps it is better to know what they are than not. But we are not actually morally responsible, or culpable, for our feelings'.

Edwin knew that the feelings that most disturbed him were those he had clearly been experiencing in France, feelings towards and about his mother. He was beginning to understand that what had happened during their holiday was that powerful forces within himself were crying out for recognition and acknowledgement. Because he had been unable to do so, he seemed to be functioning less adequately, in a less than fully human way, than he was accustomed to. Presumably all he needed was to come to terms with those feelings, and he assumed they must be to do with the way in which his mother had bullied his dad, and he himself, if he was honest, all his life, and things would improve. Hidden things would go away when revealed and recognised and claimed. It all seemed quite sensible. It made sense; cause and effect – the law of nature.

What made less sense was Libby's reaction to his news about his hospital visit. He had introduced it in the context of his report about his father's telephone call.

'I'm interested that you feel about me much as do your wife', said Libby after a moment's pause. 'You know, someone whom you spoon feed information when you've decided you're ready for them to hear it but not until. It's your choice of course. I'm just interested'.

He found her reply upsetting. He had assumed she would pour forth tender concern and reassurance but instead all that mattered to her was his reasons for telling her at this time and in this way.

What was the matter with the woman? Didn't she realise that he might be seriously ill?

He lay on the couch in silence, confused and uncertain as to what to say next. He was even aware of tears pricking in his eyes. His breathing had altered, and he had started to sweat.

As if aware of his thoughts she finally broke the silence (for the first time - was this a victory?).

'Edwin, I'm sure you must be feeling anxious about your tests, and anxious too about your father. I understand that completely and we can talk about it, but I do think it is quite important that we consider why it is that you have kept this to yourself, why you still conceal this from Sylvia, the person you described to me as your best friend, given that this may be the most important thing that is happening to you in the whole world. I suppose I was also wondering whether your reluctance to share this with me indicated a resistance, a lack of trust or what'.

It was the longest sentence he had heard her utter. He was having to think hard, and to think things he had never had to think before. He had always assumed that he did things because that was how things were and that we all function more or less alike. Of course he knew that he had not done some of the things his clients had done, but he knew enough of himself to recognise that the difference between them and himself was one of degree not something essential. A change of circumstances and who is to say how he would behave – there but for the grace of God go I, he had always maintained (except of course he probably didn't believe in God, and even if he did then he didn't believe in grace). But was she suggesting that perhaps things were not always as they seemed, that perhaps there was no simple causal relationship such as he had always imagined? That was more frightening than interesting.

He gave voice to this thought, but she interrupted him.

'Edwin, I cannot help feeling that if you wish to discuss

philosophy you could spend your money more wisely than on me. It would be an stimulating distraction but I think we should stay with trying to understand why it is that what I have said makes you feel so uncomfortable'.

'Yes, but what does it matter what I feel? What are feelings but passing moments? You're always saying that feelings don't matter'.

'I think it highly unlikely that I have ever said that feelings don't matter. I do believe that feelings just are, that attaching moral value to them is unwise and unhelpful, but I think they matter a great deal, and I think your feelings matter a great deal. To you and to me'.

'To you?'.

'Whilst we are working together, I have considerable concern for how you attend to your feelings. They matter to me, especially when you are wriggling away from any sort of attention to them. It just may be, you see, that they hold a key to a way forward'.

'Really? You really think they might provide the key to understanding what has been, is, going on?'.

'Certainly not'.

'But I thought you said... '

'I do not believe that there is ever anything which can be called the key to anything. I stopped believing in magic some time ago, but it may be *a* key, not *the* key, to the way forward. I am sure however that my role in this process is to hold you to your feelings and not to a discussion of the place of feelings, however interesting that might be'.

Only children, Edwin supposed to himself (for he felt sure she wouldn't let him muse aloud), have to objectify everything in order to understand them. It's a way they have of coping. With no one to share feelings they become accustomed to looking at them dispassionately, almost as if from outside. He often talked to himself and throughout childhood his inner world had been peopled with literally dozens of selves with whom to discuss any and everything. But that was the inner world, and when it came down to it those selves were really just himself. This was different. This was done in the presence of someone else; this was discussion with someone else, if so one-sided an exercise could be called discussion.

He became aware of his outer silence. If she had spoken more in this session, it was also true that he had spoken less, or at least that he had delivered of himself less. He felt more exposed, more (if he was honest) vulnerable, though of course his anxieties about his dad and his own tests might account for that.

Libby too must have been aware of the outer silence, sensing perhaps that inwardly there was much going on but reluctant to say more. Perhaps a first moment of recognition was dawning. If so, she showed no intent on rushing Edwin towards it.

'I guess', he said eventually, 'that it's not that I conceal things because I don't want others to know them so much as I am unsure how they will react. I know that I am always anxious about how Sylvia will react. Sometimes it's easier to avoid the anxiety by keeping things to myself.'

It was clear that he was working hard. She knew it and he knew it. It was also clear that their session did not have long left to run. Sometimes of course, as Libby knew very well from years of experience, clients waited until just before the end in order to drop a bombshell precisely to avoid having to live with the consequences of it – in the trade it was known as a "door handle moment" – which left the therapist feeling helpless. She didn't think that was true of Edwin, but she needed to be aware of the possibility.

For his part Edwin left feeling far from settled. On top of the anxieties he was already carrying, he was having to face up to something in himself that made him feel uneasy. If he was not as attentive to his clients and colleagues that day he did not have to wonder why. For the first time he also wondered whether he had done the right thing in going into therapy. Might it not be better to let sleeping dogs lie? Did he really want something that interfered with his work, for after all his work was his life?

The trouble was the dog was now awake.

4

The call came at about 2-00 am. At first, in his sleepy state, he thought it must be something to do with his dad. He was therefore a bit confused when the voice said it was the Police. Eventually he came to sufficiently to realise that although he was not the solicitor on call, the duty social worker had insisted he be called. They wanted him there, now.

A young woman had been brought in and was being questioned about the mysterious death of her baby. The child had been taken into A & E in the early evening suffering from severe bruising to the head and neck. Later the baby died and the doctors felt obliged to inform the police that although no post-mortem had yet been performed, they suspected that the child had died from injuries inflicted non-accidentally. The mother, just 19 years old had been taken from hospital straight to the Police Station. A social worker had been there dealing with another matter and recognised the case as one that would benefit from the skills of Edwin Lyons.

It was a fairly typical example of the sort of work he had been doing since he had arrived in the city. The Police respected him because he always treated them with respect even when they felt he was using the law to obstruct what they believed was their duty.

In the present instance, for example, he realised at once that the two investigating officers, both detective constables, one of them a woman whose language was as coarse as anything he had heard from any police officer, had nothing but a contempt bordering on hatred for the somewhat pathetic young woman before them. He had to remind them their job was not that of judge and jury but of investigating officers who would decide and recommend to their superiors whether or not there was evidence sufficient to warrant that the young woman be charged with the alleged offence.

'Oh, give us a break' said the young woman DC.

'I'll give you a break, Detective Constable,' replied Edwin firmly and quietly, 'when you behave in a way commensurate with your authority as a police officer and not as a bully. I would remind you that no post-mortem examination has been carried out and that the only basis upon which any of us in this room can act lies within the dictates of the Police and Criminal Evidence Act'.

Edwin found any matter to do with child, and especially baby, abuse profoundly distasteful. Indeed at times his sleep had been disturbed by dreams consequent upon accounts of injuries to which he had been subject in court or read at his desk. That made the necessity of detachment that much more important, and the law was the only means of preventing feelings erupting into what he knew could easily become mob rule. But mob rule began when law broke down and if it broke down in the Interview Room then the breach was indeed serious. The exalted role accorded to the police on television and in novels, which tended to make them the ultimate arbiters in matters of right and wrong led too many officers to assume it in reality. It was not so. Writers, viewers and certainly too many police officers themselves forgot that when Inspectors Morse, Frost or whomsoever concluded their investigations with a "result", the legal procedures, the safeguards of civilisation, had scarcely begun.

He knew that his own expectations about the character of those men and women authorised to serve as police officers were probably unrealistic. He had met enough of them over the years to be sure of that. Nevertheless, he still believed that a measure of congruence between theory and practice in the administration of the law was necessary. When he stated this point to colleagues they tended to smile at what they no doubt viewed as his naivety.

He finally emerged from the police station with only just sufficient time to get home, change clothes and get to therapy. He was almost late, but not quite.

He began by describing his night, giving Libby a warning that he might at any stage drop off to sleep even though he was sufficiently aware of his own constitution to know that this was only likely from about three o'clock in the afternoon onwards and for certain after four! He would need to be back at the Police Station later in the day following the post-mortem and his energies were also required in court for most of the morning.

He was not sure what, if anything, Libby would pick up from the account of his night's work. She had always allowed him to decide on the content of their sessions and he perhaps thought she might want him to return to the uncomfortable matters that had concluded the previous session.

If she too had hoped they might begin where they had left off she certainly did not let it show, but neither (and as he was discovering, typically) did she allow the session to consist of a discussion, or even monologue, on Edwin's work and concerns. So perhaps he was taken aback somewhat by the question when it came.

'I wonder why you need to do this work, Edwin?'.

'I don't', he replied, a little over hastily. 'I don't need to do it. I choose to do it. I want to do it. It matters to me that I continue to practice criminal law because it is the most important expression of where law and human life coincides, where law and persons most often collide, and too often to the detriment of law and therefore to the detriment of persons.'

'Yes, that sounds like a lawyer speaking'.

'It *is* a lawyer speaking', he enjoined, somewhat crossly, 'and a human being.'.

'Well if I wish to consult a lawyer, Edwin, I do so in his rooms, across his desk, and I pay.'

'Yes, but I am a lawyer. It is my life and I cannot divide up my life into neat sections. If I come here the whole of me comes not a disembodied self apart from all that it does and is.'

'And it makes you cross when I challenge that?'.

'I'm not cross', he retorted, 'simply trying to clarify ground rules and presuppositions'.

'Not laying down the law?'.

He was beginning to feel a little uncomfortable around his collar and wished he could have undone his tie. No doubt about it – not enough sleep.

'I do not believe so', he said, almost magisterially as if thereby believing they could move on to his feelings about what he had dealing with in the night. Surely, he thought to himself, if feelings are so important why did she not want now to help unburden him of very strong feelings? It seems she did not.

'And I ask again, even though clearly the question has made you feel uneasy – in fact, if I am honest, because the question has made you uneasy, why it is that you do this work? You do not need the money. You do not need to lose sleep. You probably, as much as anyone, find the work disturbing in terms of the content of that with which you are dealing. None of your partners choose to do likewise. Your wife almost certainly would prefer you not to do it. So why do you do it? What, other than your stated ideological, theoretical concerns (which I take to be genuine), drives you to this concern for the broken, the weak and those who do terrible things?'

Though Edwin had indeed been irritated by her it was difficult for him, not least by virtue of habit, to pause and consider the reasonable nature of her question. Indeed he thought it wise to do so and allow himself to withdraw a little from his passionate response to her original question. If he was to resolve the crisis, if it really was an inner crisis, he knew full well that it could only be done dispassionately.

'My school fellows', he eventually continued in even-tempered tone, 'laughed at me when we first read Prometheus because I burst into tears at what had happened to him. It wasn't the only time. It happened at the end of *Tess of the D'Urbevilles*. We had a master, an English Teacher, he was a genius, who believed that stories were meant to be spoken aloud and we read the whole of *Tess* in class. It took us almost two terms, and at the end when she was executed I burst into tears at the outrage I felt'.

'That's why I chose to read Classics at University, well Greek and Ancient Philosophy, because I felt the moral force of those ancient stories. How can someone not cry when his dog Argos recognises Odysseus on his return from the wars? How can anyone not feel the force of Antigone's love for her disgraced brother and not feel repulsed by Creon's abuse of the legal processes against her? So I guess I have always felt for those on the edges, even those who have offended, and indeed done terrible things, because I imagine myself to be in their place, and know full well that our only defence lies in the law'.

Libby waited, allowing him to continue. When it was clear that he had said what he needed to, and as gently as she could given the force of feelings he had expressed, she spoke again.

'And yet, as we both know, others in your class did not cry at Tess's fate, nor that of Prometheus or Antigone. And it seems to me that what makes you who you are, and all you are, is precisely your capacity for (I apologise for an over-used word) empathy. I am not being cynical about it when I wonder where that comes from and whether there is not something in your own past that helps account for it, something of which you might even be barely aware, but which might also account for those experiences at Christmas with which we began our meetings'.

It occurred to him in later months that this session was a turning point, at least in his understanding of what it was the therapeutic process was endeavouring to achieve. He believed that this development in his understanding was primarily conceptual. Libby Francis, in her supervision, may well have reported that for the first time her client had emerged from under the layers of cerebral protection and exposed something of his feelings, something of the passion, something of the pain that she suspected lay long hidden, long buried, but in no way dormant, and liable, before too long, to erupt.

The news from Maryport was not as bad as Edwin had feared though as always Edwin listened for what lay behind his father's account of the tests.

'As I thought, they just told me to stop smoking. Seems I've got a touch of emphysema. They want me to go on steroids or something like them. It's all to do with a thing called Coads – Chronic obstruction of the airways disease. The steroids will help the breathing by expanding the airways'.

'Can you cut the smoking, dad?'

'I'll try, son, I'll try. Mind, you wanna see the nurses going off for a quick drag when they're on duty. Hardly suggests that anybody's serious about it. But Iris says she'll help me. Nag me to death more like. Anyway I start the tablets today and we'll see how it goes..

'Did they say anything about getting exercise?'.

'You know what they're like. They're always suggesting exercise. Anyway, I'll try. The important thing is that it isn't bad news'.

Edwin ought to have asked his father if he had been fearing bad news, but he didn't think getting into a serious conversation would help either of them. In any case, as his dad had said, it was good news, so why complicate things?

'That's great dad. And we're hoping to get to see you in the summer. We're going to Argyll again and we'll call in on the way back down. Megan's dying to see you... '.

The conversation trailed off into what Edwin would have felt were the sort of banalities he and his father specialised in, but the sort of thing that kept their friendship going. He had quite enough intensity on his plate, including his own forthcoming tests, without complicating the relationship with his dad.

He had decided that when he reported his father's call to Sylvia that evening he would mention his own little problem, but she was rushing out straight after supper to a women's bible study which she was leading and was distracted throughout their meal. She was of course pleased with the news from the north but she seemed more open to concern for the fate of Jonah in his whale than that of the man opposite her and he sensed it would not be fair to burden her with something which might in any case be nothing at all.

The bleeding had continued. Sometimes it was absent; at other times he gazed into the bowl and was aghast at what he saw. Well, he would soon know as the investigations were due the following week. That evening he lost himself, after Megan and he had watched television until her bed-time, with work on his new book. He had been neglecting it of late and the publisher had informally enquired into its progress only that morning in the course of a conversation about a series of reviews that were overdue.

Edwin had a capacity to focus his attention in a way that Buddhists sometimes call "single point concentration". It enabled considerable creativity and he was able to work his way through review books with remarkable speed whilst retaining an almost complete picture of where particular sentences or paragraphs could be found. His students had always found him to be a remarkable source of bibliographical information and he would have perhaps acknowledged that sometimes he did too much of the work for them but it was a capacity he felt had to be utilised not just for himself but for others.

His own new book was a study of the theory of Natural Law, something he believed in profoundly but which he felt almost everywhere was incompletely stated. Much of the past year had been spent wading through medieval theological writers but at long last he was able to begin working towards that synthesis of ancient Greek and scholastic theory which he felt to underlie the place of Law as a fundamental principle not just of human practice but of human being. He still had at least another 150 pages to write but he was determined to complete the work in the remaining months of the year.

'I guess I was so anxious about my dad that I did my very best to keep busy that week', he confessed to Libby at their next meeting. 'Work is a wonderful anaesthetic, I suppose. But it's such good news, and such a relief.

'Yes, and I imagine that throws into relief anxieties about your self.'

'Well, I haven't really had time to think about it', he lied.

She must have known he was lying, of course, but decided to let it go.

'How is Sylvia coping with the news?'.

It was a deliberately open question. How would he respond? Predictably.

'She's pleased of course, and we're hoping to get to see him soon'.

She tried again.

'And about your tests?'

'Oh well, she's been so preoccupied this week with her work it just wasn't possible to find the time and place to say anything. But she'd be marvellous about it, I know. She really is tremendously supportive'.

'So not telling her was Sylvia's own responsibility? Her busyness meant she was preventing you telling her?'

'There's nothing to tell as yet is there? I mean it's only tests and it may be nothing at all. I think it will be best now to say nothing until after I've been done'.

Libby waited for more. In vain.

Pippa, Edwin's secretary was truly a confidential clerk. She guarded the contents of his diary jealously and it is unlikely she that would have disclosed them even to Mr Lyons himself over a telephone line without considerable evidence that he was whom he claimed to be. She took her work seriously as a legal secretary and that meant, above all, the capacity to recognise and observe a secret. She was also fiercely loyal to her employer and a great admirer of his work. She sometimes accompanied him to court or to prison to visit those held on remand and was in awe of his capacity to retain self-control and composure in the face of considerable provocation.

Even this most loyal of servants might well, however, have allowed herself an expression of astonishment at an empty Friday afternoon in Mr Lyons's diary and his further disappearance without a word of explanation as to his location should he be needed. Not that any such expression of astonishment would have been even hinted to others. Yet she was truly amazed. It was the first occasion it had had ever occurred and she felt flustered all afternoon.

The city hospital was moving to a new location on the edge of the city and Edwin had needed to re-confirm in his mind that he was due to visit the Out-Patients Department in the old building in the centre of town. His appointment was for one o'clock though the appointment card advised him that it might last three hours. The ward he was directed to seemed akin to the Marie Celeste but the clerk who emerged from a cupboard on hearing his footsteps allocated him a bed and asked him to undress and put on the gown she gave him. This done he sat there shivering.

Outside the screens he could hear the sound of an approaching trolley and then the curtain opened by a huge West Indian nurse.

'I'm Staff Nurse Spencer', she said, 'I ave to give you a henema'. A henema he could live with. 'Lie on the bed on your right hand side and tuck your knees under your chin. That's it'.

He felt her pull up the gown.

'Oh, silly man, you've still got your drawers on. Take them off.

He obliged, avoiding her eyes.

'Now when you've had this, don't rush straight to the toilet. Try and keep it in for as long as you can bear it. That way it will do its work best. In any case you are third and there are two ladies who've already had theirs and there's only two loos. So work hard'.

It was so wonderfully funny that he coped without too much anxiety with the discomfort of something being inserted and cold liquid from a freshly squeezed bag making its unwelcome entry. As suddenly as she had come the nurse disappeared though before doing so she had drawn back the curtain. One other patient lay opposite him, an elderly lady. Another bed had already shed its occupant, and in some haste from the look of things.

Edwin's capacity for holding on was somewhat limited and he felt terribly guilty when the old lady had sought the convenience only to find both cubicles occupied. He would have given anything to allow her to use it but at that precise moment he feared his insides were falling out. On his eventual return to the ward hers were another pair of eyes he studiously avoided for the remainder of his stay!

Just before three o'clock the old lady of the bed opposite returned from wheresoever and the nurse accompanying her asked him to follow her. He felt somewhat naked wearing only the gown which made him look like a Fellini extra in an ill-fitting toga but the day was warm and a dressing gown would have been too hot. He was led into a room in the centre of which was a sort of operating theatre table. Next to it a man in a gown was doing something with a long green tube which Edwin sincerely hoped was not going to be used on him. Some hope.

The man turned out to be a doctor and as Edwin lay on the bed, again on his right side, he said he was going to give him a small injection in the back of his hand which would help his muscles relax. Its actual effect was to render Edwin all but asleep for the duration of the examination.

When it was over, he was led back to the ward where the big West Indian nurse brought him a most welcome cup of tea. The other two patients had already departed and Edwin was able to look up again.

5

A key moment in therapy, as Edwin discovered again and again, were the breaks. Libby took a long summer holiday – five weeks, and that was a long gap for clients to have to come to terms with. If clients' own holidays did not overlap with her break the gap could be considerably greater. Fortunately, Edwin, Sylvia and Megan were planning to be away more or less in the middle of Libby's break. Nevertheless, as the break drew nearer Edwin became aware that he was not looking forward to it, that he was becoming dependent upon these sessions. As they had continued he had felt himself relaxing more and more, able to bring into the open feelings about colleagues for example, that until now he had hardly even been aware of himself.

Edwin's hospital test results was something of a non-event. His GP simply rang him at work and said that there was no reason to come round. Nothing abnormal had been found other than a slight area in his transverse colon which showed signs of having been tender. It might be that more roughage in his diet would prevent this. In any case Edwin had noticed that the bleeding had stopped, and he was greatly relieved that he hadn't had to worry Sylvia with it.

With the coming of Summer they tended to do more as a family – long walks in the evening in the Chalke valley and Saturday picnics. Edwin would have wished for some cricket but with Sylvia so taken up on Sundays they had to utilise Saturdays as their family day out. He didn't mind provided he could have some time on Sundays for his writing and especially for his work on the Journal. It was a quarterly and at certain times the pressure was on – chasing up promised articles, commissioning ahead, negotiating and disputes with printers about lay-out. It was vital he had time to complete the autumn edition before they left for the summer holiday in July, but that could only be accomplished by more late nights and clear Sundays. Unfortunately today he had to produce lunch and if it was sunny both Sylvia and Megan liked to go for an afternoon walk and he felt obliged to go with them. The last thing he wanted to do was to provide Sylvia with a reason for being critical of his therapy – that it was eating up his time (she didn't know just how much it was costing) or his energy. The result was later and later nights, and earlier and earlier mornings. Very often, during June and early July he was up at just after 4-30 writing and reading until he had to leave either for work or therapy. It was little wonder that he was beginning to feel in need of a holiday.

They were heading north again. In their days in Edinburgh they had found a cottage on the shore opposite the Isle of Jura on the west coast of Scotland, and it provided them with an annual opportunity to renew their Scottish friendships and passions. They took it for three weeks though the journey up lasted three days allowing for a stay of two nights with Sylvia's parents. They lived in the extraordinarily ugly (as Edwin thought it) Fenland countryside north of Peterborough, a village called Guyhirn on the busy A47. Sylvia had taken the first opportunity to flee after the delights of Wisbech Grammar School to a secretarial college in

London and every time Edwin came back to the Fens he was sure she had been wise. It was not just the flat lands, which went on further than the eye could see, so much as the dark soil and all-pervading smell either of spray or cabbages. Her parents were quiet people whom he loved. They had taken to him immediately and were immensely proud that their daughter (also an only child) had done so well for herself. Their only wish was that she lived nearer though it was marginally nearer than had been Edinburgh, if not quite so accessible by train.

Edwin used the visit as an opportunity to visit Cambridge. He still had an account at Heffer's and he always enjoyed being able to take books away and not pay for them until the last day of the following month. He equipped himself for his summer break with light reading. This consisted of a new edition of the poems of A E Housman, a new Greek edition of The Odyssey and a new book on the life and work of Duns Scotus, a medieval scholar with whose work he was familiar through his study of natural law.

They drove north up the Al and eventually arrived in the beautiful city of Edinburgh. It was Megan's birthplace and according to Sylvia the place of her own "second and most real birth". And he was the man who denied it to them.

They remained three nights visiting old friends and just enjoying the delights of the place, not least a meal in one of the best wholefood eating houses in the world, "if not the universe", added Megan.

In fact Edwin had not been especially happy in Edinburgh and was not particularly keen to chase up erstwhile colleagues. Most of those they saw there were Sylvia's friends, many of them from her church. At times he felt uneasy with the religious language and culture and felt sure he sometimes must have made some of them feel uneasy given his reluctance (as they might have called it) or refusal (as he did) to share their convictions or their expression. But Edinburgh is a beautiful city and because the Festival had not yet begun it was mercifully still free of the monstrous hordes of visitors who would soon throng, if not choke, its thoroughfares.

Eventually they departed and headed north and west, going via Stirling and Oban before dropping down the coast, there to gaze on the wondrous Paps of Jura across the treacherous, but oh so beautiful, Sound.

In July the sun hardly sets and it was still light at little short of eleven. Megan stayed up late and they all enjoyed beachcombing until just before dark. Then, if they were fortunate, they might be privileged to see not just seals, which abounded, nor even the porpoises that delighted them, but sea otters hunting late at night or in the half-light of dawn. It was one of the sights that most enriched them. This year it was Megan who saw them first, and they all slipped into the kitchen from which they had a splendid vantage of one of the finest sights in the natural history of the British Isles.

There were three otters to be seen. One was smaller than the others and stayed with, presumably, the mother, but all three fished and occasionally sang. With Jura and Islay beyond, the natural world seemed harmonious and perhaps that was why Edwin felt so sustained by it, because it was harmonious, and its harmonies reflected the laws by which all life has its being. It could be relied upon, was not arbitrary even when it was apparently cruel. It made sense, it had order.

Their days were taken up with walking and swimming. Once or twice each week one or all would go off into Lochgilphead to do the shopping. They might combine this with a visit to Oban or a drive down the coast to the Mull of Kintrye, but generally preferred to do nothing, just to relax and read and play.

Edwin loved the work of Housman, however pessimistic some claimed it to be. Yes, it dealt with dark themes, but it did so in a way that was itself the bearer of light because it did so with order and precision. He mostly disliked modern poets who, as it seemed to him, simply strung feelings together and wore them like pearls – gaudies. That was too easy. Good communication demanded effort and a concise use of words and their meaning. Housman used metre and rhyme in a way that few now did because they were lazy and because at the end of the day they were more interested in themselves than in what they were describing or those reading them. He supposed a classical education had enabled him to see this. Translation demanded much of those determined to convey not just literal meaning but nuance. His own work approximated to that very often. Some thought him occasionally pedantic in his use of language – it was always a shock to him that fellow solicitor of all people seemed unconcerned with the difference between "fewer" and "less", for example, or the use of a semi-colon – but it mattered to him. In a way it was one with the otters and the beauty about him.

Sylvia and Megan had gone to do some shopping in Lochgilphead leaving him to sleep a little later than he customarily did. On waking he made himself some toast and sat overlooking the sea. Sylvia had left one of her books by his chair and he picked it up. *Spring Harvest Song Book* proclaimed the cover, and he recognised it vaguely from having seen it, amongst others, at home. As he turned the pages he found himself becoming increasingly irritated. It was full of banal and sentimental doggerel. He didn't like the hymns which the Church of England sang but some of this was an insult to the English language as well as to such religious sensibilities as he retained. The emphasis all seemed to be on the rottenness of people from which Jesus comes as cosmic rescuer. It described a world ultimately doomed, ultimately rotten, a world he knew he did not recognise. It was if everything inside himself was rising up in rebellion at the book and it was all he could do to stop himself hurling it into the ocean.

He had been very quiet on their return and indeed all day long they had both kept asking him if he was alright. It was only after supper as he and Sylvia walked along the beach (Megan back at the cottage reading or watching television - an innovation from last year and to be regretted) that he broached the subject of the song book.

'I read that song book of yours while you were out this morning. How can you sing that stuff? Its horrible'.

He could tell at once how hurt Sylvia was. They had worked out an unofficial truce between them over the years with regard to Sylvia's faith and this was the first real infringement.

'Is that you speaking or your therapist?'.

'I beg your pardon?' It was his turn to be outraged. This was turning threatening.

'What does it matter to you what books I read, or those of my friends, or how we see the world? Why must we be measured by the standards of your superiority. No, they're not Greek. They are probably not even proper poetry but they matter to me and those who matter to me. I believe them. I live my life by them and for them. OK?'.

She stormed ahead kicking up the sand as she did so. He stood still and looked out across the sea. It was quite chilly out here and there were white horses in the Sound, but he suspected that would be as nothing to the atmosphere in the cottage.

They never argued. He couldn't bear the atmosphere of conflict and he found it almost impossible to endure any kind of alienation from Sylvia. And now he had trodden upon her most tender part, that which gave her life its meaning and purpose - spat upon it. Why? Why? Why? Maybe she was right, maybe it was therapy that had done this. Maybe he was being bewitched by the process and its apparent hope, if not actually promise. Certainly in all the time that Sylvia had been part of her church, a Christian as she called it, he had never once expressed scorn towards it, whatever his private reservations. So why now and why here - on holiday?

His apologies were profuse. He knew how tired he was, he knew that some aspects of his worldview were becoming a little less secure than formerly, he knew he was approaching that middle-aged stage when men reflect upon their lives and measure achievement against former ambition. All of these he cited in an attempt to bring peace. He didn't mind what he said against himself so long as they were able to be together again, somehow, enjoying the place they all loved so much.

And when peace returned there was still somewhere lurking within him a nagging question about why it was that once again this disturbance had happened during a holiday. It had happened at Christmas. It had happened again. And alongside that question there remained a growing unease with Sylvia's world and its certainties.

As the furies of the Sound of Jura settled and gave way again to the peaceful waters of high summer so peace again emerged between Lyons and a Christian! The holiday was enjoyed and it even occurred to them that perhaps the conflict had served to draw them even closer together. So it seemed.

The route home was via Maryport. As the car pulled up outside his father's house Edwin noticed the door open and there stood a stranger. He told Libby later that no shock in his life had been as great as this. The steroids on which the doctors had placed his father since the tests in the Spring had made him look grotesque. He was enormous, bloated, ridiculous. Edwin wanted to scream and shout and cry. No, no, no, he thought, not my dad, No! But instead he had to get out of the car, walk forwards and treat him as if everything were normal. He held his dad and inside his heart was breaking. How could this be? How could this happen? Even worse was the fact that his dad's voice had turned squeaky. It all seemed so cruel, so terrible. What on earth had any man done to deserve this?

The visit was hell as far as Edwin was concerned. It was as if he had been given a glimpse into disintegration and he wanted nothing of it. In fact he wanted to turn about and drive away immediately. To be there with this man he loved and see him as he had become was too much to bear. He thought of the days of his childhood and the fun and the laughter, the sort of thing he had just been enjoying himself with Megan, and all he wanted to do was cry and hold his dad. And instead he had to act normal, pretend and engage in conversation about the weather and the Test match which was on the television and comment on the lovely holiday they were having together. Merciful heaven, the earth should have been crying out its protest.

They spent the night at a b&b in Cockermouth before returning again on the following morning before heading south. Although prepared this time, once again the meeting with his father shook Edwin rigid. Why, oh why, oh why had his dad smoked so heavily? This was a terrible retribution. Cause and effect it may be but it was terrible to behold.

Iris had been wonderful. She had sensed Edwin's pain, perhaps more than Sylvia. She sought to reassure him that once he was off the tablets things would begin to get better. As his dad had done earlier in the year she kept repeating "It could be a lot worse".

It was clear that Sylvia didn't know quite what to say. Why should she? He didn't know what to say and it was his own father.

They made the final leg of the journey in just one stage, Iris having filled what little space was left in their car with sandwiches and cakes and drinks such that they might have been able to stop and for a little while open a new service station. They travelled many miles in silence each thinking their own thoughts. In time though, as happens, ordinary things began to be spoken, and other things took over, and they were glad to forget what they had seen.

Edwin rang his father as soon as they arrived home just to let him know that they had arrived safely. But for another reason too.

For the first time that he could recall there was something he needed to say to his father, something he had never felt able to say before, something he had not been able to say to his face that morning:

'I love you dad, you know that, don't you?. There was a muffled reply.

'I know, son, I know, and I love you too.'

And then Edwin had cried, and perhaps for the first time in ages, and for lots of things and people too, not just for himself and his dad: for all the broken people he knew and whose broken lives he had entered and whose pain he had protected himself from with his detachment and his law. And the crying was long and at the end he was exhausted and slept deeply.

And to protect himself against this happening again Edwin determined that he needed to work harder. Libby was still away and though he had one day at the Oval Test Match he returned to work with an even greater determination than before to give himself to it. Each morning he was rising before five, slogging away at his book; proofs arrived for the next edition of the journal which he read and corrected; books came for review and he read them and made notes; letters were sent and telephone conversations made; he was in court and in prison; he was in Dunton and in the city; he was at the police station and there seemed nowhere where he was not. Even Pippa seemed unable to keep up with him and the sheer volume of work that was passing across his desk and through his life. And Pippa began to wonder how long he could keep it up.

And not only Pippa.

6

At their first session after her return from holiday, it was clear to Libby that so much had happened to Edwin that he needed to discharge feelings and he seemed to have acquired energy, the like of which she had not encountered in him before. He claimed to be feeling much better, that the summer with all its ups and downs had shown him the direction of his future and that they ought to be thinking of drawing therapy to a close before long. Of course he was grateful etc. etc., but therapy was not life and he realised that his work was perhaps suffering from the energies he was having to give to it, and of course the money question had to be faced. It was all delivered at breakneck pace.

'You are quite right to raise the issue of ending', she said, eventually, during one of his breath takes. 'Therapy is not life-long, at least I hope not', she joked, lightening the sky a little after the half-implicit threat of her first words. 'We must always be monitoring what we are doing and whether we have reached a place to end, but my own judgement would be that the first session after a break is probably not the best occasion on which to make that sort of decision'.

Edwin seemed relieved that she had provided him with a step back from his brinkmanship bravado, at least if the speed of his response were anything to go by.

'Yes, I see that. Yes'.

'And from all you've told me about your holiday', she pressed on, given the slight opening she had created for herself, 'there is a great deal for us to reflect upon and seek to make sense of in terms of what, after all, you first brought – your relationship with your mother'.

'But I haven't had any contact with my mother. None of this has anything to do with my mother'.

A rising note of protest in his voice clearly suggested to Libby that she had hit the right note and she decided she had said quite enough.

'I mean, I know that Freud said everything had to do with mothers but isn't it pushing it to say that what happened on a Scottish beach and my shock at seeing my dad so deformed by illness can be related to that?'

Libby remained silent.

Edwin, for his part, was now feeling all churned up, in total contrast to how he had been on arrival and during his opening speech - just moments ago. He was forced to accept that talk of ending was possibly a little premature but how did his feelings manage to change so swiftly in just one session? He too lapsed into silence for a while as he endeavoured to puzzle out why he was now feeling so uncertain and vulnerable again.

In their sessions during September it was hard at first for him to get away from his memories of the sight of his father but they served as an excellent entry point into recollections of his childhood and the things he had done with his father when young. That also opened the door to memories of his mother. Most of these were new to Libby. Indeed, given that he had come presenting the issue of his mother, he had been reluctant to speak of her other than describing the circumstances of his parents' divorce and her remarriage.

'I think my mother must have suffered from what we nowadays call post-natal depression', he volunteered one morning. 'The family story was that she was always "bad with her nerves". To be honest I never quite knew what that meant. Anyway it did mean that for a long time after I was born she had to go away and leave me with my grandmother. I don't exactly know how long it was for but from stories I used to hear I suspect it was quite a while.'

This was all new.

'I really loved her, my grandma. I lived for the school holidays and the chance to be with her. She had a hard life. My grandad was a total bastard, probably not his fault, what with the depression and everything.'

'Depression?' she suddenly interjected.

'Not your sort. The 1930s, unemployment – that sort. He was out of work for years and he drank heavily. It was always said that he badly used her though I never saw it. But she was simply wonderful.'

It was unnecessary to prompt him.

'She had no education to speak of, was barely literate, and perhaps the best thing about her was that all I achieved meant absolutely nothing to her and so to be there was such a joy. I didn't have to prove anything. I think I always knew that no matter what good I did or achieved she would not love me any more than she did, and that no matter what bad I did or failures I caused or experienced she would not love me any less. It was such a relief. When I stayed there I just relaxed and laughed and enjoyed life to the full. There was no pressure. It was just a place of ease. And the contrast with home couldn't have been greater.'

Libby was determined to allow him to speak freely but she also needed a little clarification. 'You spent a lot of time with her?'

'Oh yes, do you know most of the things I recall from my childhood, the good things anyway, and the long summers, are memories of being with her'.

'Where was that?'

It was small village called Eglingham in Northumberland, near to Alnwick. It's still pretty remote and was even more so then, but I loved it. My grandad worked on the land, when he worked, and they had four children. They were very poor but generous to a fault. I loved it there.'

'So you went in your school holidays? Even when you were at boarding school?'.

'Oh yes, I never needed to asked twice because their house was my home. I belonged there.'

'And you didn't want to be with your parents in the holidays?'.

'No!' – clear definite, final.

There was a pause and neither seemed willing to break it. Edwin seemed lost in thought.

The time for the completion of the session was drawing near and eventually Libby asked him, 'Did you never want to know why your mother couldn't look after you when you were born, Edwin. I mean it's a perfectly natural thing to wonder about. Have you never asked her?'.

'No.'

There was something of a difficulty that needed to be sorted out in the Practice. There was a long-standing tradition that partners "in-house" would gather for tea at 3-30. It lasted no more than 20 minutes and on most days, at least, some would gather. Edwin had noticed that almost always their American newcomer was there when he was. Of course she was still building up her practice but he had expected that she would be out more than she was. But perhaps he was just uneasy, having pushed for her appointment in the first place so strongly.

The difficulty came in the form of an irate Paul charging into his room and demanding to know why the returns for July and

August had not been completed. Edwin had general over-sight of the work lists of partners and it was down to him to prepare them for the monthly partners' meeting due the following week. He was at a loss to give an answer, not least because he had asked Jayne to take this work on as part of her induction process into the practice. He reported this to Paul.

'Yes, well if she worked as hard as she engages in conversation they might have been done. I was expecting a lightening of my load when she came and it isn't happening. It isn't happening at all'.

'Paul, she's new and this is her first English practice. Give her time. Leave it with me'.

Giving Jayne time meant, in the present instance, even less time for Edwin. Not only did he feel that her excuse was somewhat lame, but she also then waylaid him in conversation on a somewhat obscure legal nicety, a lure he could not resist, and then discovered that he would have to do the work himself after all, which took more than four hours that evening, four hours he was jealously guarding for his book.

However much he and Sylvia had resolved the holiday crisis there was no doubting that they seemed further apart than before. The arrival of autumn saw both of them throwing themselves into their work with renewed fervour but Edwin did wonder whether this was because of what had happened in Scotland, that in some way they were both endeavouring to avoid whatever all that had been about. If it were so then it did at least have the virtue of being convenient for Edwin's book. At the moment the material seemed to be pouring out of him like lava from an erupting volcano. Of course he knew that the gestation process had been considerable; he had had some of these things in mind for a long time. Even so the speed with which he wrote and the quality of his own writing astonished him. He was even feeling less tired than he had been in the early summer even though he was maintaining a schedule that was probably not sustainable for too long. On some nights he was getting little more than four hours of sleep but it didn't seem to limit his capacity for creative work.

The case of the client charged with the murder of her own baby was due in court. The evidence was conclusive and Edwin's main concern was ensuring a proper presentation of the psychiatric and social reports. Grace Gordon came and gave evidence as the psychiatrist. She was impressive in court. His client pleaded guilty to manslaughter by reason of diminished responsibility, a plea the judge accepted, though the Press were baying for her blood. Edwin had been profoundly shocked when he read the medical reports of the injuries to the baby. He read them over and over, wondering just what must happen within a person to allow themselves to do such things to something so vulnerable. And yet the girl too (and she was little more than a girl) had a history of abuse and neglect that appalled him no less. The huge irony was that outside the court was a pack (and the word seemed highly appropriate) of people screaming hatred at the prison van as it took her away. But in what way were they any different? Were they not ready to do exactly the same as she had done? Perhaps it was worse in their case because they had not the cause she had.

So where did the feelings come from? How was it that across the world people in droves still attended public executions in those countries where it was still practised? It didn't make sense. Cause and effect was one thing but surely these people can't all be victims of abuse themselves?

Such thoughts occupied his mind as he drove back from Winchester. The clocks had changed, and it was already getting dark. He hated having to drive with lights in his mirror but for the next couple of months there was also the low sun to contend with morning and evening. Driving west this afternoon it was hard to see clearly. The sight of the Cathedral with the setting sun behind it never failed to move him as he began to drop down from the hills into the city. Perhaps he would get to Choral Evensong after getting back to the office.

There were five in the congregation. The choir consisted of six men (Vicars Choral he knew they were called, though as far as he knew none of them were in holy orders) and eighteen boys.

They were backed up by three clergymen though not this evening including, he noticed, the Dean (do Deans get a day off? he wondered), a verger at their head and the director of music immediately behind him conducting the Introit as he walked. Five in the congregation was more or less typical for darkest autumn. He had once heard someone justify the expenditure on the grounds that they were worshipping and celebrating Evensong simply for the glory of God not for the adulation of an audience. Edwin approved even if he wasn't wholly sure that the intended recipient was actually present. But He ought to be. The singing, the reading, the "performance" was perfect. The only jarring note was struck by the canon reading the prayers towards the end. Rather than staying with the products of ArchO'Connell Cranmer's genius he decided to add a note of informal contemporaneity to the Almighty, who, it occurred to Edwin, had he actually been earlier present might have chosen this as the moment to take his leave.

That evening Edwin finished the book he had been working on. He had already decided that he would leave the indexing to the Society of Indexers, a group of people in whom he had enormous confidence. He also knew that it would require little in the way of revision. He was pleased with it but also relieved to reach the end. He also felt that completing it would enable him to get a little more sleep (he was feeling very tired tonight) and to give more time to the family. He knew full well that he had been neglecting them. Perhaps he and Megan would have the day out together on

Sunday. Thus, greatly relieved and weary, he made his way to bed shortly before 2-00 am.

He could hear the screams before he woke. He was terrified. Sylvia was shaking him and calling out his name.

'What is it? Is she alright, is she alright?', he called out to her. 'Edwin, what's the matter, what is it?'.

Sylvia was leaning over him and holding him. 'Is she alright?'.

'Everything's fine. You must have been dreaming'.

Edwin was aware that he was soaking wet. He felt totally disorientated. 'What time is it?' he asked.

'Nearly half three'.

Was there a slight tone of reproach in the voice?

'I'm sorry', he said and lay back. 'Bad dream. Too many late nights'.

As he lay there he eventually heard Sylvia's breathing change signifying a return to sleep. But he did not, and could not. He could not get the dream out of his head nor clear his mind of the sound of the screams.

They had not often worked on his dreams. On the only occasion he had mentioned a dream in passing her interest had irritated him. He was convinced that dreams served only to clear up the detritus of brain activity and could not provide some sort of unravelling of the complexities of his difficulties. But this dream was different. He felt himself compelled to relate it.

'I was in a prison cell. It wasn't Winchester, in fact I don't know where it was. I was in there – I don't know why I was there, perhaps I was there as a prisoner. Yes, that must be it, because I can remember now', he chuckled, 'thinking that this was most surprising, me being a con, in the reverse role. And then when I turned round she was there, the girl who killed her baby, and the next thing I knew I was shouting at her that there was nobody to make it all right for her now, nobody to protect her now, and then...'.

He stopped, seeming lost deep inside himself. Libby knew well to allow him to go at his own pace.

'And then I started to hit her', he eventually continued. 'I shook her and shook her and then I started to punch her, and all the time I was screaming abuse at her. And that was when I woke up. I thought it was Megan screaming'.

'That sound really frightening, Edwin', Libby said quietly, 'really frightening. Remembering dreams is not simply a matter of telling a tale, recounting something from the past. There is something in the nature of what a dream is, where it comes from and what it is seeking to do, that means we, as it were, enter back into something of the original feeling when we recount it'.

Edwin was clearly much affected by his account, much as he might have been had the events he was describing actually happened. In fact of course they had, emotionally speaking. Inwardly he had lived those feelings and there was little difference between how that felt and how it would have done had he been recounting an event, what might be called fact.

Libby clearly believed that this dream was very important though seemed reluctant to say too much in the way of theory.

'Odd to find yourself a prisoner'.

It served to distract him from the painful ending of the dream but kept him still focussed.

'It was, and yet strangely familiar – the place I mean. You know how dreams are, they combine unlikely places and people. When I think about it, the room was not really like the cells I go to. It was more like a bedroom; except I knew it was a prison'.

'A bedroom?'.

'Yes, it wasn't unlike a bedroom I used to have, in one of the houses we used to live in when I was young'.

Libby decided to risk the question.

'What do you think the dream was all about Edwin?'.

As she had probably anticipated he was defensive and dismissed her question. He was not yet able to face the questions that were building up demanding a response. Not yet.

7

Edwin was finding it hard to function out there in the wider world. Pippa noticed a change in him. He seemed distracted, lost in thought, sat doing nothing – quite unlike him. She even wondered, albeit for little more than a fleeting moment, whether she should say something to Mr Raven. She was concerned.

At home, life continued much as ever. Megan was busy both at and after school. A burgeoning social life meant more lifts to and from here, there and everywhere and if she had noticed something odd about her dad then she, at least, said nothing. Sylvia certainly noticed that Edwin was more restless than she had ever known him, but she put this down to the completion of his book. He would soon be firing on all cylinders again she was sure. For her own part she was becoming more and drawn into peoples' lives and faith. Her work had expanded considerably and there was talk in the Church of an assistant pastor for women being appointed. She had also been asked to take responsibility for mounting a major new evangelistic project in the Spring. It was something being set up by a Church in London and they were looking for local churches around the country to run trials which they would monitor and support. It would be for women and was the first time Sylvia had been involved in outreach on such a scale. It involved a number of trips up to London for training and supervision and Sylvia was enjoying the excitement and the responsibility.

She hugely wished that Edwin was able to share in her sense of excitement. He was encouraging of all she did but then again she felt that he would be supportive of her whatever it might have been throwing herself into – water skiing, witchcraft or wattle repair (if there was such a thing).

What she wanted, and for which she prayed day by day, alone and with others, was his conversion. Not just for her own sake but his. She was anxious about his salvation. And she also knew that in her increasingly important role in the life of the Church an evangelist who had still not managed to convert her husband was as convincing as a bald-headed man selling hair restorer! But to think such thoughts, she knew full well was a sign of her lack of trust in God. Soon her mind turned towards the meeting ahead and the people with whom she would be working later that morning in London.

Across from her in the railway carriage, and wholly unbeknown to either, sat Libby Francis, herself also en route to London for supervision. The same man figured heavily in their own pondering as they gazed out through filthy dirty windows at the north Hampshire countryside, and to a certain extent the question of his salvation concerned both too, albeit salvation of a different kind: one life eternal, the other, life now.

And neither knew who the other was, nor ever would.

On that same day Edwin was in Bristol at the University. He conducted a post-graduate seminar twice a term and, on this occasion, he was giving a paper on Natural Law (he read them his concluding Chapter). As he knew only too well that it pertains to the nature of the post-graduate student that he or she remains blind to almost any thoughts other than those essential to their own research. Countenancing a different way of thinking or looking at the world is far too challenging. In consequence Edwin anticipated either silence or hostility. What upset him, as he thought about it later on the Sprinter train crawling its way down the Avon valley, was their indifference. How could people, intelligent people, not care about the larger vision, setting the minutiae with which lawyers are bound to spend their days within a greater context? How could people be satisfied with just getting on with what they did, doing a job, and not see that it mattered how things hold together? He felt depressed by it.

Sylvia returned home feeling excited and elated by the day. The keynote speaker, a young barrister-turned-clergyman focussed their minds on the kingdom of God and the harvest of souls it demanded. On her journey Sylvia had determined to pray more for Edwin, who was at home cooking for Megan and preparing to meet her train. At least her return would free him for some work. She would be on the telephone gushing all evening and he was aware that he was falling behind in his work for the Journal. It required of him a concerted effort in the next fortnight, a return to late nights and early mornings. That was not going to be easy. In the following two weeks he was going to be in court a considerable amount – not the most effective use of time travelling and little opportunity to use inevitable delays for sustained reading. Still, work was what he did best. It was what he was good at. It was what he had always been good at.

Edwin had therefore already been up for more than three hours when he arrived at Libby's door the following morning. He was tired and had been finding it difficult to concentrate. Only shortly before leaving home had he remembered that a Partner's Meeting was scheduled for 9-00 and that he would need to leave Libby's promptly. He hoped (although this hope, as he knew, was well founded) that Pippa would have everything ready for him.

'It sounds quite a performance', observed Libby in response to his description of all that he had to have prepared for the forthcoming meeting.

'We are all professionals,' he replied immediately, 'and we owe each other the best, and that includes not wasting valuable time because someone is under-prepared'.

'Do all your partners share your sense of principle? I mean, will they all be as prepared as you?'

'On the whole, yes'.

'Has it always been like this, Edwin? Was it like this at school? Edwin the hard-working? Edwin the brilliant?'

It was perhaps the first time that Edwin had felt a jarring note in Libby's words, a veiled criticism. He was surprised to find himself feeling hurt, though he said nothing about it, and therefore fell into her trap and began to talk about something he might have preferred, on reflection, to avoid.

'Actually, no'. He paused. 'In fact, quite the opposite. Oh, I was clever enough, clever though never brilliant, and not brilliant now', he added.

Libby said nothing.

'In a strange way I was something of a failure at school. My O-levels were nothing special and whilst I did enough in the sixth form to get to university it was only then that I began to do well. Indeed it was only then that I began to work hard. I really enjoyed study – classics came alive for me and a mounting sense of excitement about the place of Law in human existence'.

'Was it because you just didn't like school that you didn't do as well as you could?'.

'No. To be honest, though I wouldn't have been able to say or understand this at the time, I think I failed at school to spite my mother'.

Libby knew well enough to leave alone the silence that followed. He would continue.

'They were so ambitious for me. Well no. I think they were

ambitious for themselves. She was particularly. She was always pushing my dad to do this and get that, to get on and get more. She was a total snob, and I'm afraid I was part of her grand design. I had to go to boarding school – no, public school as she insisted it be called, because that was what she expected of the sort of person she had become or wanted to become. I was part of her project. In a real way I think my school career was some sort of fighting back. I really didn't do well for a long time – always near the bottom of the class, and although I used to be quite scared of her anger when she received my end of term reports I was also strangely pleased inside. God, I hated her'.

It was the first time, the first cracking of the ice on the river, the warning of danger.

Edwin had to move swiftly across town, collect his papers and be ready to begin as the cathedral bell struck the hour. High on the agenda was the implementation of an earlier agreement to bring in new computerisation, an issue close to Edwin's heart. They were still using an older system and he wanted to press the case for the installation of a new network and programme which he felt certain was going to be the market leader. That was low on the batting order and Edwin found himself increasingly detached from the discussion going on about him. He had been shocked by what he had said to Libby. Shocked too because it had taken him so long to admit it. Over and over, he repeated to himself his words but found as he listened that the perfect tense had given way to the present. "I hate her, I hate her, I hate her". And then he realised that there was silence about him and that they were all looking at him.

Hugh was chairing the meeting.

'Are you alright, Edwin?'.

'Mm?'. He was confused, troubled. Why was everyone staring at him? What had he been saying? Had they heard him?

'I was inviting you to speak to us about your hopes for a new computer system', said Hugh gently, as if knowing, somehow.

Solicitors have considerable experience of clients in tears and even more powerful expression of emotion. One of Edwin's partners had once been taken hostage in a magistrates court cell and held at knife-point for more than three hours. They were all familiar with strong feelings and had developed ways and means for dealing with them when clients manifested them. They were all professionals. And they all now felt acutely embarrassed because they could see quite plainly that one of their number, one of their own colleagues, was quite clearly going through some sort of crisis. Tears were coursing down his cheeks and he was speechless and looked terrible.

And terrible was how he felt. He was helpless and that made him feel even worse. He could not move and he had no idea what to say. Eventually, as the embarrassed silence deepened, he shook his head and mumbled an apology. And if his colleagues had been hoping that he might get up and go, that in this way he might spare them even greater embarrassment, they were disappointed. He did not know how to stand. And as Hugh moved business on Edwin sat there in agonising misery and wondered what on earth was happening.

The meeting was over. Paul remained in the room after the others had made a hasty departure. He came and sat next to Edwin.

'I'm sorry Edwin, I think we thought it best just to go on. Do you think it would be best if I called Sylvia and got you home? Pippa can handle your appointments'.

'No, I'm the one who should be sorry, Paul. What a mess. It was all too much'.

'Is it your father?'.

'No. Well, in part. No, I'm just doing too much, and oh, you know, getting caught up in things, and well, not getting priorities sorted. I sometimes forget that this place is number one, and then the tail starts wagging the dog and lo and behold, this morning's little episode. I need to make a change or too'.

'You do have a full schedule, Edwin. What with here and Dunton, and the University and your writings. And all the legal aid on-call work. Do you need to drop something?'.

'No, I'll get it sorted. I probably most of all need some sleep. Once I can get the Journal off to the printers, I might take a day or two away. Go up and visit the old man by train. Sleep a bit and do some walking in the lakes or something like that'.

Edwin rose and began to gather his papers together. Outside it was raining hard.

'There are still people I have to see today. Cancelling them won't make them go away. They'll still be there tomorrow and tomorrow and tomorrow.' He stood up straight.

'Thanks, Paul.'

'I still wish you'd allow me to let Sylvia know'.

'No need, honest. I will survive, you know'.

As he made his way back to his room, Edwin wondered whether this show of confidence was at all well-placed. He hoped Paul believed it because he was far from convinced himself.

News spread fast it seemed. Pippa had clearly already learned that something was amiss judging from the solicitous looks he received on returning to his office. And he knew too that it probably wouldn't be too long before Sylvia heard something, which meant more, and unwanted, hassle about therapy. Thankfully he had work to throw himself into: two clients before lunch and a prison visit scheduled for the afternoon. A barrister was coming down from London whom Edwin knew well and whose company he enjoyed. The case was relatively straightforward, and they ought to have the chance for some tea together in Winchester afterwards. Things were looking up.

As he drove over towards Winchester Edwin was listening to

Mozart's K466 Piano Concerto on the radio. He had once read that the greatest composer of all had written or said, "Oh if only all the world could feel the power of harmony" and though he had never been able to track down the source of the quotation it was entirely congruent with all that the man had created. Edwin believed it. He believed in the essential harmony of creation despite all he saw day by day to suggest that the more orthodox Christian belief in original sin had more going for it as an explanation of how things are. How could anyone believe in original sin, Edwin wondered, when they could listen to this and know perfection in musical form? He had heard that there such things as music therapists and he could understand it, for music was a source of healing - a pathway into wholeness.

That, in part, accounted for why he couldn't stand the appalling music (if that was the right word) that predominated in Sylvia's church. One evening at a dinner at Paul's house he had met a clarinettist from the Bournemouth Symphony Orchestra who was running the music group at the church. Edwin had asked him how he endured the music demanded of church life when compared with the wonderful stuff he played with the orchestra, and was appalled when the man told him that the music he played in church meant infinitely more to him than anything he played elsewhere, because "it is the Lord's music". Well, more fool the Lord then! Edwin had thought. To have made Mozart but to prefer hymns and ditties suggested the Almighty needed therapy Himself.

His afternoon with John, their incarcerated client notwithstanding, was as good as he hoped it might be. They had hardly known each other at Sedbergh, Edwin being two years older, but had played cricket together for a year at university. Over crumpets and Earl Grey in the Cathedral Gatehouse they argued the pros and cons of the inclusion of various players in the England squad that had just begun its tour of Australia. Two men who knew each other well, who worked together, who knew each other's families, and other than pleasantries their principal subject for conversation was a cricket team in which neither of them had any real investment and players that neither of them knew. Men.

Pleasantries were not quite the order of the evening at home. Paul had spoken to Betty and she had telephoned Sylvia and by the time Edwin arrived home, the Spanish Inquisition (or at least its evangelical counterpart) awaited his return. She gave him a hard time. She attacked his therapy of course, and he also felt he could detect somewhere in all she said the distant voice of Paul's disapproval of his legal aid work. Considering that Sylvia claimed to be addressing Edwin's needs, and expressing care and concern for him, it did feel a little like she was more concerned for their position in the city – and maybe therefore her position in the Church?

Edwin mostly did not do anger, at least outwardly, but he knew as he sat at his desk upstairs when he had finally marched up the stairs, that he was burning with fury. Why the hell did he have to put up with this? He didn't need it and he didn't want it. Bloody women.

Bloody, bloody women!

8

Libby began by asking Edwin if she too were among the 'bloody, bloody women'. He had been describing the terrible day and night following his previous session with her.

'After all, it might be said that I was the woman who caused the difficulties of the day', she volunteered. 'It might be argued, and I am sure one of your partners, or even you, could make a strong prima facie case against me, that I was guilty of neglect in allowing you to leave here clearly worked up. Your wife, I'm sure, attributes to me the guilt in no small measure, and I suspect may not be quite so willing to allot me the forgiveness she no doubt believes in'.

Edwin wondered what she was trying to say. Was she feeling guilty? He had no idea. Sometimes the meaning behind her words eluded his grasp completely. Nevertheless, he did want to reassure her about guilt.

'Not at all', he said. 'I come here freely. If a patient with a broken leg is run over crossing a road after he has left a hospital appointment with the orthopaedic consultant, it would seem a strange defence to argue that the doctor had a responsibility to see his patient safely across the road simply because he knew he had a bad leg.'

As Libby knew full well Edwin was now on safe ground. In the face of painful emotion, switching into intellectual mode had consistently proved itself to be a more than adequate defence. He was good at it too, and she even enjoyed seeing him do it. Her own temptation was to succumb to the lure of his voice and follow him into the fantasy garden of cerebral delights. Not today, though she did not know how easy it would be to get him out of it. "Route One", as she had heard it described by an American psychotherapist, – "if in doubt say absolutely nothing and say it loud".

She took his advice.

'Besides which,' Edwin obligingly continued, 'unlike the others you don't seek to impose expectations upon me. I'm not saying you don't have them, but you don't appear, at any rate, to force me to live up to them'.

Libby would have liked to explore the issue of their working relationship - his expectations of her - but she felt, even more, that there was an opening here into Edwin's relationships with mother and wife that could not be ignored, even temporarily.

'Yes, you said the other morning something of the terrible weight of expectation placed upon you by your mother'.

'You don't know the half. There was an edge to his voice, an uncharacteristic note of steel.

She guessed she need not respond - correctly.

'All the time and as far back as I can recall, all she wanted was for me to succeed, and even more importantly, to be seen to succeed. In public she used to shower affection upon me, use the language of doting care. But take away the audience and then – nothing. She could turn from someone smiling and warm when people were watching into a cold and calculating bitch in a flash. To their faces she was all warmth and then, as soon as they had gone, she would call them all the names under the sun. I never knew where I was with her. Except I knew when I wasn't up to the mark. God, she let me know then'.

'In what way?'

'She hit me a lot as a child. Across my head and face. She locked me in my room quite often. I remember once her doing so and forbidding me to turn on the light'.

'And did you?'.

'No. I was terrified of her. But even that wasn't as bad as the worst thing of all... '. He stopped as if the memory might be too painful to speak.

Libby waited and then gently asked 'And that was?'.

'Total silence. She wouldn't speak to me. Sometimes it lasted for two or three days. She did it to my dad as well. It created an atmosphere of total and absolute hell and misery. You know some people have described and painted hell as a place of fire and brimstone, a place of screaming and suffering, but they're quite wrong, for all those things are the things of life. No. Hell is the dead silence of non-communication, the isolation cell, the bitter cold of enforced solitude. That's what hell is'.

'The memory of it seems very alive, Edwin'.

'Oh, it happened over and over, and what made it so bad is that always it was terrible. There never was a time when I got used to it. And when my dad was away with his work which seemed to happen more and more, before I was sent away to school, there was just me to handle her, just me to bear it'.

She could see he was caught up in something powerful and painful.

'One night', he began, paused and then looked at her over his right shoulder, 'and I have never told another soul this, when I was about twelve, my dad was away. I was home from school and had gone to bed. About one o'clock in the morning I woke and noticed the landing light was on. I assumed she had omitted to tum it off and got up to do so. After I had opened the door I could hear strange noises coming from downstairs. I didn't know what it is and crept down as quietly as I could. The door to the sitting room was slightly ajar and I froze in horror when through the crack I could see her and a man on the settee. Both were more or less naked and *in flagrante delicto*.

Perhaps my mother heard me and she suddenly called out my name. I retreated in haste to my room and feigned sleep. She didn't come into my room and shortly afterwards I heard the front door close and a car start up and drive away. In the morning she came into the kitchen whilst I was having my breakfast and shouted at me "You evil little boy. You little sneak with your lies". She then stormed out and did not speak to me until the evening of the following day. That was when my father had come home. He had asked how we were and she smiled at me and said we'd been fine, "haven't we darling?" And the worst thing is that I colluded with my own torture, with my own exclusion'.

Edwin had spoken these words quietly but no longer the quiet of his dispassion but with the quiet of being on the edge of something frightening.

'Do you think your father knew?'

'If he did, and I don't know, I don't think he cared. He was, as they say, making alternative arrangements of his own in the sexual department'.

'It might well be true that he didn't care what she did. But what of his care for you? You weren't a little boy, you were twelve, but he didn't do much to protect you from her'.

'No', said Edwin even more quietly.

'So there you are, an innocent witness finding yourself carrying the burden of guilt. What did it make you think of her?'

'Actually Libby, the truth is that it didn't change anything. You see I hated her and have hated her for as long as I can remember. So it changed nothing. It simply served to give me yet more reasons for my total loathing. She was a whore, a slut, she was disgusting and always had been. It changed nothing at all'.

The anger and contempt was evident in every syllable he uttered. 'But you didn't reveal anything of this to her?'

'No, I just went along with it, longing either to get back to school or to my grandma in the holidays. And I can't forgive myself for that. How could I have done it? How could I have let her get away with it?'

For the first time in therapy, and already there had been a lot of sessions together, tears were flowing down his cheeks. He quickly reached for a tissue from the box that stood by the chaise and began to wipe them away.

'I'm so sorry', he said, 'how silly of me. Please excuse me. It's so ridiculous. For crying out loud this was twenty five years ago. It has nothing to do with now'.

'Well, maybe crying out loud is not such a bad description of what you need to do, however many years it is since it happened. The pain and the feelings are real enough and perhaps those tears have been waiting twenty five years to get out'.

It was difficult for Edwin to have to go to his office after this session. He thought of telephoning Pippa and feigning an illness but duty took him across town. He had always been possessed of considerable acting skills and they stood him in good stead this morning. His colleagues did not, however, act quite so well and he could see from their forced cheerfulness when they encountered him that they were wary of his presence. Most managed to be busy at coffee time; they must have known he was likely to be there. Not that Edwin blamed them. He felt terrible about what had happened and wondered how he could make it up. It was hardly surprising they wanted to avoid him; what else did he deserve? Still, it meant he would not waste time. There was so much to be doing: clients to be seen, papers to prepare, articles chased up, books to be read and reviewed, and two essays from students to be assessed. He resolved to give himself wholly and utterly to his work for the remainder of the day. Perhaps now that he had got it all out into the open he could begin to live again, and live for the Law he loved.

It was the weekend. Sylvia and Megan were going to do some shopping in Southampton for the day. Edwin had no desire to accompany them. A confirmed bachelor friend had once commented to him that he had no desire whatsoever to commit matrimony until it came to the time to write Christmas cards. Edwin was more than happy to allow his wife to deal with Christmas – cards, presents, turkeys, whatever. If she spent a fortune today he would still think it a price worth paying.

He worked for most of the morning then at lunch-time had gone for a walk across the water meadows. The cathedral spire had disappeared beneath scaffolding - some dangerous brickwork had been recently discovered and they were talking in terms of millions of pounds for restoration. His partner Hugh had been hinting at the possibility that their firm might be invited to manage the legal work involved. Edwin supposed that Hugh's friendship with the Dean made it likely that he shouldn't handle it himself. Alistair would no doubt enjoy it, however. He was a keen conservationist. Paul too would be over the moon if the contract came – good for the prestige of the firm, even though he knew full well that Paul with his arch-evangelical non-conformist principles almost thought of the cathedral as the domain of the anti-Christ. Still what were principles if they couldn't be shored up with scaffolding and bring in both income and prestige?

Edwin thought the spire looked sad: metal and plastic against a heavy and threatening grey sky. It had been raining heavily for weeks now and the water-meadows were flooded. They matched how he felt and as he looked down into the water all he could see was a yet heavier sky bringing more woe.

He worked hard all-day Sunday. Megan had gone to church with Sylvia, and from there onto a friend's house for the day. Sylvia was having lunch at church. It was a study day for leaders of the forthcoming evangelistic outreach mission and she had to give a report on her recent visit to London. That allowed him space to play music as loud as he needed to and on that day, he needed to. Perhaps, he thought to himself, I'll drown out the voices speaking inside. During the afternoon, and at something like maximum volume, he listened to the Karajan recording of Siegfried.

Normally he didn't care much for Wagner, but he liked to work his way through the Ring at least once a year. Today it was part three. But if he was hoping that the music might lift his mood it signally failed to do so. Not that he used music like that. On the whole he chose music because it reflected how he felt rather than the mood he was seeking. He began feeling low and some three and a half hours later felt no better (some would say that after three and a half hours of Wagner that was hardly surprising!).

He worked until late. Megan and Sylvia had both returned full to overflowing with reports of their respective days. He listened dutifully and endeavoured to show interest in what they reported, but his mind was elsewhere. During the evening he found himself reading and then re-reading almost every sentence of the book he was ploughing through. He was, he felt, truly distracted by distraction. As he made his way to bed shortly before midnight he was aware that he couldn't remember anything of what he had read all evening. He just felt very, very tired.

He slept until just after three. It was a dream, a dream in which he was running down the length of a train. Outside it was dark and the train was moving fast. He knew he was looking for somewhere safe, somewhere he could hide. But all he could recall was a sense of running and being unable to find a refuge. Then the dream had changed and he found himself inside a large room. It had a high ceiling, the walls were darkly painted and had no windows. He could hear water lapping against the side of one of the walls. Then he could footsteps coming and a voice shouting out to him "No hiding place, no hiding place". That was when he woke up, sweating and terrified.

He lay there, his heart pounding, striving to be as quiet as he could. Sylvia was deeply asleep next to him, and he didn't want to wake her. In the first place it wasn't fair to her. But also, he didn't want a further cross examination. He thought of trying to creep out of bed to get himself a cup of tea but decided instead to remain there and try to get back to sleep. He had a busy day scheduled ahead and he was feeling so tired. So tired. So weary. He would give anything to get to sleep and it totally eluded him.

On arrival Edwin told Libby that he had not had much sleep. Perhaps that accounted for how he was feeling. Or maybe it was just another Monday morning. Or was it the dream? Or was it work? Or what was it?

As he recounted the dream he quickly found himself once again experiencing the frightening emotions that had awakened him. He could almost feel the motion of the train and he was aware that he was running backwards, against the direction of travel. The faster the train went, the faster he ran. He didn't know who was chasing him, nor at first did he recognise the voice calling out to him in the dark room. Then he did. Then he knew. It was his mother. And he recalled too that the words she had used were the title of a television programme when he was young. It had been about policemen from Scotland Yard and all he could recall of it was a sense of being frightened by the title - for what would happen if there was no place that was safe?

When he left at ten minutes to nine Libby wondered whether he was going to be capable of work. He looked more tired than she could recall and it was self-evident that he was now in touch with a seam of memories that were threatening him and would need all her skills to help him manage.

In later days people sometimes asked Edwin what a breakdown was like. The question made him smile. Not that he was capable of anything approximating to a smile on this particular morning. He closed the door behind him as he left Libby's house and made his way towards his office. It was the same route that he took every Monday, Wednesday and Friday morning. He walked along her road, turned right and dropped down towards the City Square. All very familiar. He reached the square and waited for a car to pass him before crossing the road. He reached the pavement on the other side and stood where the market was held on Saturdays - that was when it happened.

Edwin looked about him. He knew something was odd for the buildings were all moving, not violently but gently from side to side. And then he realised that he had no idea where he was. He was completely lost. He noticed a police care parked on one side of the square and he began to walk towards it. They would help him, they would tell him where he was and which way to go. But as he approached it drove away. Now he began to be a little afraid. He set off walking, determined, indeed now increasingly desperate, to go somewhere. But he didn't know where. He had no idea where anything was, and in the days that followed he marvelled how he had managed to cross the road safely (and his amazement was well-founded for he walked out into the road without any sort of awareness of traffic for both mercifully and unusually at that moment there was none). He had reached the comer of the square. Before him there was a door - a house, a shop, an office, – he had no idea what it was. He went towards it and rang the bell to the left of the doorway. It was opened by Anthony Whitmore, a solicitor from another practice in the city.

'Edwin?' he said, amazed.

Edwin stood there, and then suddenly fell forwards into Anthony's arms, and began to cry, and cry, and cry, and cry.

A chair was found for him. He couldn't speak. At first because he could not stop crying – it was as if he was having to cry all the tears blocked over the years and he felt as if he might cry for years. Then he became totally numb. He stared out into nothing – could hear nothing, see nothing. Just how long he was there he did not know. He wasn't even sure where he was.

A telephone call to his home had simply resulted in a message being left on the answering machine. Sylvia had a Bible Study group at that moment in the sitting room and did not want to break the atmosphere which she thought was going so well. She could hear something about the need for an urgent call to Anthony Whitmore's Chambers but preferred to continue the Bible group. It could wait.

Anthony decided to ring for a doctor. It was clear to him that Edwin was in trouble. He then rang through to Paul Raven.

'Oh no', was Paul's response to the news. 'I'm so sorry, Tony. This has been coming. I'll come straight round and get him home'.

Ringing off he rang home and told his wife to get round to Sylvia's as fast as possible.

The doctor was diverted to Edwin's address and arrived moments after Paul had come with a silent and clearly unwell Edwin. Sylvia was flustered. The Bible study was still going on when Edwin had arrived. Even now she couldn't take in what she was being told about Edwin. What had happened to him? Was he ill? Had he had an accident? What was the fuss about? Paul insisted that the group should be asked to break, and Sylvia was in with them explaining that her husband had been taken ill, and leading them in a final prayer when he arrived.

Paul led him straight upstairs and into the bedroom. They were followed by a young doctor who received a brief report on what had happened before suggesting that Paul left them alone. Colin Nuffield was a member of the practice with which Edwin was registered. In his late thirties, he had survived a serious car crash three years previously which had left him partially sighted. There were those who said, however, that a half-blind Dr Nuffield could see more than most other sighted doctors put together.

'May I call you Edwin?' he asked gently. A slight nod of assent and he continued.

'I'm Colin Nuffield, I'm a doctor. Something's happened to you, Edwin, and we need to try and work out what it is and how we can best address it. Ok?'.

Edwin was still standing, mostly looking out of the bedroom window but seeing nothing at all.

'I think it might help if you sat down'. The doctor positioned himself with the window behind him to get the fullest benefit of the light.

'Edwin, I need you to try and tell me what has happened this morning. As much as you can remember'.

As he finished the door burst open. It was Sylvia.

'Edwin, what's the matter?'

The doctor rose and introduced himself. Edwin looked up but seemed almost incapable of saying anything to his wife. The doctor saw Sylvia's fear and anxiety.

'I think Edwin's going to need a bit of time to process what's happened. At the moment he's sort of switched off some of the normal functioning mechanisms just so that he can cope. It's alright. He'll just need some time'.

The doctor helped Sylvia undress Edwin and get him into his pyjamas. It was whilst they were doing this that he heard Sylvia mutter something to Edwin about "that damn therapy". He waited until they had got Edwin into bed and then asked to be shown the bathroom. Outside the door he asked her what she was referring to.

'He's been going to a psychologist for about six months, and a fat lot of good it's done him. Dr Grace Gordon had recommended her to him'.

'Is he a patient of Dr Gordon's?'.

'Oh no, nothing like that. Edwin works with Grace's husband and it was just a chance conversation, and she said she knew this woman, Libby Francis I think she's called, and Edwin went to see her and he's been going three times a week since then. And look where it's got him. I knew it was wrong'.

'When did he last see her?'.

'This morning at 8. Always at 8, Monday, Wednesday, Friday. It's ridiculous'.

'Ok', said Dr Nuffield. 'Look I need to make a phone call and I think Edwin needs a warm drink. Can you heat some milk for him'.

'I'll have to go and get some. We've had a group here this morning and we used it up'.

'Fine', replied the doctor, relieved that it might allow him some much-needed space with his patient. 'You do that, and I'll try and get through to Mrs Francis.'

'Do you know her?'.

Did he know her? Did he know her? He had sometimes thought in the past three years that without Elizabeth Francis he would never have had the courage to go on after the accident.

'Slightly', he lied. 'Anyway, enough to respect her abilities'.

Eventually persuading Sylvia to go and get some milk and keeping his (only) eye on Edwin who was lying on his bed eyes wide open, lost somewhere, Colin rang Libby. Inevitably he got the answering machine.

'Libby, it's Colin. Ring me urgently. It's about Edwin Lyons'.

He returned to Edwin and sat on the windowsill.

'I gather you saw Libby Francis this morning'.

The name seemed to earth him. His eyes rolled towards the doctor.

'Mm'. A slight nod.

'Is what has happened to do with that, with what you and Libby have been doing together? I mean, that would make sense to me. I could understand that'.

'I just can't take any more' said Edwin, slightly puzzled by why the doctor's eyes seemed to be looking in different directions.

A mobile in Dr Nuffield's top pocket started to give off its call, much to the puzzlement of Edwin.

'That's just my phone', he explained, rising and making for the landing where the surgery informed him that Libby Francis was able to take his call now. He rang her and told her what he knew about what had happened. For her part, she explained as briefly as possible that what had happened to Edwin was almost certainly not a psychotic event which would require hospitalisation but (as he had thought) a stage in therapy in which he had hit some things so terrible that his constitution needs to stop completely to enable himself to come to terms with them.

'Frankly, Colin, what he most needs today is sleep. If you put him into the psychiatric hospital it will make him ill. He is not ill now. He is becoming well'.

Colin Nuffield needed no convincing.

'I will need to talk to you though, Libby,' he said, 'if I'm going to be of any use to you in this. I don't need details but I do need more information'.

'Of course', and they agreed to meet later in the day.

By the time Sylvia had arrived back, Edwin was fast asleep.

'I've given him something to relax him and help him sleep', he said trying to prevent Sylvia force feeding her husband warm milk.

'He'll need that later. What he really needs now is sleep'.

Edwin heard nothing of this. Edwin was not there. Edwin was somewhere safe. Edwin was, at last, in a hiding place.

For now.

9

Edwin remembered the days that followed whatever it was that had happened on that Monday morning as some of the most peaceful he had ever known. It was if he had suddenly been freed from a terrible burden. He recalled that one morning as he lay in bed, long after Megan had gone to school and Sylvia to whatever event the Church was providing that day, he suddenly noticed the sunlight playing on the remaining leaves on a tree in the garden. And he noticed that he noticed.

And it struck him that it had been such a long time since he had done that, such a long time since he had taken the time to stop and look, such a long time since had taken the time to stop, such a long time since he had taken the time.

One of the joys of those days was reading *A Village Affair* by Joanna Trollope. Pippa called to see him and he had asked to borrow her copy. He had seen her reading it earlier in the summer. It struck him that other than Enid Blyton and Agatha Christie it was the first book by a woman writer of the twentieth century that he had read. He found himself powerfully moved by the story and noted with some surprise that it was set in a nearby village. After years of the sort of books he had been reading (and writing) this was joy upon joy – a book about real people and real feelings, and he knew instinctively that a man could not have written it. He went to read others by her and other women. How, he found himself wondering as he read, did they know all this about human beings, about how they really operate? How had they found such things out? How were they so open and tolerant of it all? And more, importantly, why had he missed out on all this until now? Well, perhaps now he could learn to live differently himself.

In the first two sessions after the happening' (and neither wanted to give it any other title) Libby noticed a lightness bordering on light-headedness in Edwin that had been hitherto noticeably lacking. He put this down to "having solved all my problems". She allowed that to pass. In part he was benefiting from what Dr Nuffield had described as "state of the art" sleeping tablets; in part it was clear to her that his brain was still in self-protect mode and not allowing his conscious mind access to the pain that had produced such an effect as he had simply made his way into work.

'What arrangements have you made with regard to your work?', enquired Libby, somewhat disingenuously given that she had herself encouraged Colin Nuffield to sign him off for a good long period.

'The doctor has given me a sick note for a month. "Nervous exhaustion" he wrote on it. Is that what you would call it?', he asked, suddenly turning to cast a glance at Libby.

'I rather suspect the important thing, Edwin, is how you can make sense of this for yourself. That's much more important than what Dr Nuffield or I think of it'.

'Well it was such a relief on when I saw him in the surgery that it was dark – we could only get an appointment late in the day – I couldn't face the possibility of being recognised by anyone, or seeing anyone I knew. And I keep thinking, ludicrous I know, that I never want to go back to work again. So I guess something must still not be quite right. I mean they are hardly my normal ways of being. So I suppose he had to write something on the certificate and I guess that's the formula in such circumstances'.

'Edwin, there are a number of important things you have just said that we ought to give some thought to,' said Libby. 'I'm not sure whether worrying about the wording of a sick note should be one of them. Whatever words the doctor uses the important thing is that they are going to keep you out of work for a while. Much more important are your fears or anxieties about being seen, and of course your feelings about your work'.

'Oh I wouldn't describe them as fears', Edwin immediately retorted, 'it's just that I did not want to have to give some sort of account to anyone I met as to how I am. I mean, for Christ's sake Libby, how am I? I don't know and what could I say?'.

She allowed him to continue.

'You should have seen Tony Whitmore's face when I fell in his doorway. He was shocked of course, but I am sure that more than anything else he was completely embarrassed. Now it will have done the rounds and everyone will know. I suspect there will be quite a few solicitors in town desperate not to see me. I've let the side down'.

'That sounds somewhat harsh. Surely solicitors are human too and subject to the normal vicissitudes of existence'.

'Of course. They can get drunk and have affairs - many do, the latter often a consequence of the former, I might add. But that's alright - almost expected in some chambers. However certain things are not acceptable. One is a hand in the till. That's absolute. The other is to do with mental stability'.

'Is that what you think has happened to you Edwin? That you're now mentally unstable?'.

'It's what they will think. After all the story will have grown in the telling and accounts of my performance last week at the partners' meeting will have been recounted. Most of them will picture me in a straitjacket already, I expect'.

Libby welcomed this expression of feeling not because she thought for one moment that Edwin was actually concerned about his peers' judgement but because of what his words expressed about his own judgement of himself: was he mad? was he mentally ill? Perhaps the time had come for an expression of honesty from her.

'I think I should have told you before, and I apologise for not doing so though there did not seem any pressing need until now, that on Monday afternoon I met briefly with Dr Nuffield, and together we spoke on the telephone to Dr Gordon. I was able to say to Dr Nuffield that in my opinion what had happened to you in the morning was not a psychiatric event per se, and that in consequence I did not believe you needed or would benefit from a psychiatric assessment. When we telephoned Dr Gordon and described what had happened, she accepted my opinion and suggested that Dr Nuffield continue to monitor your progress but not interfere in our work. That relieved Dr Nuffield of his immediate responsibility for you. You were by now his patient. It also did not place obstacles in the work we are doing'.

Edwin considered her words.

'Thank you', he replied. 'You have helped me greatly by saying that. Yes. I was anxious about what had happened, that in some way I was, am, cracking up. It had occurred to me to wonder what might have ensued had I actually gone to that police car in the square'.

'I'm confident that you can rest assured that you're not suffering from a psychiatric illness, but I do think we need to give thought to trying to understand what has happened. And yes, you are going to have to get used to people feeling uneasy around you. Its quite scary what has happened to you because people think it might happen to them too. It's not unlike bereavement. It touches people in a vulnerable place. And that isn't going to be easy for you. That's why, well it's one of the reasons why it is important for you to have time well away from work, so that you don't have to waste energy worrying about how people are reacting to you'.

'I don't want to be there anyway', said Edwin with determination in his voice. 'Do you know, there's been a recurring fantasy in my mind in the past twenty-four hours. It's about going into the room where all our casebooks and textbooks and journals are stored – it's a kind of mini-library – it's about going in there and pulling every book off the shelves and leaving them in a huge pile on the floor'.

'That sounds a pretty violent fantasy'.

'Not violence towards people you understand, except, well, I suppose it would be to whoever had to clear up the mess afterwards, but you don't think about that logically. It's just a powerful feeling of some sort or other'.

As Edwin made his way home the commercial world was beginning its morning opening, part of the frenetic rush in the weeks before Christmas. Shop windows were full of tinsel and lights. As Edwin looked at people on their way to work or the shops, he wondered what their lives held.

Some faces seemed pained, indeed at that time in the morning there was little joy, even of the festive kind, about. What sort of lives did they live? What dramas made up their days? With the imagination of a writer perhaps he could look and visualise their homes and work and anxieties and joys. What might Joanna Trollope make of them? But then what would Joanna Trollope make of him? Probably very little, for however much he was enjoying and being truly moved by her writing he couldn't entirely escape the sense that her female characters were much more real than the men, who often seemed quite wooden. Or was it that she was in fact quite accurate: that men really were more wooden than women? After all, as he was becoming aware day by day, he had only to consider how out of touch with his own feelings he had become to realise how wooden he had become. And when he thought of the nature of his friendships with men he was struck by how often it was that men dealt in superficialities, especially of the cerebral kind. No doubt it was safer though, as he knew, all too often, especially in the academic world, those apparent wholly cerebral exchanges concealed murderous intentions and jealousies. And the thought struck him that perhaps in some way he was a kind of living dead person, that certain of his vital functions continued but that others, most notably those concerned with feeling, were hardly in use at all. Perhaps that was how he had succeeded for so long in avoiding some of the pain of the past. Was that why he worked as he did? But if so, what did that mean for the future? What future?

At home Sylvia too needed her defences. She was puzzled and troubled by what had happened and was happening to Edwin. She was troubled too about how those with whom she worked, at her church, were taking it. She, and they, felt it had everything to do with his rejection, or at least non-acceptance, of Christ. If only he would become a Christian, then he would discover so much. It would also make her life easier. Circumstances hardly made her the best advert for all she proclaimed and sought to live. If you can't convert your husband, should you really be leading a mission to convert others? she wondered, and so, increasingly did some others, not least those she knew what to do it instead. Of course, she was also receiving a considerable degree of support and love from the Church and without that she didn't know how she could have continued. She knew that many people were praying for her and that was wonderful, but she also didn't like it, she didn't like being in that position and, if she were honest, she kind of felt extremely angry with Edwin for putting her into it. Above all she reserved her violent hatred for this woman whom he went to see. Sylvia was quite convinced that she was the source of the problem.

When she had talked it over with the pastor he agreed. They both felt that Edwin would be much better off seeking help from a

Christian counsellor, and he had furnished her with a couple of names she might be able to persuade Edwin to consider.

Although initially Betty and Paul Raven had been kind to her, she also felt a distinct distancing on their part which she found unsettling, especially as they were members of the same Church. And although she hadn't commented on it to Edwin, she had been disappointed for him that no one from work other than his secretary had been to see him or even telephoned. She felt he ought to be back at work as soon as possible. It was not him at all sitting around and reading rubbishy novels and going out for walks in the dark. It was also difficult for her to have the groups round with him there. She was so conscious of his presence. She had been aghast when he had told her the doctor had signed him off for a month "at least". Surely he would be better off active, the devil making work for idle hands (and the hands she had in mind were of the woman possessed of evil thoughts that had so influenced Edwin).

Edwin was dreading Christmas. Apart from the intensity of religion oozing out of Sylvia in its approach and the schmaltz of life in the city, he knew that Libby was having a break of a fortnight, and he began to be anxious as to how he would survive it. The initial sense of release was beginning to give way to anxiety and unease. He had also noticed that he was becoming quite neurotic about not being seen as he made his way to and from her house, and that he was now only going out for walks in the darkness that mercifully fell earlier each afternoon.. Then, bizarrely, one morning on his way back home he had gone into a post office to get some stamps for the Christmas cards (he had taken on their writing) when he noticed through the window one of his colleagues advancing towards the shop. Immediately he threw himself to the ground and rolled under the window. The people in the shop looked round in amazement. One wondered whether he had been taken ill and rushed towards him. He had simply looked at her in horror, risen and fled.

In therapy too, the ease of the immediate aftermath had given way to struggle. Libby noticed that for the first time in their months together Edwin was speaking less. Silences were becoming longer. He seemed more withdrawn. She was not at all surprised. Indeed she had anticipated a change when the mind began to allow some of the pain to re-emerge. She also wondered about how Edwin would cope with the forthcoming break. And she wondered whether he wondered about this. She had determined to raise it, however obliquely, at the next session, but the sight of Edwin at her front door when she opened it made her realise that something had happened, something important, something pressing.

'I had a terrible dream last night,' Edwin began even as he was taking his place on the chaise. 'This morning it must have been. It woke me at about 2-30 and I haven't been back to sleep since. It was horrible, horrible'.

Libby knew she need say nothing.

'It was unlike anything I've ever dreamed before', he continued, barely pausing to take breath, 'because I was two people in the same dream. Or at least I was me but I was in the dream as me twice over. That is I was a small child me and also me now'.

Libby shifted slightly in her seat sensing that a vital moment had possibly arrived.

'I was standing by the window looking at the bed – this was in a house we used to live in when I was young – and on the bed my mother was lying totally naked (and I immediately felt really sick as I saw her there, it was just like it was last Christmas, I was repulsed by her) but I was also there as a the little child (I don't know, perhaps 18 months old) also naked lying on top of her as if playing.

She was holding me/him and they/we were laughing as if in play. And then... '. He stopped, finding himself having to fight back the feelings of revulsion again.

'And then?' prompted Libby gently, as if trying to establish a sense of something objective, here and now, outside the dream.

'And then it was different'. Edwin suddenly spoke in a cold, slow way. 'Then she was rubbing me/him against herself, and I could see from her face that she was becoming aroused, and so was I'.

As Edwin spoke the final words he suddenly burst into hysterical tears.

'And when I woke up', he said, slightly gulping for air, 'I was aroused then too. And it's horrible and I think I should die. God, I hate myself, I'm so vile. I just want to be dead'.

It is a first rule of the sort of psychotherapy practised by Libby that there should be no physical contact between therapist and client, and in the present context that rule was absolutely necessary – heaven only knows, thought Libby, what would happen if I was to touch him now – but it took a monumental effort on her part to remain in her seat. She had hardly ever seen anyone so distressed. She was profoundly distressed herself and her eyes were welling up with tears. But she had a job to do and never more so than now.

'That sounds absolutely terrible, Edwin. I'm so sorry that you've had to experience that'.

She was appalled by how trite her words sounded but what else was she to say?

The tears continued to course down Edwin's cheeks though he was quieter now. And if Libby had been asked directly some weeks or even months ago what all this with Edwin was about she would probably have said that one day something was going to emerge, and the something she might have described would have been akin to what in fact had now surfaced. But she had been scrupulous never even to hint at this to Edwin. She knew full well that claims were sometimes made that therapists were responsible for introducing ideas of sexual abuse into the minds of clients. Even now she was uncertain what she was dealing with. Edwin was presenting a dream. But what was it? Was it possibly a memory, or was it a fantasy, a wish. It was vital for her to continue to remember that the material with which they were working was the product of Edwin's mind. Whether there were or had been corresponding experiences back then in the physical world was a question that could not and perhaps never would be answered. The present reality, however, was before her in her client.

In mythological terms she knew full well that Edwin had a hidden monster to be faced. As in the old story of Theseus, he had to enter into the labyrinth and seek out, face up to and overcome the minotaur – half-human, half-bull, which held everyone in terrible thrall. Her own part was to be like Ariadne, providing little more than a ball of wool which he could slowly unwind as he entered into the twisting darkness, and which could, were he to prove victorious, use to find his way out again. Would she be up to it? Would Edwin?

'What I think most interesting in your dream', she said eventually when he seemed to have calmed down a little, 'is the fact of there being two of you. You were observer and participant. You were child and adult. We might even want to think of it in terms of then and now, both happening simultaneously. Dreams do that. Time is not quite so linear'.

'Yes, but what disgusts me is that the adult/observer me woke up aroused. The baby was being abused but the adult seemed to be a voyeur'.

'Yes, let's think about the baby,' replied Libby, endeavouring to shift him, for the time being, away from his sense of self-loathing. 'What you described, which may or may not have happened as you saw it – remember that dreams seem to manufacture all sorts of things and most of the time we don't assume that the things happening in them ever happened in what we call the real world.'

'True,' he acknowledged.

'Well, what you recounted was something being done to a baby by an adult. Something which most of us would feel instinctively was wrong. Something which you have come across time and again in the course of your work'.

'Oh yes'.

'You know, and I suspect you knew in the dream, that what you were witnessing was wrong, that a profound assault was being made upon the person of that little boy, that it was not something that he would forget and be of no account in later years, but something which we both know can exert a profound effect upon a person's life. And we both also know that many of those who were abused or claim they were abused in their early years feel guilty about what happened to them even though no guilt whatsoever can be laid at their door. It was like you discovering your mother with her man friend. You felt the guilt of her act, and wholly inappropriately.'

'Yes'.

He was listening intently and she knew it, and was determined that whilst she needed to say these things it was also vital for them to remain with the painful feelings of the dream and not hide away in their heads. She needed to stop speaking but must finish what she had to say first.

'Well, all I'm saying is that regardless of the feelings that might have been engendered in the adult of the dream, you can recognise that the child was wholly free of guilt, wholly free of blame. If what you described had happened, and we do not know that it did or did not, at least you can keep telling yourself that the child Edwin was not responsible or guilty in any way at all'.

Edwin nodded without speaking. The silence lasted a while. Eventually he broke it, removing his glasses and rubbing his eyes as he spoke.

'I'm so tired. I just want to sleep, sleep and not wake up, and sleep and not dream either'.

'It's an important practical matter, Edwin. Did Dr Nuffield not give you some tablets to help you sleep?'.

'Yes, but only a few and I've used them up. Anyway I don't want to become dependent on sleeping tablets. That's not much use'.

His head had rolled forward as he lay there and he ran his hand over and over his forehead.

He looked as agitated as he was feeling.

'I mean I'm not doing anything to tire me out. I just don't feel much like walking outside, besides which it's so unpleasant and cold at the moment, and all I do is sit and read and feel sorry for myself and worry about what the hell is happening and how I am ever to go back to work and about how much I never want to go back to it and about what the future holds. And then, when Sylvia and Megan come in, I just try and concentrate my energies on being normal. Sylvia says I've got to try and remain as normal as I can for Megan's sake. And she's right of course'.

'Megan presumably knows that you are off sick and however much you try she is bound to be seeing something somewhat radically different in your ways of being'.

'Yes, but Sylvia insists that we've got to try and keep any emotional stuff hidden away. And she's right - it isn't fair on Megan'.

'And that no doubt suits Sylvia too?' It was a question, and he ignored it.

The session was drawing towards a close and Libby knew that she still had not broached the issue of how Edwin was feeling about the forthcoming break.

'I know that you are feeling pretty ghastly as a result of the dream, Edwin, and I am sure that your response to it has been exactly as it would be in anyone, but I want also to say that I feel it is an important staging post on the pathway to your health and well-being. I'm not saying this just to make you feel better. I believe it. And whilst there are hard things to come, and having a break over Christmas might be one of them, I know from my experience that there are signs of life here. It may feel much like a bulb immersed in the in total darkness of the earth but I think we are seeing some shoots emerging which suggest the possibility of new growth and new life'.

And as she spoke Libby wondered whether Edwin was any more convinced by her words than she was.

10

Edwin made his way home slowly. He felt as exhausted as he sometimes did after a long day in and out of court, in and out of meetings. Yet it was not yet nine o'clock in the morning. He used the back streets as far as possible – something of a circuitous route – to avoid seeing or being seen. He hoped that Sylvia would be gone when he arrived home. The day was dark. December. He remembered some words from a story he used to read to Megan when she was small: "always winter but never Christmas". Yet this year he felt that Christmas too was part of the darkness, nothing more than an illusion in which we invest so much because we know deep down it is a chimera, even if we desperately hope it isn't. It had become like a fake picture: the more you paid for it the more you had to believe it was real. But he knew it was unreal. He had no doubts about it.

Sylvia was still there when he arrived home, busying herself with preparations for a carol service for young mums and toddlers. He longed for her not to say anything or ask about his session.

'How was it this morning?'.

Edwin guessed that the question was not one inviting a serious reply, much like "how are you?" on meeting someone – the last thing you want, or expect, is an honest reply.

'Alright. What time's your thing this morning?' It didn't work.

'How much is this costing us, Edwin?'

'What, therapy you mean?'

'Therapy, being off work, doing nothing. How much is this costing?'

'You know that being off sick costs us nothing at all – I get paid in full'.

'Yes, but how long can that go on? And how long are you going to be seeing this woman? If you don't mind my saying so, it doesn't actually look particularly therapeutic. If anything you're looking even worse than you were before you started. Don't you think you'd be better off going back to work? At least your mind would have something to occupy itself and your sense of self esteem would be higher than it obviously is. And maybe you should consider another therapist. I know of one in Southampton who's done some wonderful things with people. You would probably only need to see him a few times at most'.

He didn't need this.

'I'm really sorry Sylvia. You don't need this, I know. I just have to work my way through it'.

'Yes, but are you?'

He detected a note of anger in her voice.

'Are you working through it, or are you not just wandering round in a sort of maze, getting nowhere? You may not have a great deal of time for what I do, Edwin, but I can tell you this for absolutely certain, we have people in far worse states than you whose lives are transformed by God. People with cancer healed, drug addicts cured – all sorts of things. Why won't you realise that you could be better?'

She had drawn near to him and taken hold of his hand, pleading, beseeching.

Edwin did not know what to say or do. He wanted to yell at her that if it was true that her God could do those things she claimed, and he doubted that completely, why couldn't such things happen all the time and on a larger scale? Why didn't God intervene when children were dying of cancer or being abused or gassed in concentration camps or burnt to death in house fires? Instead he shrugged and attempted a smile.

'I'm sorry', he said and sighed.

After Sylvia had gone, Edwin sat in the small bedroom which they had converted into a study and gazed at his books and computer. His mind was a blank for much of the morning and he just gazed and gazed, mostly at nothing at all. It was most odd. He was so tired – he had not gone back to sleep after the dream.

He did nothing and barely noticed the fact. He could see papers and letters and journals, and his own writings, the things which had sustained him for years, the things which had given life meaning and into which he had poured all his energies and commitment, the things which had always given him a buzz. Now as he looked at them he saw nothing but pieces of paper.

He could not get away from the feelings engendered within him by his dream. Even if he was not thinking consciously about it, and indeed for the most of the morning he could not honestly have admitted to being aware of thinking about anything, nevertheless he continued to feel the dream. He felt sick with self-disgust, however much Libby had sought to reassure him. What if, he thought with a mounting sense of horror, his dream had been a memory of something that had happened? As a former student of classics he knew Sophocles's myth of Oedipus and whilst his own circumstances were quite different, at the back of his mind there was a profound unease as he recalled the consequences of that ancient story which threatened to be a terrible part of his present.

For her part Libby would have welcomed the apparent shut-down of Edwin's mind as he lived with the aftereffects of his dream, whatever its origins. She knew she had to be sceptical about any sort of interpretation Edwin gave to the dream. What was real however, and of immediate concern to her, was the effects of the dream upon Edwin. She found herself wishing that she was not having a break from supervision in the Christmas season.

She too found herself reflecting upon the Oedipus story. She recalled a lecture she had attended in London. It had been given by an American from Harvard, a classicist, who from the beginning made it clear how much he resented what Freud had done to the story. It was not, he maintained, so much a story about incest and patricide, but about freedom. Oedipus had the choice: did he discover the truth about himself or not? Against the advice and appeals of others he presses on, a quest for the whole truth and nothing but the truth (Libby recalled these precise words in the lecture and how appropriate in the case of Edwin, she reflected). That he discovers tragic, even terrible, things is far less important, so the Professor had maintained, than that he marshals together the courage, intelligence and perseverance needed to pursue the truth. "That is what makes human beings great" – the very words with which he had concluded his lecture.

After supper he set out and walked a circular route across the water meadows and back through the Close, beneath the great cathedral. One evening he was aware of voices as he walked over the small park by the bridge over the river, one of which he recognised as belonging to one of his colleagues. He hid behind a tree. Heaven knows what they would have thought if they had seen the figure, hood pulled over his head concealing himself in the shrubbery.

He had lost his appetite and was aware that he was avoiding the bathroom scales. At mealtimes he played with his food and sought to concentrate instead on asking the others questions about their day. Sometimes in an attempt to be normal his behaviour was so wholly abnormal as to increase their anxiety about him. To some extent Megan took it in her stride. It was the run-up to Christmas and she was busy in and out of school. Sylvia, however, was deeply troubled and unsure how to express or attend to it. She had spoken with the pastor but she felt something of a failure and did not like to show that in the context of her position in the life of the Church. Anxiety betokened lack of faith but "taking no heed for the morrow" was not easy. She also felt guilty about feeling so angry with Edwin. All she could so was hope that doctor would encourage Edwin to go back to work as soon as possible and allow normality to creep back into their lives.

When Edwin arrived for his next session Libby noticed at once how ghastly he looked. He had bags under his eyes from an obvious lack of sleep, he was unshaven, and his clothes looked almost as if he had slept in them. He went up to the room and lay on the chaise and she took her place behind him to his right. Normally this would be the cue for him to begin speaking. This morning he said nothing, just continued gazing into space. It took all her skills and self-discipline not to break the silence but felt it essential that she did not do so.

The minutes went by. At one point she quietly leant forward just to reassure herself that he had not fallen asleep. No, his eyes were fully open. There were, she knew, different sorts of silence, but this was quite frightening to endure, akin perhaps to the silence surrounding someone working on an unexploded bomb.

As the 50 minutes ticked by and the end drew nearer Libby finally decided that she had to say something.

'Edwin, I rather think the time has come to consider the possibility that you may need some assistance to help you cope with what it is that you are currently experiencing'.

Silence.

'What I mean is', she said, finding herself forced to continue, 'I think it might be helpful for you to go and see Dr Nuffield and discuss the advantages there might be for you in certain types of medication'.

'Anti-depressants you mean?', he said wearily.

'Possibly. But something to help you with your sleeping patterns. It's difficult for us to make the most of our time together if you are so utterly weary that you have nothing to bring, nothing for us to work on. And I suspect that if this is how you are here it may be that you could benefit from help for how you are at home. Plus, as I'm sure you are aware, we are due to have a break after next week and you may be wondering how you are going to get through that.

'Medication is only medication, but it can help provide some support. It's like having a back-up battery in an alarm clock, for use when there's a power cut. Well, you're having a period of current alternation and it just might help you. It does so for quite a lot of people'.

It was unlike her to be so directive in her words but she was truly anxious about how Edwin was going to fare in the days to follow. He seemed to detect this note and it served to make him think that perhaps he should take notice of it. He said he would make an appointment to see the doctor after he got home this morning.

As he left, Libby thought that he looked almost drugged already. In the ancient myth Oedipus, having unknowingly murdered his father and married his mother, blinds himself and lives out his days as an outcast. In a way Edwin could no longer see outside himself and was evidently concealing himself successfully from others. If, however, he was to follow the ancient hero on his journey with the truth about himself he would need help just at the time when she was about to withdraw it, if only for a little while.

She decided to telephone Colin Nuffield herself before the arrival of her next client. The receptionist told her that he was with a patient.

'This is urgent – put me through please, now'. It was not just the stentorian tone of the command that made the receptionist obey. Dr Nuffield had once told her that if ever Mrs Francis called, she was to be allowed to speak to him whatever the circumstances though that had been in the days when he needed her for his own survival.

'Libby', he said warmly, 'how lovely to hear from you'.

'Colin, it's about Edwin Lyons. I've suggested he make an appointment to see you. He needs medication – a matter of some urgency I would think. He said he would call to make an appointment. Is it possible to ensure he gets a swift appointment? I'm sorry to be pushy but we have a break coming up and I am genuinely concerned for him'.

'Oh, I'd be very surprised if you are sorry to be pushy', he laughed gently into the telephone, 'and I know about breaks. Leave it with me'.

As soon as he had finished with his patient, he called the receptionist and told her that if a Mr Lyons rang for an appointment he was to be fitted in this morning no matter how much of a nuisance that was.

Mr Lyons did not call. Dr Nuffield therefore decided that he would have to do a home visit. At the end of surgery he gathered together his list, patient's notes, case and flask of tea and set off to his car. He was still very self-conscious of the disabled sticker on his car and wondered what it did for the confidence of those he visited. Ah well, it was better than being dead.

Edwin opened the door.

'Dr Nuffield, hello. Come in'.

Colin Nuffield could not but notice the state of the man before him and the contrast with the patient he had first encountered some weeks earlier. Libby had been right to notify him.

'I suppose Libby told you to come'. It was not an accusation, but Colin felt duty-bound to protect his own former therapist's reputation.

'No, she didn't,' he replied truthfully. 'But when you began therapy, I expect she asked your permission to contact your GP if necessary?' He wasn't expecting an answer. 'All she did this morning was to telephone and ask that if you called for an appointment could I make sure it was soon. She said nothing more than. When you had not called by the time I left the surgery I decided that I should perhaps take the initiative and check up on my patient. And I think it's probably a good idea that I did'. He paused and smiled. 'You're not looking too brilliant'.

'Libby said she thought I might need some sort of anti-depressant. To be honest I feel so ashamed about it that I just couldn't call the surgery.'

'What do you think?'

'I suppose she's probably right. Perhaps not knowing you need them is a sign that you do. I don't know. To be honest I'm past caring'.

'Are you sleeping?'.

'Fits and starts. I still get to sleep but I'm waking most mornings at about 2 and I struggle to get back to sleep. My mind races and yet I have no idea what, if anything, I'm thinking about'.

'Do you sleep in the day?'.

'No'.

'Appetite?'.

'Can't be bothered really.'

'What about exercise? Do you get out?'

'I walk to Libby's and back. Otherwise, I only go out in the dark, I just don't want anyone to see me'.

'And what about your therapy? How's it going?'.

'To be honest it feels like I've fallen into a deep pit and I have no idea how to get out. I'm not sure how I could manage without Libby and yet I know I've got to. She stops work for Christmas and I'm dreading that'.

Colin sat quietly for a while.

'I think anti-depressants could help you, Edwin. What I have in mind would certainly help immediately with your sleeping. They're not sleeping tablets, but they do contain a sedative which will give you more sleep than you're getting now. That will make an immediate improvement. Unfortunately, their anti-depressant effect has to build up and really it takes about three weeks for you to feel the benefit of that. All the same I do think you might well discover they can give you a little bit more of yourself back. They don't work miracles I'm afraid, but they might just help you in difficult and dark times.'

Edwin held his hand under his head as if it would fall off without proper support. There was a brief and barely perceptible nod.

'I also think Edwin, and here you have to take your doctor's word for it, that you need to have a further period of time not just off work but without having to be thinking about when you ought to be going back. I shall give you a prescription for some tablets. In the first week just take one tablet about two hours before you go to bed, and then in the second week increase the dose to two. They're non-addictive and I want you to stay on them for at least six months.'

'Six months? You're kidding, aren't you?'.

'I'm told you are a very good lawyer, Edwin, but as far as I know the study of pharmacology is not one of your skills. Six months – minimum. They have a job to do, and they can do it, provided you let them do it properly'.

Edwin was in no state to argue.

'I am also writing for you a sick note for a further period of twelve weeks. I know that sounds a long time but it isn't and I think you are going to need that time – for you'.

Before he left, the doctor arranged for Edwin to come and see him each week in the period when Libby was not working.

'Thank you so much' said Edwin to the doctor as he opened the front door for him. 'I feel so guilty about this'.

'Yes, I know', came the reply. 'Been there. Survived too. So will you. See you next Tuesday'.

Edwin decided to walk to a chemist shop he had seen on the other side of town. He didn't want to go into the local shop. They knew him there – he had represented the pharmacist in a case of some kind – and he felt so ashamed going to collect his tablets. When he arrived at the shop, he kept his face well down and the collar of his coat well up as he handed over the prescription together with the money. He had wished the assistant had not had to call his name out aloud when she brought the tablets but at least only she and the pharmacist (and perhaps only him) knew what the matter with him was. He took the bag and fled. Now he had to face Sylvia.

'Where've you been?' she asked when he arrived back.

'To the chemists'.

'The chemists? I didn't see you when I passed. Anyway, why did you go to the chemists?'.

'I went for a walk and just called in on one I was passing'.

'What for?'

'Dr Nuffield called round and he's given me a prescription for some tablets to help me. sleep'.

'Sleeping tablets?' – she'd been very uneasy about him taking the original ones.

'Er, well, no they're more of a sedative'. He was trying to busy himself and wanting to change the subject. 'How was, er, whatever you were doing this morning?'

'Edwin, tablets are an answer to nothing, surely you realise that. You can't live on tablets. You just need to get back to work and get shaved and properly dressed. You'd soon start to feel better about yourself again, and so would we'.

Oh hell, hell, hell, thought Edwin, shit and hell. He sat down on the bench by the kitchen table.

'I'm afraid I'm not going to be going back to work for some time.

The doctor's signed me off for another three months.'

'What?' He felt sure they must have heard it next door. 'Three months? You're joking, aren't you?'

He felt battered by her.

'Look, shout if you must. But it doesn't change how things are. I've been told that I am suffering from depression. I have been prescribed anti-depressants which contain a sedative to help me sleep and quite frankly at the moment I would like to sleep and sleep and never wake up'.

He had risen as he spoke, and on completion walked out of the kitchen and into the sitting room where with a deep sigh he allowed himself to fall into an armchair. When Sylvia followed him, she could see tears on his cheeks.

'What's gone wrong with us Edwin? Why is this happening?'.

What could he possibly say in reply? How could he even begin to explain and recount what he was facing?

'Nothing's gone wrong with us. It's not us at all; it's me. It's me that's gone wrong. I'm the cause of all this and I wish I were not'.

Tears were pouring down his cheeks and Sylvia had come and perched herself on the wing of the armchair.

'I just wish I could spare you and Megan this', he continued. 'I didn't know what I was likely to get into when I started all this. All I can say is that I still believe I have to see it through and that I need the time and space to do so'.

The tears broke through whatever barrier Sylvia had in place and she took hold of her husband's hand. She had never seen him like this before. He looked terrible: unshaven, dishevelled, sunk in misery. She could not stop herself thinking about the man in the gospel who outwardly had everything but who, when the moment of truth came, discovered that he had nothing at all. It was hard not to recognise Edwin in him, the Edwin who was so good at all he did, the achiever, the writer, the brilliant lawyer – but what good did it do him now? And in that moment, as she held his hand, she prayed for Edwin and his salvation and thanked God for the opportunity she now had.

And he was thinking that for the first time in ages she was showing him some loving care. Not loving but praying.

11

When Edwin arrived for his next session with Libby it was clear to him at least, that the sedative effect of his new tablets had not yet worn off. It had been hard coming to when the radio alarm came on and his mouth was unbelievably dry. He had slept however, though the kind of heavy sleep which leaves you almost more tired when you wake up than you were before falling asleep. At least it meant no dreams and that was a blessing. No wonder, Edwin had thought at sometime in the past twenty-four hours, Hamlet feared sleep for the danger of dreaming. But had it been a dream? That was the question.

'I'm afraid I'm a bit dopey this morning Libby', Edwin said as he lay down. 'It's the effect of the tablets Dr Nuffield gave me'.

'Have they made a difference?'.

'Well to my sleeping yes, though he told me they didn't work on the other thing until three weeks had gone by'.

'You've been sleeping?'.

'Oh yes, have I not? I could barely wake up yesterday morning and it was a real struggle to get out of bed this morning'. He yawned the sort of yawn that almost threatens to suck in a fair amount of the room's furniture with it. Libby seemed not to mind.

'Well you needed some sleep. You've been through a great deal and turning completely off even for some of the time must have helped a great deal'.

It was a statement masquerading as a question - therapist's gambit. Edwin was capable of little in the way of defence.

'Yes, but now I keep falling asleep even in the day time and I am beginning to lose my sense of what and when, and I can't afford to do that. Megan breaks up this week and next week is Christmas. I haven't bought a present or even a card for Sylvia yet. So what will happen when I double the dose next week?'.

'It's amazing how our bodies can adapt to medication and its effects. Do you take your tablets at night-time?'.

'Mm'.

'Well try and take them earlier in the evening and go to bed earlier. You'd got into a pattern of going very late to bed. It might be better for you to sleep earlier and feel more alert in the morning. I don't know, but it's worth a try'.

Libby was not wholly sure that Edwin was still awake. She coughed and saw that it had roused him a little.

'You haven't spoken about what sort of contact you've been having with your mother during this past year, Edwin. I wondered whether she would have been expecting you all to go to France for Christmas again'.

The subject matter seemed to stimulate him.

'No, last Christmas was a one-off. In fact over the years, I've had very little contact with her. She telephones about once a month or so. Sylvia tells me that when I'm on the phone to her I become a different person'.

'What does she mean by that?'

'I tend to freeze up, let her do all the talking – she's very accomplished at that – and reply monosyllabically. It reminds me that when Sylvia and I first met she brushed something off my shoulder and I visibly froze. I just couldn't stand being touched by her in that sort of way, not in public'.

'I'm not sure I understand why the public nature of that should so affect you'.

'No, well, when I was young my mother was always putting on a good show in public. The only times I can ever recall affection from her were in public, when others were there to see. Then she could be sickly warm and touch my hair or run her hand across my shoulders. Not only did it make me want to be sick – and I can recall a real feeling of nausea – but what I always found so disconcerting was that once we were alone again, afterwards, the warmth disappeared. I used to dread being alone with her after others had gone. She would start slagging them off when moments earlier she'd been all over them, or even worse would start criticising me. I used to feel so confused by the contrast, especially when I was very small, though she still went on doing that all through my teens'.

'I should think that was so difficult to live with'.

'God, I hated it, hated her. I was made to feel as if I was an exhibit and anything I achieved was really there for her reflected glory. I never told you but when I got my finals' results – they were telephoned through because I had done so well – her response, and I can picture it now, she was in the kitchen and I walked through to tell her, was to say, "Aren't you pleased for all we did for you?". She never once ever said "well done" or congratulated me though that evening she was on the 'phone to all her friends boasting as if it had been her and she was determined to get the best seats for the graduation ceremony. The fact is that I don't think she would have been able to spell "classics" let alone know anything about it'.

'That must have been very distressing for you'.

'I'd learned to handle my distress and let it pass'.

'Yes, but at quite a heavy cost Edwin. Isn't that you've been discovering in the past twelve months, and rather painfully in the past month? What Sylvia describes about the you who speaks on the telephone to her, your reaction to a harmless and caring touch on the shoulder to brush off a speck of dust, the way you have been handling your feelings for years, they're all indicative of the way in which you have been doing considerable harm to yourself when some might argue that the person you should have been doing harm to is your mother'.

'I couldn't do harm to her. She's so pathetic. I mean it's such a tragedy for her that her life has been as it is - what she's done and what's like - what kind of living is that? It must be terrible'.

'Yes, and it's extraordinary when I reflect upon it - and you may not agree with my observation - that quite a lot of your working life has been spent and still is, defending people who have behaved as some might say your mother did with regard to you. Do you remember the young girl earlier in the year who murdered her baby? I don't understand it but I am certain there is a link between your own experience of a mother whose behaviour was considerably less than adequate and your need to put yourself out in the way you do to defend those like her'.

If Libby had hoped that her words might be a source of comfort to Edwin, a way of helping him feel better about himself, of helping him understand himself more and accept it, she was mistaken.

'People don't always know why they do things. It must be terrible to damage your own child. They need love and support especially the kind of detached concern and care I can bring. Getting the passion out of the situation, and it is not easy with the police and in prison, is so important. The law is the only way it can be done'.

'Do you remember telling me about the time you came across your mother with another man and how you were made to bear the guilt inflicted by her, though she was the one who committed the offence, as it were, and then asked you to collude with her in her defence when your father came home? Well, what sort of justice was that?'.

'I couldn't do anything. Who would have believed me? And in any case, suppose it had broken up my parents' marriage? Added to which I had to live with her. There were going to be many other times when my dad was away and I had to survive them. The thought of not agreeing with her and then having to be alone with her later was too awful to contemplate. But I guess that what you're pointing out is my cowardice, my failure to do what was right'.

'Oh Edwin I would not suggest anything like that at all. Quite the opposite. Indeed I'm somewhat in awe of the way in which you have handled all this for so long. I honestly think many if not most others in a similar situation would not have managed to deal with this as you have'.

Edwin remained silent. Libby too paused a while before continuing.

'Some schools of therapy don't describe the sort of thing that has happened to you as a breakdown', she began (the word was spoken for the first time), but as a breakthrough. It's a little akin to knocking down a wall in a house only to find on the other side a hidden room. There's lots of chaos and dirt to be cleared away when you first get going and much remains to be done to make the new room habitable and hospitable but essentially it's a move towards something new. Perhaps you can begin to think of what's been happening to you in the past year, last Christmas just as much as our work together, as being like that, the opening up of something new, bringing fresh air into what had been lost and sealed away. But the most important thing of all is that you've done this. This is your achievement, not hers, and certainly not mine'.

'It doesn't feel much like of an achievement, if you don't mind my saying so. In fact it feels like a disaster. Maybe you feel better for telling me how good it is, but it doesn't do much for me. 'You see', he continued, 'whilst you go on with your theories and your attempts to encourage me, what I have to live with is not only the knowledge of what happened to me at some stage in my life and I don't know whether my dream was just the tip of the iceberg or not, but also the profound sense of self-disgust I feel about my reaction to the dream. Also the disgust of what I have been a party to – however innocently, that doesn't matter. I feel dirty and disgusting beyond any capacity I have to describe it. And then there's a lurking feeling that my whole life has been a great lie, a great cover-up, a false world erected by my need to conceal from myself the reality of the shit hole which I am and into which I have been plunged'.

As he spoke the tears had come again and he reached for the tissues.

'Have you found yourself thinking about the dream a lot?' she asked eventually.

'Not the content, but the feelings it left me with just won't go away and the fact is that I recognise those feelings. That's how I know what I was dreaming was not just a fantasy and much more like a memory. You see, these feelings of disgust I feel are how I have reacted to my mother for as long as I can remember. I have hated being near her, hated ever having to kiss her or even accidentally touch in passing her. I've been like this for as long as I can remember and now I understand why. And whilst I hate her all the more, I hate myself too. I am loathsome'.

'I understand why you feel that, and yet the fact is that you have sought, albeit unconsciously, to put your experience to the service of others. Look at the way you have given yourself to caring for and defending the vulnerable in the legal processes. That's not a fantasy either. That is what you have been doing and doing well, whatever the reasons for it'.

'But it isn't like that. It's not so long ago that I dreamed I was in a prison cell beating the hell out of that woman who murdered her baby. That's obviously what I was really feeling. And how much more have I been covering up – smiling and caring outwardly but inwardly and unknown to me wanting to murder them? I always believed that there was something higher in this universe, the law, the foundation of all that matters in civilisation, and what I am discovering is that all along I was living a total fantasy. I am just as corrupt as all those who scream for revenge outside the court-houses or who beat prisoners up when the screws' backs are turned. All I've been doing is using my so-called intellectual equipment to pretend that I was part of something different from that. But it isn't true. You see not only have I discovered terrible things about myself and my past but I think I'm losing completely the whole world-view by which and according to which I have lived all my life'.

The session was drawing to a close. An important part of Libby's discipline was in allowing clients finish a session without her having to make everything alright for them. Edwin found himself wondering whether this caused her any tension. The 50 minute hour was seemingly unbreakable. The unreconciled had to remain so.

Whatever tensions and anxieties she might have had about Edwin the discipline triumphed.

'Edwin, we have to stop now. We have one more session before the Christmas break. We shall need to think about how best to enable you to manage that'.

It was raining as Edwin left her house and he undid the hood on his coat and pulled it up. That was something of an advantage because he knew he had to use the morning to get some Christmas presents for Sylvia and something for Megan which was from him. He was not looking forward to going into the shops and hoped that by being able to do so early he might avoid most people though, as always, a former client might appear anywhere and Edwin was even dreading having his hair cut but could not put it off much longer – "Any plans for the Christmas holiday, sir?"!

He went into a bookshop. Megan had a great passion for the work of the Pre-Raphaelite Brotherhood, and he unearthed a first edition of one of the best accounts of their work full of prints superbly reproduced. The cost was steep but given how useless a father he was being to her he happily paid up. He tried to find something for Sylvia there but his search was fruitless and so he left the shop, crossed the road and entered the cathedral bookshop.

He really had no idea what he was looking for. It felt an alien world. The covers of so many of the books on display seemed to consist of garish titles and the exposed teeth of a smiling author over-doing sincerity. The blurb was of little help – far too many adjectives and superlatives. The reality was that most of these books would be remaindered within twelve months and permanently forgotten a year after that, but here and now they were being hailed as the best books ever written. He remained sceptical. In the end he asked the assistance of the manager who turned out to be a delightful fellow as sceptical as himself of the hyperbole of the Christian book world. Having explained the particular brand of his wife's religion, the manager was able to guide him towards a couple of books which he thought would appeal. One was on healing which he thought best left alone but he took the other which he intended to supplement with perfume and an unusual hanging lamp he had seen in a shop window. He also bought Sylvia a very religious card in the shop though he felt profoundly uneasy with it himself. Still, it would hopefully show her that he cared for her and her concerns even if he did not necessarily share them.

It was raining even harder as he completed his shopping and began the walk home. It was one of those December days when it never really gets light and looking down as he tramped through the streets he caught the reflection of the hideous decorative lights the council insisted wasting money on. He decided to bypass the Close and return by way of the water meadows. He was getting wetter by the minute but having ensured the books he carried were safe within their plastic containers he did not mind. He had been reduced to tears so often in recent weeks that he felt an unusual affinity with the rain which, by the time he had crossed the town path, was now doing a good impression of a torrent. Sylvia had been telling him for some time that he needed a new coat. She was right, he was drenched. And did not care. Indeed, felt the better for it.

There was a car outside his house which he did not recognise. Sylvia had not mentioned that she was hosting a meeting or study group of any kind (she had mostly had to find alternative venues for them of late – something he felt guilty about). As he opened the door he could hear a quiet male voice speaking. He opened the sitting room door and popped his head through. Sylvia smiled at him, pointed towards her visitor on the settee opposite and said to Edwin 'You know Jeremy Bullen, our Pastor?'

'Of course', he replied, 'nice to see you. Look, I'm somewhat soaked to the skin. I'll leave you be and get dried off and change'.

'I was expecting you sooner', said Sylvia, almost in a tone of accusation.

'Ah well, secret Christmas type things to do', as he closed the door firmly wondering what kind of secret Christian conversations would now ensue.

Edwin took his time changing and then went to look at the post which Sylvia had put into his study. Mostly circulars, of which solicitors seemed to receive considerably more than their fair share, but one he had been dreading. It was from the publishers of the Journal. It said baldly that they had heard he was not well and probably not able to complete the work on the current edition of the Journal. With his agreement they wanted to appoint a temporary assistant editor to ensure they went to press on time. They named someone whom Edwin knew from the academic legal world who already edited a lesser legal magazine. Edwin could not question his suitability but began to wonder whether this was a sign of something to come, and he wondered how they had found out what was happening to him. Oh, he didn't care.

He had hoped that the pastor would have gone by the time he came back downstairs but the smile greeting him as he came through the door disappointed him.

'Coffee?' asked Sylvia, unusually solicitous.

'I'll get it', said Edwin, determined to free himself from the necessity of a solitary conversation with the pastor.

'Not at all', she replied with determination in her voice, 'sit down'. She was already in the kitchen as she finished the sentence.

'Your busy time, I suppose', said Edwin. He smiled back.

'People often think that but actually in some ways it's easier for me at this time. People are so busy they don't really want visits from the pastor, and of course I'm not a vicar, having to put on carol services to feed sentimentality when they themselves don't believe a word of the story'.

'Yes, I can understand people not wanting a visit from the pastor. Do people really address you as Pastor Bullen? I mean, isn't it really like the title 'Reverend' – strictly speaking it's an adjective? They should not be called Reverend Smith, but the Reverend Mr Smith. Pastor is a job description. Shouldn't you be the Pastor, Mr Bullen, or the Pastor, the Reverend Mr Bullen?'.

It seemed too much for the man.

'Titles don't matter, do they Edwin?', (who had said he could use his first name?), 'it's what is inside us that counts, don't you agree?'.

'If people use titles, and obviously you do and the members of your church seem to be encouraged to speak of you as Pastor, it would seem sensible to use them correctly though. Either that or get rid of them completely'.

Sylvia had returned with a cup of coffee for her husband at whom she was looking daggers.

He took it, and the daggers.

'Jeremy just called round to see how you were getting on', she said.

He smiled inwardly. He had enough experience of evangelicals to know how readily they used "just" and "really", especially with the neologism "wanna" in their prayers to the Almighty.

'Thank you', he replied meekly, leaving it to the pair of them to decide whether the gratitude was for the coffee or the visit. There was an embarrassed silence which he had no intention of ending.

'We're obviously concerned for you and Sylvia and Megan, and sorry to hear that you have been having a rough time', volunteered the pastor.

'I sometimes think I must be something of an embarrassment to Sylvia at your Church. After all she has a key position and yet here am I, not a Christian', said Edwin.

'You go to the Cathedral', interjected Sylvia. And Edwin wondered whether she had to use that to safeguard her position.

'Yes, I do from time to time, though I suspect that in your Church that would not necessarily count as the sort of faith you seem to suggest we ought to have if we are to be accounted real Christians as you define them'. He was addressing the pastor.

'Surely the thing that matters Edwin', and here he paused and then looked earnestly at Edwin, 'is whether what we believe can be for us a source of new life especially when the old one begins to fall apart'.

Edwin had had enough.

'Well, thank you for your concern. I'm not sure waiting until someone is down before seeking to convert them lends credit to what it is you say you believe, but then again I don't believe it, so I cannot really comment. I'll leave you be to finish your chat with Sylvia. Bye'.

As he was speaking Edwin rose and walked to the door, opened it and with as insincere a smile as he could muster, disappeared.

Later, after he had heard the front door close and the strange car start off and pull away he joined in the study room by Sylvia. He could see she was angry.

'You humiliated me', she said, 'and you were extremely rude to a guest and a friend'.

She was right of course. Indeed, since he had sat down he had been enveloped by a sense of guilt as to his behaviour. It wasn't fair that what was happening to him should be having such an effect upon his family. He certainly had no right to exacerbate the situation. There was nothing he could say – he felt wretched.

12

Christmas came and went. It had a kind of momentum of its own which carried Edwin along even without his sessions with Libby. He had joined Sylvia and Megan at her church carol service much to his wife's surprise – a peace offering, and a costly sacrifice too, he thought to himself as he sat there enduring the excruciating agony of the music and the sincerity with which everything was done. And if another person smiled at him with *that* look in their eyes, he thought he would probably vomit.

He was sleeping well and still deeply enough not be troubled by disturbing dreams. Waking was still difficult and the dry mouth with which he greeted the day was horrible. But he did begin to wonder whether the tablets were also beginning to have an anti-depressant effect. Certainly he got through Christmas day happily enough. It was very mild and they had taken a walk in the afternoon. Megan had been over the moon with her present. Sylvia had been stunned by hers and he could see from the look in her eyes that she was convinced that all hope for Edwin was not yet gone.

In the evening his mother had telephoned. He had said nothing to either of his parents about being off work. He was as cold as always replying mostly with a yes or no to her questions and comments. He could feel hostility oozing out of himself as he held the phone. Mercifully she was not on long.

Sylvia's parents rang and were full of Fenland cheer. They had been to a special service in Ely Cathedral called a Christingle, the heart of which seemed, from their report, to be about sticking pins into an orange. Edwin was increasingly convinced religion was getting barmier. Perhaps Hieronymous Bosch was correct and the world really was coming to an end. They were looking forward to seeing them for the new year festivities.

In recent weeks Edwin and his dad had spoken even less frequently than usual, and then mostly about the cricket (England had already lost the first test against Australia by ten wickets), but he had been pleased to note that his voice was less squeaky than it had been and Iris had told him that since coming off the tablets his dad was much thinner again. Nevertheless, Edwin felt there was a strange tone to his dad's voice as he spoke about nothing, and he wondered if his father felt the same about his.

Their days over the new year in the Fens passed by happily enough. Edwin had seen Colin Nuffield twice and that was helping in the absence of Libby though of course it had only been for ten to fifteen minutes on each occasion. Unusually Edwin expressed no wish to go to Cambridge and Sylvia's parents had both mentioned to their daughter that Edwin didn't seem his usual self. But Sylvia had said nothing and laughed it off.

The difficulties began in the car on their way back. Megan was staying with her grandparents for a few extra days and going to a pantomime in London before returning home. Sylvia was in the driving seat.

'So, are you going to go on with your visits to this therapist?'.

It was a stark question.

'I expect so'.

'Even though you've managed perfectly well without her for nearly a fortnight now?'

'Yes'.

'And what about work?'.

'You know I'm signed off for another ten weeks'.

'You don't have to stay off though. You can go back, you know, and I really think it would be best for you. Look how you've been at mum and dad's and over Christmas with things to occupy you. You've been fine. I really think you should go back to work'.

'I haven't been fine', replied Edwin. 'In fact, for much of the time I've felt so absolutely awful inside and it's only the tablets that are keeping my head above water'.

'You can't live on tablets' - her voice rising. She was driving faster too, putting her foot down.

That he did not respond seem to enrage her.

'For heaven's sake Edwin what's the matter with you? Don't you take seriously your responsibilities towards Megan and me? We have rights as well as your clients. You made us move from Edinburgh, we didn't want to come, we did that for you and is this how you intend to repay us?'.

'What do you mean?' It was turning into a full-blown row. 'What's happening to me doesn't affect you. I still get paid. My job's quite safe'.

'When will you realise that it has nothing to do with money? Is that all you can think about? We want, we need, more than that. We don't want people sniggering behind our backs about a husband and father. We don't want to be with someone who yawns all the time and mopes about the place looking scruffy, who stares endlessly into space and spends all our money on something that seems to me is only making you worse'.

'I thought you said it had nothing to do with money?'

'Sarcasm doesn't become you'.

Sylvia must have looked at one of the bank statements. Normally she never bothered with them and Edwin always paid Libby with a cheque. He preferred to divert her attention from that.

'So all that matters to you is people sniggering? Which people? Wonderful Christians at your church?'.

It was, Edwin later thought, little wonder that wars broke out. In their car Sylvia and Edwin were launching verbal but no less deadly forms of missiles at one another Most of the rest of the journey was spent in a silence smouldering with bad feeling.

They had not been in the house for more than ten minutes when the telephone rang. It was Iris.

'Edwin, I know we should have told you before, but we didn't want to spoil your Christmas. It's your dad. He's got something the matter with his colon. They're talking about a growth of some sort – they won't be more specific. He's got a lot of pain and is getting a lot of bleeding from his back passage. He's going into hospital tomorrow for some tests'.

Edwin didn't know what to say.

'What, where, how long..?' he spluttered.

'He's going into Carlisle. He's a nice man the doctor. Dr Boxer I think he's called, no Mr Boxer, that's right, because he's a surgeon'.

'Is dad there?'

'I'll just get him for you'.

It was typical that the news had come from Iris rather than from his dad, but then again Edwin had not told his dad anything about what was happening to him. How could he? And when his dad came onto the telephone he just laughed it all off and said that he might have to have a small op, but that it would be ok afterwards and that Edwin needn't worry. But Edwin was shocked, and Sylvia detected the sound in his voice and no matter how difficult it had been between them for hours at once she was there beside him.

He wanted to go at once up to Carlisle though Iris and his dad had insisted that until they'd got the results it would be a wasted journey. Sylvia too said it would be best to wait. But Edwin was in a panic. He needed to do something. He needed to be there for his dad.

Despite his tablets Edwin slept fitfully and kept seeing his father's face, and he wondered how he was feeling as the local church clock bell struck the hours. He knew that his father would be struggling and frightened however much he had feigned a relaxed detachment when speaking to his son. And then they had actually discussed the cricket. Edwin was ashamed as he lay there.

There were still three days before he was due to see Libby again so he decided to take advantage of the remaining free time to go north. He determined that he would leave first thing. But the effects of his tablets determined otherwise and it was not until after ten o'clock that he arrived at the station to catch the train to Bristol with the connection on the afternoon train to Glasgow, arriving at Carlisle station just after eight. Iris was there to meet him.

'They've done the operation and Mr Boxer says it went quite well though they've had to remove a section quite low down which might mean that eventually he'll have to have a colostomy. He'll not be pleased about that'.

'What did they find?'.

'They won't know until they get the results back from the lab tomorrow but it's obvious that it's a tumour of some sort. Let's just hope that it's benign'.

It was too late to visit that evening but first thing next morning (Edwin did not take his tablets and hardly slept at all but that did mean that he was relatively wide awake early) he set off for Carlisle.

'What are you doing here?', said his dad, but obviously delighted to see his son. He was in a side room for the present though he had been told he would be moved into the main ward later in the day.

Hugs over, Edwin asked the usual questions about how it was feeling and what did he remember and were the nurses pretty. His first feeling was one of relief because his father looked so much more back to normal than he had on his last visit. This he put down to his being off the steroids; it did not occur to him that there might be a more sinister explanation. Then, inevitably, their talk turned to cricket and the dismal performance of England in the second test match in Melbourne. With a new test due to begin in Sydney, father and son were gloomy about the prospects. Neither said anything about the big realities of their lives: lives falling apart – they talked cricket.

His dad had to be cleaned up and his wound attended to. Edwin decided to use the time to go and see the ward sister. He knocked on her door and introduced himself to her.

'Have you any idea when you will know what it is?', he asked. 'Oh, we know that already, Mr Lyons'.

'I thought you had to wait for the result of the tests'.

'Tissue samples are always sent away for examination but according to Mr Boxer's notes... ', she stood up and reached for his father's notes, 'yes, carcinoma of the bowel, obviously malignant. Some evidence from manual examination of secondaries in the liver. Not good'.

Edwin felt as if the world had stopped turning, yet through the window he could see a teenage couple walking hand in hand and laughing. Life going on and life ending.

'I take it my dad doesn't know yet. Or Iris, his wife, she doesn't know either?'

'No. Mr Boxer will be in later this morning. He'll need to discuss chemotherapy and radiotherapy with you all. He has a ward round and he'll make time at the end of that for you to see him'.

Was that it? The death sentence passed and then the lunch menus to be done. He thanked her and left the room slowly, stopping outside the door and wondering how the hell he was ever going to be able to say anything at all to his dad. He now knew the truth. His dad was going to die. Had cancer. His dad.

He walked back into his dad's room. He was sitting up in bed with the paper before him.

What on earth was he going to say?

'Any news?'

'You're the one with the newspaper', he replied limply.

'I don't know why I bother with it. It says here that England go into the third test without a great deal of hope. I already knew that'.

'Er, the sister said Mr Boxer will be round later. He'll be able to give us all the gen. But it's clear they've done a big job on you. She said they'd had to remove quite a bit of your bowel'.

'Oh well, it's best gone if it's rotten'.

Edwin paused. Was he going to say more? Was he going to have the courage to tell his dad the real news, that he too was about to begin a test without much hope. Only this was no game; this was death.

'They say he's one of the best', continued his father.

'I'm sure'.

'So are you going to pop back and collect Iris? She'll want to see the doc too.'

'Yes', replied Edwin with undue haste, standing up from the bed on which he had perched himself.

'Yes, I'll do that, then we can be back in good time for his ward round'.

'Yeah, you do that, son. It'll give me a chance to have a bit of a snooze too. I'm still feeling a bit groggy from the gas'.

As Edwin went down the stairs and towards the car he found himself wondering whether in fact his father already knew and was actually trying to protect him from the pain of the truth. And if that was the case just how much his father known all life through and done nothing about it, said nothing? Even now, staring death in the face, all they could discuss was a stupid game on the other side of the world. How often had they done so in the past in order to avoid other painful truths? And why hadn't his dad protected him from her when he needed it?

As he drove back to collect Iris he had turned on the radio. The music was a piece by John Tavener and featured a cello and orchestra. It was hauntingly beautiful and Edwin had suddenly to pull over to the side of the road because he had become aware of tears streaming down his face.

'Oh, my poor dad. Why, why, why? I love you so', he wailed, as the cello played on and on.

He had recovered his composure by the time he had got back to collect Iris. As they drove back towards Carlisle, Edwin said to Iris, 'It may be bad news we're going to hear this morning'.

'Uhuh'.

Even now, even with Iris, Edwin found it impossible to say how it was. Most of the journey was passed in silence, each enveloped in their private world.

On arrival they found that Mr Boxer was already well under way with his ward round. Edwin's father had been sleeping for most of the time he had been away, though the nurses had awoken him and tidied up the bed ready for the arrival of the consultant. Edwin left Iris with him for a while and sought out the visitor's loo. His own guts were playing him up this morning. He was dreading the next few minutes of his life. What minutes of his life did he not now dread?

They did not have long to wait. The entourage of doctors and nurses were gathered outside his father's door as Edwin returned. At their centre in a white coat was a tall man with jet black hair. They were speaking quietly as Edwin came towards then. Then they stopped, smiled and waited for him to enter the room. There could be no doubt then!

'All set?', said Edwin as he pushed the door to behind him.

What a stupid thing to say. But then again what wouldn't be? And Edwin wondered what sort of things solicitors and barristers would have said to their clients in the days of capital punishment as they awaited the return of a jury.

The door opened and in came the doctor together with one of his minions, a young woman.

'Good morning. You must be Mr Lyons's son' he had turned to Edwin and held out his hand before turning back to his patient.

'So, any pain at all this morning?'

He had pulled back the sheet and was gently prodding his abdomen around the dressing over the wound. Even the doctor wanted to avoid the moment.

'No, but they've been giving me something for the pain just in case'. Cheerful. Helping the doctor.

'Good'. He pulled the sheet back up, paused and then delivered the verdict and sentence. 'I'm sorry to say that the news could be better'.

Jesus! thought Edwin.

'We got in and found that the lower part of the descending colon, this bit here... ' (he indicated on himself) 'was diseased and we removed it. To be honest I thought we'd have to give you a colostomy, but we managed to get the bits back together. We have a new instrument, a Chinese staple gun, and it does wonders. So you're spared a bag and all its complications. And I think we got everything we could see away. But I fear that we may have got in there a bit too late. Thing is, that sort of cancer... (the word had been spoken at last) tends to spread its wings a little, and I was able to feel clear evidence that it had got to your liver. We shall need to do more tests to find out just how much is affected, and we shall need to talk about treatment. But I'm afraid that once it's in there we tend to run out of things to do. I'm very sorry to have to give you this bad news but I felt you should be told the truth'.

'How long have I got?'. His father's voice was surprisingly strong. Perhaps it was no news at all.

'It's impossible for me to give an exact figure, Mr Lyons. There are so many factors to take into account, most of which I don't know anything about'.

'Roughly'.

'Six months, maybe a little more, maybe less. I honestly can't be more specific than that'.

The doctor said that they would need to wait to discuss further treatment until after they had heard from the laboratories. Also it was vital for them to have some time to reflect before they could think clearly about the next stage.

Edwin could not help admiring how the doctor had handled it.

'Thank you doctor', said his father as Mr Boxer got up to leave. 'I suppose I knew it might not be good. I'm sorry to have had to put you through this'.

The patient protecting the doctor.

Iris was crying quietly and holding her husband's hand. Edwin felt he should leave them and said so, but they insisted he remain. Strangely, now it was out in the open it all seemed so much easier to bear though it might also have been, thought Edwin, that they were all just numb.

'Well son', said his father after a long period of silence, 'compared with some of our batsmen I've not had a bad innings'.

Edwin smiled and hugged his dad's hand to himself. He felt that they had never been closer. He would even have liked, in that moment, to tell them about himself, but thought better of it. After all they had a huge burden to face and worrying about him would only make it worse.

Edwin eventually left them alone and sought a quiet place in which to call Syvia, but was answered by the machine. He left a message saying he would call back later in the afternoon. He then rang British Rail to find out about overnight or late evening trains before returning to the ward. As he walked towards his father's room, he met Mr Boxer.

'Hello Mr Lyons. I'm so sorry about your father'.

'Thank you for handling it so well. I think we all appreciated your frankness. What I guess we need to do now is talk over with you the options. I suspect the most important thing for my dad and Iris – she's not my mother you know, my parents were divorced, though I think the world of her – is that they can have some quality of life. If things are as you say, can you keep the pain and inconvenience of things as small as possible?'.

Mr Boxer led him into a room off the corridor and closed the door before replying.

'Best not to have conversations like that in public', he explained. 'When secondaries are in the liver there is not a lot of point in too much active treatment. Cytotoxic drugs – chemotherapy – might slow things down but the side-effects might even be worse than what they are treating. It's the same with radiotherapy. After he recovers from surgery your father will have a lot less pain than he has been putting up with for what I suspect has been a long time. Had he come to me a year ago it might have been different. But there will be pain and other symptoms. These we can treat. There's a good hospice and excellent home care nurses who will support him. I have every reason to hope we can keep him pain-free throughout. One of the things I want to discuss with them, perhaps tomorrow, is a referral to the hospice home care team. They are very good'.

When Edwin returned to the room, his father and Iris were sitting holding hands quietly together. Edwin smiled at them, though whether to make himself or them feel better he was not sure.

'You'll be needing to get back, son'.

'Yes, there's a late train to London and a sort of milk train which will get me home in good time for tomorrow. If Iris can run me to the station tonight I'll do that. Presumably you'll only be in here for a day or two. I can come back easily enough'.

'Don't be silly. There's no need for that. Anyway you've got your own life to be getting on with. You've got a very important job and that has to come first'.

Edwin decided to leave them for a longer period together, and drove back to their house to collect his things. He also wanted some time by the sea – just to be there. It had timeless qualities and as he gazed across the Solway Firth he could see the first lights in the gathering gloom in Dumfries and along the coast. Nature always helped set things in perspective for him in a way that religion never had. At school he had found most of what the Chaplain and others came out with almost bereft of meaning whereas all around Sedbergh the hills cried out to him and he heard. With the sound of the powerful waves of the sea beating upon the jetty and his ancient Greeks ever with him, he even found himself feeling he could survive all that was happening. It was a first moment of hope in a long time. The irony of it being on the very day he had learned that his father was soon to die of cancer was not lost on him.

He telephoned Sylvia again before setting off back to hospital. She was shocked by the news and genuinely anxious for Edwin. She arranged to meet him at the Station even though it would have been more sensible for him to get a taxi at what would be five in the morning.

His parting from his father was inevitably low key. Neither man had much in the way of surplus energy left by evening. Iris gave them some time together but they were largely unable to make much use of it for anything other trivialities. Feeling somewhat guilty about this, Edwin comforted himself that though Eliot had maintained humankind cannot bear very much reality it was not necessarily a criticism; it might be sound sense.

13

Edwin could have waited until the following day to return home, and his journey would have been much easier (and he had also discovered that his return ticket was not valid for the journey as his outward journey had been via Bristol and he was returning via London), but he was anxious not to miss his first session with Libby after their break. Were he to do so he would have had to wait until after the weekend before seeing her and that felt just too long to wait. He thought it best not to take his tablets and as a result most of his sleep was fitful and haunted by the memory of his father's face as he left. It had seemed so empty, so bewildered. He had wanted to take him in his arms and hold him and make everything alright. And he could not. No one could now.

He was cold and feeling tired and miserable by the time the stopping train out of Waterloo arrived back in Wiltshire. He had crossed London by cab and then had to wait on the concourse at Waterloo for almost two hours. Several people were sleeping rough even within the station and the police seemed to turn a blind eye provided they were quiet. Edwin looked at some of the waifs and strays that increasingly seemed to make up the population of London and wondered what had brought them to this. And what of himself? He could understand how it might be to run away in the hope not necessarily of a new beginning, for truth to tell he was sceptical about that possibility, but of just not being who he was with all his baggage. He even found himself wondering whether that was why some people drank so much. He had never been much of a drinker – the odd glass of wine and an occasional scotch being his limit – but maybe, just maybe, people found release in it.

Good luck to them.

It was just after half past five when he arrived home. Sylvia made coffee and toast for him while he had a wash and changed his clothes. She was clearly trying hard to offer him understanding and support in the face of the news, and he appreciated that though he found himself holding back in terms of his feelings. He merely described to her the events of the previous twenty four hours. When she had suggested that he go to bed he told her that he was going to therapy this morning and sensed a slight if momentary prickliness in her. She made no comment. A dark early January morning was clearly not the time for either to express feelings.

Edwin thought that he might be saving them for his time with Libby but it proved not to be so. He described all that had happened but seemed quite incapable of emerging from emotional first gear. He was very tired and assumed this was the cause and by the end of the session he found himself wondering whether it had been worth the effort of getting back. Even worse was the reception at home. He had left for Libby's before Megan had awoken and Sylvia clearly no longer felt the need to hold back her feelings.

'I think you have got your priorities all wrong Edwin', was her greeting as he closed the front door. 'Your daughter should have come first, not some stranger who only sees you because you pay her. Do you not think that she cares about her grandfather and about how her dad is and deserves attention? She was desperately upset when she found you weren't here'.

Edwin felt he had nothing to offer by way of mitigation. He was feeling sick and just wanted to be left alone.

'I know, I know', was all he could say as he tumbled into an arm-chair.

'Did you tell your dad that you're off work?'.

He shook his head.

'What are you going to do this morning?'

'See if I can get some sleep. You?'.

'I've always got plenty to keep me going, and if you want my opinion that's what you're going to need in these next months: work to occupy your mind. Otherwise you'll just get worse and worse as you think about your dad. He won't thank you for that you know. He's always been a busy person'.

Edwin said nothing.

'I was talking to Hugh last night - he rang to find out how things were – and he said he was sure you could go back part-time if need be. You could make life a lot easier for yourself without your legal aid on-call work for a start. But you'd have a focus and it would do you good to feel that you were contributing again'.

'What would do me good this morning is sleep', murmured Edwin as he endeavoured to raise himself from the chair. 'Thank you for caring. It isn't easy, I know that. And I'll make lots of time for Meg over the weekend'.

He touched her hand briefly before leaving the room and going upstairs.

He decided to do "total immersion" rather than just lie on the bed. The last time he had been in his pyjamas and in bed during the daytime was on the day his 'event' had happened. He felt no less tired today but found that once he was in bed, head on the pillow, he could not sleep. He could see the hospital and the ward and his father. He could see the tramps on Waterloo Station. He could see his office and his colleagues, and he wondered what they might be saying about him. He could see countless people whom he was failing and letting down. He could even see his mother and he began to wonder whether he should let her know about his father. And as these images came and went he felt nothing about any of them. They were just there, preventing sleep, and devoid of content.

Edwin worked hard over the weekend to make everything alright for Megan and Sylvia. His tablets had at least enabled him to get some sleep at last, but he still felt the effects of them into the middle of the day. He was not yet conscious of them helping his mood however. Not that he felt especially gloomy. Indeed he hardly felt anything at all. It was much more as if he was in a state of 'under-drive'. He was unable to see or appreciate the beauty around him; he had no wish to listen to music; a television programme could be on and he would hardly have known what it was. It was as if a barrier had come up (and it certainly felt as if it arose out of the earth rather than descending upon him as a cloud) and placed itself between him and the outside world. It was akin to acute deafness or extreme myopia, but of the spirit. Things were there, but that was it, they were things – not people, not places. On the inside his mind raced but arrived nowhere. He was unable to settle, unable to read. He often sat and then found he had been doing so for almost two hours and had not noticed the time passing. He played with his nails and looked out of the window. He found the dark of January oppressive but feared the light more for fear that he should meet someone who knew him. On those occasions when he had to take to the open air he did so warily.

From the beginning of their working relationship Libby had noticed a reluctance bordering upon refusal for Edwin to speak about his wife. And of course, Edwin, not Sylvia, was her client but on the subject of his marriage Edwin's silence intrigued her, especially given the nature of what had happened to him as a child and the possible consequences of that for relating to women. She found herself wondering how Sylvia was reacting to the very depressed man she was herself encountering session by session. Indeed she found herself wondering a great deal. It was now far harder to get Edwin to speak and whilst occasionally his cerebral responses were almost normal there was a clear cut-off with regard to expressing and, probably, experiencing, feelings. She decided she had to ask.

'You say very little about how your wife is handling all that is happening'.

As had become customary, Edwin was slow in replying.

'It's hard for her. She doesn't know anything of what we've spoken of. She doesn't understand what's happening. All she can see is me looking terrible and inevitably she thinks I'd be better off going back to work and trying to be as normal as possible. And I know I fail her'.

Libby decided to ignore the last comment.

'Do you think it is significant that you don't tell me anything about her and don't tell her anything about me?'.

'I don't know what you mean'.

'We've spent a long time now working together and it took a long time before you were able to disclose something that was a secret, indeed so secret you were not even sure whether you knew it yourself. And it was a secret to do with your mother. And keeping secrets, or confidences and not least about women clients, has become something of a speciality to you. And I wondered what it was about'.

'I would have thought it's pretty obvious why I don't tell Sylvia anything about what we have been dealing with'.

'So you prefer to keep her in a state of confusion and misunderstanding? After all what kind of sense can she be making of this if you don't try and tell her something about it? It must seem utterly perplexing'.

'I couldn't tell her that. It's vile. I can barely face it myself.

'But maybe to Sylvia it would be the key to unlock the door of her confusion and misunderstanding. It might help her considerably. And I dare say she's not totally stupid. Maybe she suspects something'.

'She'd be horrified. I couldn't do that to her'.

Libby could see that Edwin had become highly irritated. He was moving around on the chaise as if he itched all over.

'And I'm not saying you should tell her, Edwin', she responded. 'I offered an observation. I am still wondering why it is you do not often speak of her here'.

'Because it's me we're dealing with, that's why', he replied crossly.

'I seem to have touched a raw nerve'.

'No, I'm sorry'.

'What for?'.

'Becoming irritable with you'.

'I was irritating you. Being irritated seems quite an appropriate response'.

'Oh, I don't know. The thing is I can barely cope with all this myself, what with my dad being ill as well. The thought of having to try and handle Sylvia as well just feels too much. In a way it's far easier just putting up with the hassle about going back to work and the things she says about therapy'.

'She's unhappy about your coming here?'

'Very'.

Libby waited for Edwin to continue.

'I mean, I can I understand why she feels as she does. It isn't just that she thinks there are magical Christian solutions to my woes but the fact that she doesn't know what I am having to face. She really does feel that if I would only try a bit harder I'd be better'.

'So is she being an irritation to you too?'

'In a way, yes, but it's not her fault'.

'Is it ever a woman's fault, Edwin?'.

'What do you mean?'.

'Well, either you are very gallant or you really do believe that women can do no wrong'.

'I've no idea'.

It was clear Edwin had decided he had no interest in pursuing this, try however hard she might goad him into it. But it was also clear to her that this resistance was there for a reason and she suspected it had to do with Edwin's inability, at present, to face the issue of his marriage. She decided to change tack.

'What's the latest news about your father?'.

'It's somewhat ironical. Although he's been told the worst he says he's feeling better than he has for some time. He's pain free and able to eat normally again. I think he's beginning to wonder if the doctor has got it right after all'.

'Do you share that optimism?'.

'No. Apparently after surgery there's quite often an immediate obvious improvement in symptoms – that's why they do the operation – but it doesn't change the basic diagnosis, nor, alas, the prognosis. It's just that the course of the cancer in the liver makes itself felt more slowly'.

'Have you told your mother yet?'

'No. I need to ask my dad first. Maybe he won't want her to know. Anyway, it's nothing to do with her'.

'And have you said anything yet to him about how you are?'

'No way – he's got more than enough on his plate'.

'You do need to carry everyone don't you? What about allowing them all to care for you?'

'What's happened to me isn't their fault. Why should I have to burden them with my problems?'.

'Because they care for you?', suggested Libby.

Edwin made no reply.

At the beginning of February the proofs for Edwin's book on Natural Law arrived for him to check. This book represented the expression of his deepest thinking over many years. It embodied the basic philosophy by which he had sought to live. Religion per se had never worked for him. He once said he didn't think he had inherited the gene that makes some people find meaning in an organised faith. He also knew that his own philosophy was akin to much that had been expressed in different religious traditions over the century. Perhaps the religious tradition he felt closest too was that of the ancient Greeks. Not that he believed in Zeus any more than in any other divine figure, but neither, so he believed, did the greatest of the ancients. For him, and for them, these personal descriptions of the divine simply served as a kind of focus for their highest aspirations. His beloved Homer (whoever he was and his supposed identities were as manifold as those of Shakespeare) wrote about history in the context of eternity. Whether Homer believed in the existence of the deities of which he wrote did not matter. The important thing was that he described human events as being on a truly heroic scale. The lives and events of humans matter to the Gods and therefore even the most apparently insignificant event matters. He wholly endorsed the Roman Terence's dictum: "I am human and count nothing human alien to me".

For Edwin the greatest human achievement was law – the ordering of life according to the measure of justice and right. Above that, and here his philosophy almost bordered on the religious, was the pattern of all existence which he maintained was what could truly be called the fundamental Law. He believed that human beings carry within them an intrinsic sense of right and wrong that is not merely the product of social conditioning.

In speaking of his beliefs, he often used as an illustration something he had discussed and then had the chance to test out on children in a Primary School. He had told them a story about a small child saving up to buy a new book. When the day came when he had the exact amount, he got up extra early, full of excitement, in order to be first in the queue at the bookshop that morning. When the shop eventually opened it turned out that there was only one copy on the shelf. As the little boy was getting his money out a bigger lad arrived, pushed him out of the way and bought the copy. As he told the story Edwin had seen the children identifying with the little boy and his excitement. No less did they identify with him in the experience of being pushed onto one side. It was not just sentimentality. They all described what had happened in terms of right and wrong, in terms of absolute justice. And that, Edwin maintained, was the product not of social convention but of a fundamental law of existence, a natural law.

In his book Edwin had not only outlined the historical development of the understanding of natural law from earliest times to the present (when it was much neglected) but sought to relate it to the actual practice of law – as it affects both the legislature and the judiciary. It was in itself a Herculean task. He had given most of the previous decade to thinking about it, planning it, and finally writing it.

As he opened the package (and printers, he mused, seemed determined to waste huge quantities of paper) his initial feeling was the one of thrill all writers experience when they first see their work set out. It was not his first book and he had seen himself in print regularly but even his depression could not prevent him enjoying that moment. He even set to with determination and found himself in the first minutes of enthusiasm wondering whether Sylvia wasn't right after all, that he would be better back at work. But the enthusiasm lasted only a few minutes and he managed to read only the first two pages before discovering that without him being aware of it more than an hour had passed and he had read no more.

It was a bright morning outside and he had enjoyed the cold on his face as he had returned from Libby's. He decided he would go out for a walk. Heading south up the hill and across the back of the local School he could be in the fields and woods out towards the racecourse in no time and, with luck, at this time in the morning he would not meet anyone he knew. There had been a lot of rain during January, so he put on his wellingtons and headed out into the country.

Edwin had written much about the laws of nature being congruent with his understanding of natural law. This morning no such thoughts entered his head. In later days he felt that this walk was highly significant in that instead of spending his time engaged in internal colloquy, thinking about the natural world, he found himself directly engaged with it. He looked and he saw. He listened and he heard. He could smell and touch and feel the wind upon his face and all without interposing an intellectual framework. He walked on and on.

He reached the racecourse. It was deserted and somewhat weather-beaten, akin to a seaside resort in winter. It was, he knew, though he never attended, a flat racing course and therefore only used in summer. And perhaps it was the sight of something so forlorn that began to bring about a change in his mood or it may have been that he ran out of energy. Whatever the cause Edwin was increasingly aware that he was feeling uneasy. He was no longer aware of the outer world save as a series of obstacles in his path. The woods and fields of even twenty minutes earlier had become a kind of labyrinth that threatened to overwhelm him. He began to panic. What would happen if he couldn't find his way home? What would happen out here if he had another experience like that in October? He began to sweat profusely. What was he to do?

He hadn't brought his mobile but mercifully came across a telephone box behind one of the grandstands and he rang home. There was no reply. Even the answering machine was not turned on. He put the telephone down and wondered how he could possibly get home. What had felt like a good walk of about a mile and a half across lovely fields under a blue sky on the outward journey now took on the aspect of a life and death struggle. Each step seemed to drain him of yet more energy. He was aware of feeling hungry and thirsty. More than anything he now felt totally imprisoned within his own head and was therefore having to work extra hard to make his body function. Each step became a deliberate effort. He was now on the road on the other side of the racecourse and headed down the hill. He did not know whether he was going to survive. He began to look round at each car that passed him, pleading silently for help. And when no help came, not least because he gave no indications to drivers that we was anything other than someone out for a walk on a lovely late winter's morning, he felt worse and worse.

How long it took he never knew but eventually he reached a telephone box on the edge of the town by the newsagent's shop. He was in fact no more than 800 metres from home but he did not believe he could make it that far. Sylvia answered.

'Where are you?' she cried out, 'I've been going out of my mind with worry'.

He told her, and she was with him in a matter of minutes. She could see he was having difficulties. It frightened her and she wondered whether she needed to summon help. This was how he had looked when he had been brought home following his breakdown. Just what was the matter with him?

She got him home and suggested he change his clothes whilst she made some soup to warm him up. Mostly he had said nothing. She decided to ring Paul Raven. He knew Edwin, was wise and kind, and a member of her church.

'Oh, I'm sorry to hear that, Sylvia', he said after she had told him the story. 'Perhaps calling the doctor would be best'.

'Oh, Paul I'm so scared. Do you know I think he looks worse than on that day in October. And the proofs of his new book have arrived. Can't you please come and see him and try and get him back to work. I think it's the combination of this so-called therapy and not having enough to do. It's destroying him. Please do what you can. I know he's not actually a member of the church but surely the Lord wants good things for him, not this'.

'I just pray that through all this Edwin can come to see his need of the Lord, Sylvia. He is the only solid ground any of us can have and Edwin needs something solid on which to stand. I praise God that he has you to be with him'.

Sylvia rang the surgery but Dr Nuffield was out. The receptionist said she would try and find out where he had reached and endeavour to contact him but that it might take some time.

Edwin was glad of the soup. They sat together at the kitchen table. Sylvia was wholly at a loss to know what to say. Her own emotional levels were running low, and she was overjoyed when on answering the doorbell she found Colin Nuffield on the doorstep.

'Oh, thank God you've come, doctor', she said, almost manhandling him into the house.

She hurriedly sought to recount the morning's episode. They met Edwin coming out of the kitchen.

'Hello Edwin', said the doctor, 'I hear you've had a bit of a rough episode this morning.

'Yes', replied Edwin, 'I cut my leg on some barbed wire or a bush or something', and he pulled up his trouser leg to show them, 'but it's nothing that you need to worry about, doctor'.

'Oh, that's good news', replied the doctor, and indicating one of the chairs went on, 'do you mind if I sit down?'.

'Not at all', said Sylvia hastily, 'I'll get you a coffee'.

When she had gone into the kitchen the doctor looked up at Edwin. 'You don't look too brilliant. What's been happening?'.

The doctor knew how important a question this was even if he also knew Edwin could not possibly answer it. For the first time he had to give serious consideration to the possibility that Edwin was experiencing a psychotic episode. If that was the case he was going to need a quite different approach and some psychiatric input.

'Oh, I think I just did too much. Used up too much energy, and that on top of getting proofs of my new book which I found pretty disturbing. I guess I was having to try and work something through, and went too far for my own good'.

'I don't want to intrude upon your work with Libby, so don't feel you have to answer, but what was it you found disturbing in your own writing?'.

'Just the fact of it. It's my magnum opus and so much of my life and my hopes and my longing have gone into that. I've sacrificed so much to make it possible. I've invested a great deal, if not most of myself in it and this morning when I opened it, I just thought it worthless'.

Sylvia had come back into the room with the doctor's drink into which he poured some milk.

'It must quite hard for you Mrs Lyons. This sort of experience may be horrible for your husband, but you too must wonder what's going on. It would make any of us extremely anxious'.

'Oh doctor', she cried out, 'I feel totally at a loss to understand what's happening. I feel I'm losing my husband'.

Dr Nuffield nodded gently and said nothing. What was there to say in any case? Sylvia had burst into tears and now sat with her left hand trying as it were to hold her face together. Edwin had got up to take hold of her other hand.

'Oh God, what a mess', he said.

14

Colin Nuffield had himself paid a sustained visit to hell and he recognised some of the furnishings from Edwin's descriptions. He remained concerned about Edwin's state of mind and needed to speak to Libby about him. It was an area fraught with potential misunderstanding and conflict of interest. His own work with her was but recently completed and he knew they both had to respect confidences with regard to Edwin. But he had to know whether Libby felt this recent episode and the original event were indicative of a psychotic illness that required different and specialised help.

Libby had not seen Edwin since his walk to the racecourse and was therefore a little taken aback by the report from the doctor. On the whole she felt that what Edwin had told the GP about how he had tried to do too much and then withered rang true to her own reading of his present state.

'I don't think we are dealing with a mental illness, Colin,' she maintained. He respected her judgement.

'Ok', came his reply, 'but I think he needs careful monitoring. It may be that a change in medication would help'.

'It does strike me', she commented, 'that I might telephone Edwin myself and say that I have heard from you, and offer him an extra session'.

'Yes, I think that would be helpful'.

He made no mention of Sylvia. That was for Edwin to do, he decided.

After the doctor had left, Edwin and Sylvia had gone upstairs to lie down on the bed. They listened to The Archers, something they had not done together for a long time. Sylvia had fallen asleep. Edwin wished he could do likewise. When the telephone rang he answered it quickly in the hope of not waking his sleeping wife.

'Hello, Edwin, it's Libby Francis here. I heard from Dr Nuffield that something had happened to you and I just wanted to make contact and find out how you are'.

'Blimey, he was quick off the mark'.

'It isn't easy when two people are both involved with the same person. Lines get crossed. To be honest he wanted my opinion as to whether what had happened to you might be indicative of a psychotic illness. I told him that I very much doubted it. And I want to reassure you that I have told him nothing whatsoever arising from our work together. That's also a two-edged sword because he has equally told me nothing about this morning other than that you went out for a walk and had strange experiences which alerted your wife to summon him. So my purpose in telephoning is to say that if it would be of help to you I could see you in the morning for an additional session'.

Edwin was conscious of Sylvia next him. Was she awake?

'Yes, I would like that', he said quietly.

'It would have to be earlier than usual, I'm afraid. Seven'.

'Ok. Thank you. I'll see you then'.

He put the phone down.

'Who was that?', came Sylvia's voice behind him.

'It was my therapist', he replied. 'Dr Nuffield had apparently rung her asking whether she thought I was suffering from a psychotic illness. She told him she didn't think so and she wanted me to know that he had called her'.

He waited.

'She also offered me an extra session tomorrow morning so that I can try and make sense of what happened this morning. I said yes, even though it will have to be at seven in the morning'.

'I need help to make sense of it too, Ed. I meant what I said to the doctor, I am really scared that we are going to fall apart. It wasn't easy before all this, what with my church work and yours being based on different principles and so on. But this is just getting worse. And I keep wondering why you won't talk about your therapy to me. It's tom our life and home apart. It's almost as if you had a mistress – I'm not suggesting she is – but I don't know anything about it. And I don't know how we can survive this in one piece'.

She had started to cry again and Edwin did not know what to do. He wanted to run away and hide and, if possible, die. He couldn't cope with a hurt and damaged Sylvia, especially as he was the cause of it all.

He took hold of her hand.

'Oh my love, I'm so sorry to be the cause of all this. I would give anything, anything at all, for it to be different'.

'Why won't you tell me about it, Ed?'.

'Well perhaps the time has come when I have to. If it will help you understand'.

He released her hand and shifted his position so that he was looking away from her towards the ceiling.

'The thing is', he began, and then paused, 'is that it isn't very nice'.

'Is it to do with your mother?'.

'Yes. It's to do with something that happened when I was small, something that for most of my life I have deliberately and necessarily chosen to forget, but which has been there all along, like the hidden parts of an iceberg. That time in France the

Christmas before last was, if you like, the tip. I had a violent reaction to being near her'.

'You've always been odd when she's around. You want to see and hear yourself when you speak on the telephone to her'.

He nodded.

'Just before my breakdown in October', he continued, 'I had a vivid and unpleasant dream, at least I think it was a dream but it may have been a memory, of something that happened when I was small, something she did to me, and maybe not just once but repeatedly...'.

'Oh no', cried Sylvia interrupting him, 'that's horrible. She couldn't have'.

'I think she did, and I think that's why I cannot stand to be near her, and I'm afraid it's plunged me into depression. I feel so ashamed and worthless and dirty and horrible'.

He would have welcomed being able to know the relief of tears himself at this point, but they would not come. Sylvia held him and the tears she shed were certainly more than enough for the pair of them.

'To be honest', began Edwin, early the next morning, 'I have no real idea what happened yesterday. I was feeling so good as I walked across the hill and out towards the racecourse. Then it changed and it was as if there had been a sudden change in the weather. We used to experience those when I was at school in Sedbergh. I used to go walking in the Howgills and sometimes you could set off in bright sunshine and then suddenly, and I mean in less than ten minutes, clouds could appear and envelop you. It could be quite alarming. Well, yesterday was like that'.

'It sounds very frightening'.

'Then I was in a death-like blackness and bleakness. It was like two different places yet they weren't, they were one and the same. Something triggered the ghastliness inside me. I don't know what it was, but I'm not at all surprised that Dr Nuffield reacted as he did. To be frank I was beginning to wonder myself whether there isn't, you know, well, something wrong mentally'.

'I'm not a psychiatrist, Edwin, but I would have thought that one of the sure signs in what you say is your anxiety about it. I suspect that if you really were experiencing psychotic episodes you most certainly wouldn't be aware of the possibility. But you are right about something triggering the reaction. Perhaps we could go over all that happened after you left, up to the time when you knew something was amiss'.

Edwin described in as much detail as he could the arrival of the proofs and his elation turning rapidly to ambivalence, if not worse. He then described the experience of his outward walk and his sense of being close to nature, before arriving at the racecourse and seeing how dilapidated and shabby it all looked.

'One element stands out for me in what you have said, Edwin', said Libby, once he had completed his account, 'and that's the way in which something good, even wonderful, all of a sudden no longer is. It is transformed from being light into darkness, from nourishment into poison. Your life-work is suddenly seen by you to be apparently worthless (though I am sure it is not and I trust you will also be able to see that again), the beauty of the natural world giving place to a frightening heartless world where people do not stop to help you when you need it. There is also the racecourse: like the seaside it is wonderful and exciting on its day, but at other times, and especially in winter you see it as it is without the make-up: decayed and decrepit.

'I wonder if it was the sight of the racecourse in that state – its "fallen from grace winter appearance", which triggered off internal reminders of what is happening to you at this time, which could also be said to be an experience of falling from grace, and certainly a decline from the heights of principle and purpose into something apparently squalid'.

'Is that how you see it?', said Edwin querulously. 'Well, I wouldn't be totally wrong, would I? Because however much you might want to dress it up and tell me how courageous I've been, the fact of the matter is that I've discovered I'm a fraud. I've been living something for years and all along it wasn't at all what I thought it was. All I was doing was covering up for something disgusting in my life and because I didn't have the guts to deal with it I set about building something that's nothing at all. Yes, it is a fall from grace. It's a fall into emptiness'.

'I can understand that this is what you feel, Edwin, but your feelings may be somewhat awry. After all you have truly accomplished a great deal: academically, professionally – in all these ways you have real achievements behind you, things of which you can rightly be proud. It is possibly true that what you have discovered is that your motivations, the driving force which has provided the momentum for some of this is not quite what you thought it was, but that was only the fuel in the engine. You have been driving the car and making a great deal out of something that others might not have done. That isn't flannel. It's a fact'.

Edwin remained silent, reflecting upon her words, but it was hard for him to get past the force of his feelings of worthlessness. They were like the current of a fast and furiously flowing river in full spate.

'Nevertheless', continued Libby, endeavouring to give him support, 'your entire physical and mental system has undergone a terrible shock and I suspect that means you are not yet able again to function in the rational way once you did. What is most real to you, both unconsciously and consciously, is the force of feelings that are rising up from within. I believe they were responsible for what happened to you yesterday, and though I didn't say so to him, that's what I implied to Dr Nuffield'.

'Well, one of the benefits of his coming yesterday was that it provided me with the means of being able to say something to

Sylvia about what has been happening'.

'Oh?'

'I didn't go into detail, but I said that I thought I was dealing with things that had happened to me a long time ago, things which only now was I recalling and facing'.

'How did she respond?'.

'Well at first she was shocked and very sympathetic. Later she seemed more distant and quiet, and by the time I went to bed I found it hard to read how she was'.

'And are glad you were able to say something to her about it?'

'I don't know. The thing is that I have come to see that we think in very different ways about things. She has a system based upon her rigid evangelical faith. It's all-encompassing and bound up with the ways in which others in her peer group also think. That's fine. The problem is that I do not share her basic presuppositions. Maybe once we did, when we were first married. Now I think we have moved in very different directions. While all was outwardly well we got away with it because I was too busy to notice how far apart we had grown. Now it has become obvious to both of us'.

'And how do you think she's going to play it now?'.

'That's the point; I don't know. And I don't know because we have been operating on parallel lines, doing our own thing and not meeting. The things that matter to her, and they do so with a kind of passionate intensity, mean absolutely nothing to me. In fact, it's worse than that, for I feel only contempt for them. And her reaction to my being off work and in therapy tells me that from her perspective my concerns and life are far removed for hers'.

'Do you still love her?'.

'I care for her enormously and feel a profound concern for her well-being. I am also aware that I have been a cause of pain to her. We moved here totally against her desires and now this has happened I can see, and feel, how anxious she is about our future. She is settled and wants to remain so'.

'Yet you have both changed. Perhaps her more than you until now. What is happening to you is a major shift even though I suspect that even you, let alone others, have not yet grasped how seismic the change is going to be'.

Edwin turned to look at Libby, something he rarely did. 'What do you mean?'.

'Something considerable has happened in your life. Already you are aware of that. Your unconscious self is perhaps more aware of it and is striving to protect the outer persona but I think that already you are becoming aware that you are looking at the world differently and that the future may look quite unlike the past'.

For the first time in weeks Edwin returned home via the main streets of the city. He entered the Close and looked over towards his office before continuing, past the wonderful sculpture of a walking woman, under the west end of the cathedral and on towards home. There were few people about as it was not yet eight o'clock, though a canon in his green cassock sprinted, obviously late, across the grass towards the early service.

The Close represented constancy. The very building which dominated it had stood there for centuries and whilst now undergoing considerable restoration would go on standing for many more. At its heart was the practice of a tradition and faith that went back hundreds of years and focussed its attention about that which it claimed was unchanging and eternal. This morning he felt as if these things, stones and practice, were calling him and his life into question. Measured against the building he was tiny and insignificant. Measured against the years he was nothing at all. And that was how he felt. But was it so? Was he just something blown hither and thither, soon to be no more? Christianity seemed to claim that it was only in seeing our relative insignificance that we can rise to our full stature, but was it right first to demean and diminish a man in order only then to restore his dignity? Edwin thought not. He had always found the repeated emphasis on sin and redemption so dispiriting. Why begin there? Why not take glory as the measuring stick rather than failure? Edwin thought of the greatest of human works – music, art, medicine – and did not feel that an account of mankind that ignored them and started with human misery worth the candle.

Home was busy. Megan was running late for school and never at her best first thing. Sylvia was attending a day conference in Southampton and busied herself gathering together the various books and bibles she would need. Edwin decided that keeping a low profile would be the wisest course. Once Megan had departed for school Sylvia felt able to ask Edwin about his session.

'Well, she did reassure me about yesterday. I certainly won't be repeating the trip out today, so you don't need to worry. I will have to look over the proofs.'

'I've been puzzling over what you said yesterday. I'm not in any way doubting you but sometimes children experience things in a particular way which isn't always how adults understand them. Is it possible that this is what has happened to you?'.

It was a difficult question to answer. At one level he knew full well that she was saying something that he knew and understood. He had seen it time and again in court when accusations of abuse based on memories were challenged by barristers. He also knew that even Libby refused to be dogmatic about what he had recounted from his dream. He could not deny that. But he was simultaneously shocked and hurt that she was questioning him, that in effect she was claiming that possibly he was the offender, that he was the one making unsubstantiated charges against his mother. He felt as if he were a volcano about to explode.

'I don't believe I'm hearing you say this', he said, holding back the lava flow, but only just. 'I'm not doing this for the air miles you know. I've been going through hell, having to face all sort of ghastly possibilities about my life, seeing everything fall about me, and that's all you can say'.

He got up from the kitchen table, overturning and spilling his coffee.

'Oh shit, shit, shit, shit', he yelled and walked out of the room, through the sitting room into the hall and up the stairs to his study room. He slammed the door closed behind him and sat at his desk looking at the waiting proofs with an animosity that bordered on the murderous.

15

'My parents used to argue a great deal – at least, she used to argue a great deal. Sometimes I would cry myself to sleep as I heard them at it'.

Edwin was speaking about his previous day and evening. 'That must have been so hard for an only child'.

'It's certainly left me feeling so uneasy when there is conflict around. Like last night. I made such an apology when Sylvia came home. And yet part of me knew that while I was grovelling and trying everything to make it alright I had not been in the wrong. And it reminded me that time and again when I was small I used to do that. I was always the one who sought to make peace by apologising'.

'Perhaps it's not so surprising that you have found such a refuge in the law. The idea of a certain and true judgement as opposed to the more arbitrary system of rough justice must be a very deep need within you'.

Edwin smiled.

'But', she continued, 'it is not necessarily a virtue, is it? For the fact is that you act out of your own inner need and not out of a sense of what is just. Why should a child have to put up with the vagaries of your mother's behaviour and be made to feel responsible for them, and why should you constantly have to be the one who bears the guilt and responsibility that in fact lies with others?'.

Edwin sighed and gave a rueful smile.

'To be honest I wouldn't know how else to act'.

'I'm quite sure of that. I suspect that unconsciously you took responsibility for your mother almost immediately. That she went away after you were born – I know not everyone would agree with this but I have seen it too often to doubt it – may have left you feeling unacceptable and therefore the cause of her going away. And if she did suffer from what we would now call post-natal depression, which the family called her "bad nerves", it may be that she made you feel responsible for having caused it. You see, I suspect that as you grew up she became wholly adept at thrusting responsibility onto you. You became the bearer of so many hopes and therefore also of failures. And with your father so often away who else was there? You had tobe the man in the relationship'.

'Even to the extent of what I dreamed?'.

'We cannot know, but it would fit, and even if it did not happen as you dreamed it, perhaps that is exactly what it felt like. After all she wanted from you satisfaction and good feeling'.

Edwin was suddenly aware of feeling very defensive, and not a little awkward.

'Does that imply you think I have made this up, about the dream, that I wasn't remembering something that happened but have created it out of my own sick and sordid imagination'.

'Edwin, I am not your mother, and it sounds to me like you are playing back to me things you think she would say to you. You do not have a sick and sordid imagination. You are someone who has had things done to him, of whatever kind, that no child should have to experience. But what you described to me was a dream. You have never claimed that it was a memory. It may be, and as we know, as we have been considering this morning, it would be entirely congruous with her behaviour towards you'.

'So am I left then not knowing, never knowing because I cannot know?'

'How could you do otherwise?'.

Libby seemed uneasy with her question.

'I could ask her. It's becoming fashionable in certain circles to encourage victims to face their abusers. Perhaps I need to do that, to redress the balance, to put things right'.

Libby shifted uneasily in her seat, perhaps wondering where the conversation was leading.

'And what effect does it have, these confrontations between victims and offenders, do they make things better, do they redress the balance, make things right?'

'They cannot undo what has been done certainly, but it is sometimes claimed that in many cases they do at least leave the victims feeling somewhat better about themselves'.

'Though these would be different from your own circumstances, wouldn't they? In the cases you refer to I imagine that they come about after a clear legal conviction for a certain offence and I assume that the circumstances are such as to provide maximum protection for the victim. For you to confront your mother with an accusation such as you might want to make, to do so in an uncontrolled environment, at a time when you are not exactly functioning at your best, that would be quite different'.

'Are you saying that I shouldn't do it? If so how will I ever know what has happened? How will I ever find any reconciliation within myself or peace about it?'.

'I just want you to be aware of the sort of undertaking that might be involved. And I think it possible that even were you to do so it might not produce anything in the way of a satisfactory result. After all your mother has proved herself more than capable of defending herself by attacking back. There is a sporting phrase I came across which expresses it neatly: "getting the retaliation in first". You do not need me to recall the times when that has been the case'.

'There's also a phrase in Sophocles: "One thing could hold the key to it all, a small beginning gives us grounds for hope." Isn't that the point?'.

'Is that from Oedipus?'

'Yes, from near the beginning as he sets out to find the truth'.

'And was his final state, when he had actually discovered the truth, better than his first?'

'Greek audiences might have thought so, but then again, Greek writers always valued truth above ease. Besides which, I have to know. How can I face Sylvia without an answer to her question?'

'I fully understand your wish to know the answer to that one particular question, whether what you dreamed had ever happened in fact. But that would be to focus all the attention from what we have been seeking to do in therapy onto one issue. We have been dealing with a whole history of emotional abuse. Sexual abuse is terrible, of that there is no doubt, but is it really worse than other kinds of abuse, and is it worth focussing upon that one issue especially when, as I suspect, you are not going to get your mother to admit to anything at all, and ignore the rest, of which we have certain knowledge? After all, your breakdown experience preceded the dream. What was going on inside you was happening without it'.

'Yes, but only consciously. Surely you've always said that unconscious forces are not only just as powerful as the conscious but usually even more so?'

'Indeed, and I'm not saying it is not so. I suppose I'm just a little uneasy about a process in which you would be handing over so much control to the most unstable participant. Perhaps I am being over-protective towards you but it is only a couple of days since you had an unusual and unpleasant experience which drew you to the edge of a grimpen. I suppose I am counselling caution'.

Sylvia had suggested they spend the day out in the countryside. She had a day away from her church work and it was one of those times in late winter when spring advanced its energies, mild and sunny. They drove out towards Dorchester which Edwin always loved because of its associations with Hardy. There was a supermarket there in which they could get some shopping done before going out of town for a walk and a picnic. Mostly Edwin let her talk about her work and a host of names, most of which were unknown to him. He limited his own contributions to observations on nature and a discussion about what they would do during half-term. Sylvia and Megan would be going to the Fens for a few days and he felt he had to go to Cumbria.

It was Sylvia who eventually broached the matters of the days behind them.

'I need to say sorry to you, Ed, for what I said yesterday morning, you know, about what you told me about you and your mother'.

He wanted to reassure her that such was unnecessary.

'No, let me finish,' she said. 'I was deeply shocked by what you told me but as I've thought about it, and I also read something I saw in Southampton, I have to try and get past those feelings. I can't understand how it must feel. But I can see what has been happening to you, not just in the last weeks, and not just even since that awful trip to France, but always in your relationship with your mother. So I am really sorry for appearing so cruel in what I said. I'm on your side even if I'm at a bit of a loss to know just what side that is'.

Edwin took her hand in his and sighed.

'To be perfectly honest neither do I. When I get out here into the countryside and see spring arriving it all seems so stupid and insignificant. Here I feel so much at ease, even with whatever it is that has happened and is happening. It was like that when I walked up to the racecourse – I was feeling so good again, better than for a very long time. Of course I know full well that it doesn't last. I can't live out here and even if I did I would catch up with myself pretty soon. So somehow or other I have to go on with this and try to get it and me sorted. But if I have your understanding then it makes all the difference in the world'.

They kissed lightly, held hands more tightly and enjoyed a rare moment of oneness.

Edwin was pleasantly surprised by how well his father looked. He had spent a large proportion of the journey north trying to prepare himself for an emaciated figure waiting for him on the platform at Carlisle and was astonished to see that his dad had clearly put some weight on since the operation.

'I'm beginning to think you're nothing but an old fraud', he said to his father as they drove out of the city.

'Fraud definitely; old, never'.

They laughed and the conversation, inevitably, turned to real matters: cricket, and the Rugby Six Nations. If England were faring badly with bat and ball, at least the nation's rugby team were faring well.

Edwin had travelled up after his session with Libby on the Friday and was intending to remain until Sunday. On the Saturday morning he suggested to his father that they might like to go and watch Aspatria play rugby in the afternoon, a suggestion to which his father warmed instantly. The game was very ordinary but Edwin enjoyed being out with his father and there was much laughter and banter in the tiny grandstand where they sat. It was odd, thought Edwin, that it took a life-threatening illness to bring a father and son close together.

On the way back Edwin broached the subject of his own health..

'Actually dad, I've been off work for a while'.

'Oh?'. There was deep concern in his father's voice. 'You're not in any trouble, are you?'.

'Oh good heavens no. Well not like that. But trouble of a sort. They're treating me for depression'.

Silence.

'I've not been so good for a while, to be honest,' he continued, desperately hoping his father might say something soon. However the silence from his father persisted and Edwin drove on without glancing to the passenger seat. This was getting to be uncomfortably like therapy. They must have gone three or four miles in silence before his father spoke.

'Reckon you've been watching too much cricket. That's enough to make anyone depressed'.

Edwin smiled, relieved to hear something, anything, from his father but also pained that it was such a remark. He decided to press on further.

'It's to do with my mother. To do with how she was with me when I was small. To do with how difficult I find her'.

'There's a pub about a mile ahead', said his father. 'Stop there and we'll get a drink'.

Edwin bought a pint for his dad and a glass of wine for himself and they sat down in a quiet comer. There was only one other customer. It was early.

'She tricked me into marriage', Edwin's father began without any prompting. 'When I look at you of course I cannot regret that. But she tricked me. She told me she was pregnant. In those days that was a big deal, not like now. She had a terrible reputation as a teenager. Do you know, her father even told me that – your grandad. I suppose you would say she was a tart. I don't think she particularly liked it, sex I mean, but she liked the power it gave her. I fell for it. By the time she admitted she was not pregnant the marriage had been arranged and I was trapped. I think she saw me as her route to money and position'.

Edwin had heard nothing like this from his father. He had no intention of interrupting.

'I knew from the beginning that I had made a terrible mistake. She could be foul; you've never heard a woman use language as she did. She was ruthless in her ambition, mostly pushing and driving me. She was never satisfied, always wanting more and always wanting position. She had only wanted a girl and rejected you when you were born, It was your gran who took care of you.

'Our relationship changed. For someone who'd once been so sexually active she was never much interested. I put more and more of my energies into my work and I was ambitious too. The business expanded. We had more money than ever before. Macmillan was quite right when he said we'd never had it so good. Yet for all that we had in terms of money I was miserable. I have to admit that I did have affairs. I know she did. She had a job for a while working as a secretary - this would be in the early 60s and I know full well what she got up to with the directors. And actually I didn't give a damn. Divorce wasn't really possible in those days and she wouldn't have wanted that because she stood to lose too much. I was beginning to do well and she liked that'.

There were so many questions that Edwin would have liked to ask but he feared what might happen if the spell were broken.

'I neglected you, I know that, and I wish it had been different. My mother said she was concerned about how your mother was with you. I never knew what she meant by that but I guess I always knew that things weren't exactly right. She used a lot of violence against you, again and agin she would hit you, and mind, not just a smack on the legs but with force across your ace. Once she hist you so hard she sent your glasses flying and broke them. Then at other times she was all over you.You became her project. We knew you were clever and she wanted the reflected glory of your cleverness. But that was how she was'.

He paused and took a drink.

'I wanted to be with her less and less. She liked the money I was making and the prestige as the company expanded. So I stayed away and made money. What she got up to I never knew because I never wanted to know. We used to argue a great deal because I could never be doing enough to satisfy her. She always wanted more, to move to a bigger house, to have a bigger car.

And if she didn't get what she wanted, well she could be foul beyond words. I came to hate her. That's when I decided I'd had enough. You were getting older and it didn't seem to matter that we stayed together any more. In the end she screwed me for as much as she could get, but I didn't care. It was the best thing I've ever done, getting rid of her'.

They sat quietly together for a while. Finally Edwin realised that his father had finished.

'Thanks, dad. It matters to me a great deal'.

'Yeah and what you've got to do, son, is to get rid of her as well. It doesn't surprise me what you say about depression. I don't understand it of course but I'm not surprised. All I can say is do what I did and get rid of her out of your life completely'.

By the time they arrived back for the tea Iris had prepared the conversation had returned to cricket and rugby. There would be nothing more from his father, because in a way he had given everything he had. On the following day as they embraced at the station, Edwin murmured 'Thanks, dad'. It was an enigmatic smile that he received in return.

Edwin was returning to an empty house and for that he was grateful. He felt that he needed the space and time to process all he had learned from his father. It wasn't easy hearing all he had been told. Who could possibly find it easy to be told that their mother had a reputation for promiscuity or prostitution? And however much he valued his father's reluctant honesty he could not escape feelings of anger towards him for having failed to defend and protect his son. But how do you express anger to a man with a terminal illness? And what good would it do in any case? How do you possibly change the past by being angry in the present? But more than anything else he remained perplexed by the issue of how he might possibly be able to find out whether what he had dreamed was true. Clearly his father could not have answered the question. Yet there were hints and suggestions in what he had said which were consistent with the possibility of abuse. He found what his father had said about the link between her use of sex and power most intriguing because at the end of the day control was what he believed she was most interested in.

Libby noted how energised Edwin seemed by his weekend visit at their first meeting after his return, but from previous experience of highs followed by lows she almost certainly noted it with caution.

'But where does this new information leave you here and now?', she asked.

'I'm not sure what you mean', he replied with a clear tinge of frustration in his voice.

'I mean that you are no further on in trying to find out whether what you dreamed might have happened. You knew before that it might have been and you knew too that your father was unlikely to be able to furnish you with evidence, for I take it that was what you were looking for. I'm not a lawyer, Edwin. Indeed the nearest I have ever been to court is watching Rumpole, but even I can see that you still have no evidence whatsoever. And I simply wonder where that leaves you now. It may or may not be part of your past. But what about your future?'.

Future? It was not a word that had been in Edwin's mind. What future?

16

Edwin was unquestionably beginning to feeling better. The return of light as February moved towards its end fortified him. He had returned his proofs and was beginning to feel bored which he interpreted as a positive sign. He began to feel he ought to be doing something again. And he knew full well that at some stage he was going to have to face people once more. The future, raised so painfully by Libby in their session after his half-term visit to see his father, was pressing upon him in the form of his work. He ought to begin again.

He discussed it with Libby but was not able to perceive what she might be thinking. Of late he had felt that she was more withdrawn than formerly – perhaps because he was getting better. Even Sylvia had softened her line about his returning to work. In the end he decided to do it because he needed to do something and this was the only something he knew.

Pippa was delighted when he telephoned with the news that he would be coming into the office for the first time to begin to look over his mail and prepare for a return to work. Typically she kept the information to herself so there were a number of very surprised faces when he appeared one morning.

He had no real idea how his work was to begin again. Many of his on-going clients had been redirected to other partners and his post had mostly been dealt with day by day. Indeed, much to his surprise, there seemed little for him to do. He knew, however, that things would quickly pick up once he was back in full harness.

He found meeting people very difficult. He wondered whether it was his own difficulties that predominated or theirs. Even his partners seemed somewhat circumspect in their dealings with him. Not having enough to do he tended to linger longer over coffee and go for wanders around the Close in work time, something totally new to his experience.

The most obvious thing for him to pick up was his academic work but when essays began to arrive he noticed he no longer had much in the way of interest in their content. He had arranged to meet with Jayne Callard to go over her project which he was supervising. She needed to complete this satisfactorily in order to conclude her qualification process in England. He decided he would take it home with him and work at it over the following weekend prior to their meeting.

Sylvia was delighted to see him working again. She knew he was still on medication and attending therapy but felt considerably less anxious about the possible consequences for them as a family. In any case she was now in the middle of the major evangelistic mission and she felt she was able to direct all her energies towards this now Edwin was getting better. She might have wished that his experience had led him to a deeper understanding of his need for God but she knew there was still time.

As he sat down to look it over at the weekend Edwin found Jayne's work unexpectedly disappointing. Much of the research was inadequate with far too much weight being placed on flimsy and insufficient evidence. Her central argument was insubstantial and his overall impression was that the work had not really been done anywhere thoroughly enough. She was coasting. And though that was not an uncommon process with students he knew that he would have to say this unequivocally to her. The difference was that she was also a colleague. That could make it uncomfortable but he hoped to make it as positive an occasion as possible and he began to think of clear guidance and help he could offer her. After all, she had taken on some of his work during his absence. It was the least he could do.

Throughout the period since his breakdown Edwin had continued to receive telephone calls from his mother each month. It would have been quite impossible for him to say that he was noticeably colder towards her as a result of his therapeutic experience because, as he knew full well, he had not been warm towards her for as long as he could remember. But every time she rang he wanted to ask her about his dream and he wanted to say things to her about the past. And every time he failed to do so. This was not her week to call, but on the Sunday morning he sat down and wrote a letter.

Dear Mum,

I am writing this to you only and not to Claude as well because it concerns matters to do with your past and mine and no one else's.

Last November I had what can best be described as a sort of nervous breakdown, since which time I have been off work and being treated for depression. I have not said anything about this to you because it seems that much of the cause of what has happened lies in my childhood and I have wanted to be more clear in my mind about it all before I could say anything to you. That goes also for my dad, though obviously his illness also meant I could not say anything to him until I saw him a week or two back. In therapy it has become clear to me that a major source of my unhappiness and pain originates in my earliest years. Inevitably that has meant exploring the relationship between you and me and I must confess that at times this has been bewildering and painful.

I know that after I was born you suffered from what is now called 'post-natal depression' and that your own needs were so pressing that they inevitably took precedence over mine. But it seems to have left me with a considerable vulnerability in certain areas of my life, all of which now seem to have conspired together to bring about my ill health. I derive no pleasure from describing any of this. Indeed my life has been turned upside down by it and I am struggling to make sense of it all. I do know however that it is important for me to communicate this to you, not because it can change the past but so that in some way its hold upon me can be diminished. I would hope too it might find in you a place of recognition and from that place you can offer me some compassion and understanding. I do not want to blame but to understand – you as well as me.

I know this letter will be difficult for you, but it is, I believe, essential to my healing and towards there being any possible kind of future relationship between us.

And of course I remain your son. Edwin.

As he read it over he realised how general it was and he wondered he should begin again and deal more with specifics. In the end he left it as it was because he wanted it to be more about a new and different kind of future than with raking up the past. She presumably knew all about that however much she might have conveniently have forgotten much of it. He sealed the envelope and addressed it. It was posted on his way to therapy on Monday morning, and he made no mention of it to anyone.

His meeting with Jayne was scheduled for the period immediately after coffee. To be honest he had little to do before it. Work was slow in coming in and he recognised that such was the penalty of long absence. He thought that perhaps he ought to let the social services and police know that he was back but decided that he was perhaps not quite ready for that yet.

He met Jayne in her room. That seemed much more friendly. The conversation opened on light matters: how she was settling in, her work load, how she enjoyed the life of the city. Then he turned to her work.

'I've given your project a lot of time over the weekend, Jayne. Completing qualification over here is so important to your future that I thought I should give it my full attention'.

'It's ridiculous Edwin. I had a busy and, if I may say so, highly successful practice in the States. The idea that I have to do this sucks. It's like being asked to do rookie work all over'.

Edwin was sympathetic.

'I'm sure it must be extremely frustrating, especially to one such as yourself with the academic training you have had. The only problem is that it does nevertheless have to fulfil the requirements demanded by the Society and verified by the University. And it's a problem because, and no doubt for very good reasons, as it is, as it stands now, it doesn't meet those standards. Now I think we can probably agree certain areas where you will need to work at it and I can probably direct your focus on a number of key weaknesses ... '.

He was not allowed to continue.

'What do you mean "doesn't meet those standards"?'. Her tone was aggressive.

'I mean that as your supervisor I have to see evidence that your research is sufficient to satisfy the university criteria... '.

She stopped him again.

'Are you saying my work is crap?'.

'Of course not, simply that as a piece of academic work required to meet certain minimum standards it does not yet do so, but I am sure that we can get them up... '.

'What gives you the right to sit in judgement on me? I mean what gives you the right to adopt the high moral ground with me? Because your shitty little English standards are so pedantic? Get real Edwin, I'm way out of this class and shouldn't have to be doing it in the first place. It's a total insult. And I bet you wouldn't be saying this if I was a man'.

'Jayne, I know this is not ideal... '.

'You bet your fucking last dollar it's not ideal. You want my advice? Take my project Edwin and shove it up your fucking screwed up arse. Ok? Now just piss off.'

She was now shouting. Edwin was feeling profoundly distressed and on the verge of tears. He stood and walked to the door, opened it and as he walked out felt as if he might faint. Behind him from the open door a voice shouted out 'Just fuck off, schmuck, and when you've got your brain back in one piece, if ever, stay away. Nobody wants you back here. D'you know that?'.

The door slammed.

He did not know whether anyone had heard. He desperately hoped not. He was shaking as he made his way down the stairs to his first floor office. He closed the door and burst into tears. That did not help, for moments later his door opened and Paul entered.

'Are you alright Edwin? Oh dear, I'm so sorry. Perhaps you had better go home. I heard some shouting and wondered what it was'.

'I'm fine, Paul, just had a bit of a difficult conference with someone'.

Thus it was that in trying to protect Jayne by not telling him the truth, he found himself providing Paul with the ammunition to take to a meeting of partners later that day which he would use to persuade the partners that they should be encouraging Edwin to resign. Paul maintained that Edwin was causing them to lose business. He was unlikely to get any work himself because his breakdown was common knowledge in the city and other solicitors advised clients against using him. Now it was clear he wasn't emotionally able to manage such work as he did have. Jayne Callard added that she had significant evidence that his academic judgement was seriously impaired following his illness, and that she had gained the impression from her university contacts that Edwin might soon be asked to leave the faculty. The partners agreed that Paul should have a private word with him. They all felt that the best course for Edwin would be to re-establish his practice elsewhere once, that is, he was better and Paul's report of how he had found him suggested that was far from the case at present. Jayne supported Paul's testimony recounting how Edwin had simply got up and walked out of the room during a discussion with her when she had simply questioned an aspect of his judgement. "It was very unpleasant", she had reported.

His encounter with Jayne plunged Edwin back into despondency. He had been feeling so much better, looking forward, experiencing a resurgence of strength and hope. He had left his office almost as soon as Paul had departed and walked out across the grass towards the cathedral. Already the hordes of visitors that choked the Close each summer were returning. The scaffolding on the central tower and on much of the spire now denied visitors the delights beloved of generations.

What would Constable have made of this?, he wondered. Though he also knew that when Constable had made his famous painting of the spire it was not just picturesque Britain that he was recording. The world had been changing, his beloved wife had recently died and Constable feared for the future of his country, not least the Church of England, in the light of the impending Reform Act of 1832. When he painted the spire from the meadows it was not a spire in sunshine but under a dark and stormy sky. Such hope as he could muster was expressed in the famous, rather emphatic, rainbow overarching cathedral and landscape alike. But what now? Edwin could not manufacture a rainbow and even had he been able to do so what sort of spire would it now hang over? In its present state it seemed a poignant but wholly accurate symbol of a church in disarray and, ironically, over the loss of its masculinity.

There was no rainbow for Edwin that morning, nor a way into the cathedral. Turnstiles had long been in use in the cathedral and Edwin could not accept them. He had no stomach for argument or bad feeling, and headed instead for home.

He was still shaking when he arrived home, rehearsing over and over in his mind the disagreeable encounter. He could not believe that she could have behaved as she had. It had been his advocacy that had won for her a partnership. He had continued to defend her when she had seemed to be struggling. How could she have said what she had said to him? And to what extent did her comments about his "brain" reflect those of his other colleagues? Were they all thinking such thoughts? And was that why there was no work for him?

He decided to telephone Libby. They had met earlier that morning but he needed to speak with her, just hear her voice. As if by magic it was not the answering machine.

'Libby, it's Edwin', he blurted in response to her greeting. 'Look something's happened, something awful', and he went on briefly but at breakneck pace to recount the events of the morning. Before she could say anything he then added, 'And I have done something which I haven't told you about: I've written to my mother'.

As was her style on the telephone Libby did not deal with the content of what he had said but directed both their minds to the process of attending to it. She offered him another early morning session for the following day, to which he eagerly consented.

Edwin was relieved that he would have the chance to see Libby again in the morning, but in the meantime he had to try and settle his nerves which were still all a-jangle. He headed out across the water-meadows, not by the visitors' route, but by a back way that headed out towards the little village of which George Herbert had once been incumbent. Unfortunately that little village was now just a suburb of the city and the lovely walkway ended up passing an abattoir but the little church was always worth a visit. Edwin liked old churches. He had no time for those who said that faith had nothing to do with buildings and he endorsed Larkin's description of them as "a serious house on serious earth" whilst simultaneously feeling excluded from the adolescent theoretical framework within which their present day tenants conducted themselves. Perhaps in another age faith might have been possible, but not now. But standing sub specie aeternitatis always provided a measure of stability to him, and it did so even within the rough currents which had home him to this particular "serious house".

'What are you doing here?'.

Not the warmest of greetings from a wife.

'It's going to take time to build up the work again', he replied. 'There's no point just sitting in my office doing nothing. So I've been out for a walk'.

Sylvia was regarding him as if she knew he was being economical with the truth. 'There's a message for you on the answering machine from Paul'.

'Oh?'.

He tried to sound disinterested. She knew otherwise and he knew she knew.

"Edwin, Paul here. I am concerned about you. Clearly things were too much for you this morning. I wonder whether I might call round to see you – what about first thing in the morning? Say 9-30. Let my secretary know if that's no good. Otherwise I'll see you then. Bye!".

'What's he referring to?', demanded Sylvia, 'what things were too much for you?'.

Edwin did not need the third degree from Sylvia; he had only just begun to recover from the morning's mauling.

'Nothing was. It's just Paul over-reacting and quite unnecessarily. He thought I couldn't handle something and I could and did. I think they're all a bit over-protective towards me. They'll stop'.

'So why's he coming here in the morning when you should be there?'.

'I have nothing first thing and I must have mentioned that I was doing some work at home?'.

'What work? You have no work here'.

'Well I'm beginning to get the Journal back up and running again, or at least I'm trying to catch up with all that has happened with it'.

He did not like lying to his wife. He did not like lying at all, not least because he knew full well that it is always harder to remember lies than the truth. But to protect himself he felt he had no choice at this time. Why should he have to speak about what he did not wish to, even to his wife?

The shock of his meeting with Jayne had not left him even by the time of his session on the following morning. He began with an account of all that had taken place and his brief encounter with Paul afterwards. He still could not get past his sense of disbelief that someone whose appointment he had so vigorously supported, who had needed and received his continuing commitment when in office and whose ability he still felt sure of, could behave towards him as she had done. He was also very hurt by the comments about his brain and her statement that no one wanted him back. He just did not know how anyone could behave in that way, and he expressed himself horrified that a solicitor, and especially a woman solicitor, could have used the sort of language she had employed. All in all he felt that the real pain of the occasion had been the breach of trust.

Libby heard him without comment. She knew he needed to offload. Eventually he stopped.

'Trust is an important issue in all this, Edwin, you are quite right about that. Your track record has not been all that positive especially with regard to women. Your colleague's betrayal of your trust and support, and she did not know that even after she had done her worst you would go on excusing her behaviour – and we might well try and work out why on earth you should have done that – repeat the pattern of your mother's betrayal of you. Even though it was a horrible event in itself, no doubt your experiences which you continue to carry about within you will have made it even harder to endure'.

'I have no idea why I said what I did to Paul. Actually I wasn't in a fit state to know what to do and I just said the first thing that came to mind'.

'Which was of course never to blame a woman, even though she had just given you considerable abuse'.

Edwin said nothing.

'And I keep wondering how this is related to the other issue of the day, also to do with trust of a woman, and that is the question of why you should write to your mother and yet not share that with me, even though we had a session either immediately before or after you had posted your letter to her'.

'They're hardly related'.

'Oh, I'm not so sure, Edwin. Indeed I think they might well be closely related because they both have to do with trust in relation to women – you know, those people who abuse you, who make a nuisance of themselves to you, who ask difficult and uncomfortable questions'.

If her intention had been to make Edwin feel guilty she had succeeded, and he could feel his ears burning.

'Surely I am free to do as I choose. I don't have to obtain your permission to write a letter'.

'Of course you are. Most definitely. But why, when we have spoken so much about it, has it been necessary for you to avoid telling me. After all therapy isn't a contest of wills. It's meant to be about discovering the possibility of healing so that for the future you have life rather than death staring you in the face. For that to happen we need to consider and work at your relating to women, including this woman. You don't have to do so of course. In that sense you are free not to come, but if we are to work together we have to think hard about why you have acted as you did. I really believe it is most important'.

'Yes, I'm sorry, I should have mentioned it to you'.

'But Edwin what you do is not for me to judge. In that sense your sorrow is entirely inappropriate. I neither care nor care less about the fact that you have written. I care very much about understanding why you did not tell me'.

'I suppose I feared you might not approve. I thought that you didn't think I should write. So I decided to do it without saying anything to you'.

'Until when?'

'I don't follow'.

'Well presumably at some stage there will be a response or none at all. Either will affect you in one way or another. We would then have to look at it and presumably that would have been confession time'.

Edwin was now feeling singularly crestfallen as Libby could see clearly.

'But what matters now' she quickly continued, 'is that we try to make sense of what has happened. You have done what you felt you needed to do. That can only be good and I dare say it was a costly thing to have done. In time we shall indeed have to consider her response. All I am saying now is that there are big issues involved in the way you have done it that we need to think about and reflect upon. And also we need to think more about how you handled what happened with your woman colleague. How she behaved is beyond our capacity to change. How you handled and responded to it may not be'.

Time and again Edwin had gone into therapy expecting one thing only to receive another. Perhaps it was that he expected it to be analgesic only to discover that Libby had a quite different agenda. The problem was that he just did not know whether he had the strength to do the hard work. Sometimes he just felt overwhelmed by the pain he felt.

Before their session ended Edwin had confided to Libby the content of his letter to his mother. She agreed with him that its contents were not too specific but she felt that it probably would still have a considerable effect. She feared that Edwin still had more pain to come and that he was by no means ready for it.

As he made his way home on a lovely sunny March morning, on which the birds sang even in the city, he felt grateful for all that he was receiving through his therapy. He felt sure that before long, as he re-established his life in this beautiful city, it would prove to have been so valuable.

17

Sylvia had decided she ought to be with Edwin when Paul came, though had she been asked why she would not have been able to give any kind of logical answer. It was not that she did not trust Paul so much as she felt she could not wholly trust Edwin. He so easily gave way in his dealings with colleagues. He might well hold onto his own beliefs and principles but she knew full well how he often sacrificed himself when others were involved.

Paul arrived on time. After the customary pleasantries Edwin suggested they went upstairs to talk but Sylvia insisted that they remain in the sitting room. By seating herself firmly in an armchair she also made it perfectly clear that she also intended to be present.

Edwin was hesitant.

'I suspect it's about work that Paul has come to speak, Sylvia', as if that was her cue to disappear.

'Oh well', she said, not moving a muscle other than to speak, 'if you get down to detail I'll go'.

'It's fine for you to be here Sylvia because of course it affects you as well', Paul began. 'Well, I'll come straight to the point. Yesterday afternoon we had an informal chat, those partners present that is. We were thinking about you, Edwin, and how best to enable you to get back into the practice of law. We've missed you, and not least your capacity to make us think hard about what we are doing. I think we all feel something of the pain of what has happened to you.

'I'm sure you've noticed that most of your existing work has been taken over and that at the moment there's not a lot in your in-tray. Obviously we didn't know when you'd be back so it has been essential for us just to get on, though of course hoping that you'd be able to be back sooner rather than later. But the way things have worked out it isn't quite so straightforward. I fear that your, er, incident, er, in October, you know, round at Anthony Whitmore's chambers has had something of a knock-on effect. You know what people are like; they can be odd with things to do with, well, you know, things like that'.

Edwin was now feeling very uncomfortable. What was coming?

'I'm afraid', continued Paul, determined, now he that had begun, to complete his mission, 'the somewhat public nature of what happened has become common knowledge. It has meant that people are somewhat assuming that it means you will not be up to working again'.

'But that's ridiculous', protested Sylvia.

'Of course it is', agreed Paul, a little too swiftly. 'Of course it is. But that's how people are. They can be so cruel. And that is how they are being. With our firm too, not just your work Edwin. There's no doubt that we are losing work at present, and I think we all feel that however unjustly and wholly lacking in compassion it is, the reason is your, er, condition'.

'Edwin's not the first solicitor to suffer from depression, Paul. I bet quite a few in this city take stronger tablets than he does and many of them drink a great deal more than he ever has'.

'Oh I know, and it's tragic that it is so. Ours is a stressful occupation, Edwin. I know that. The difference, however, is that most of them don't have happen to them what happened to you. We don't stumble into a rival chambers and collapse publicly. We bear out stresses and strains a little more discretely'.

Edwin was feeling strangely numb all over. He did not speak because he wasn't wholly sure that he could speak, and he was stunned too by the anger implicit in Paul's last words.

'I don't believe I'm hearing you say this Paul', said Sylvia with more than a little menace in her voice.

'Hear me out, please', appealed Paul.

Sylvia continued to look daggers at him but sat back.

'We have to live with what is, not what we hope might be. This is a small city and professional life has a high profile. In London none of this would have been an issue, but it is not London. We cannot act as if this has not happened and we all have to endure the consequences, however painful'.

'It seems to me, Paul, from what you're saying that some of us may have to endure them more than others', said Sylvia.

'Yes, I think that is so. I think, to be frank, that it is unlikely that Edwin will be able to practice here again'.

Edwin noticed that he had been excluded from the meeting by both of them, and that in the last words Paul had referred to him in the third person, almost as if he were not there. And he began to wonder whether he was there or whether this was just a dream turning into a nightmare. He gazed out of the window and could just see the top of the spire. It was a blustery morning and as he looked he saw the clouds scudding across the sky behind the spire. And as he gazed and found his mind entranced by the beauty his eyes surveyed he was aware that somewhere else a conversation was continuing but one that he had no part in. It was a sudden and rather pointed silence that drew him back in much the sort of way it is sometimes said the dying are drawn back from light into the awful reality of resuscitation.

Sylvia and Paul were both looking at him expectantly.

'I was looking at the clouds behind the spire', he volunteered.

Sylvia could have despaired at that moment. Paul simply felt a sense of sad satisfaction; how could someone in such a state work again?

Edwin rose.

'I need to be getting on. I think I'll go out for a wander. It's such a nice morning'.

He opened the door and collected his coat before heading out the front door towards the water meadows.

Before the door had closed Sylvia was in tears. Paul moved to comfort her and she let him hold her hand.

'I'm so sorry Sylvia. I cannot imagine what this must be like for you. We have prayed for you every day and hoped and hoped for a sudden improvement in Edwin's condition but it just isn't happening. Yesterday I came across Edwin after a conference with someone and he was in tears and shaking. I fear he might also have lost his temper with a client because there was shouting heard. That's no basis for beginning again and I fear word travels very fast. I think he needs treatment of some kind'.

Through the tears Sylvia murmured something about psychotherapy but added that she thought that was also the cause of what had happened.

'I think we both know that's not the treatment Edwin needs. We both heard that wonderful sermon in which psychotherapy was quite clearly numbered amongst the devil's weapons', came the sympathetic reply. 'I wish we could have got him to a Christian counsellor and perhaps also to a Christian GP. It would have made such a difference.'

'And what's to happen to me, Paul? My work? My life? and Megan's school?'

'We must trust in the Lord's guidance, Sylvia. We both know that is where our only true hope lies'.

'But why would he want to stop me from doing what I am doing here. There's so much happening and so much to be done'.

Paul had returned to his seat.

'It is not always easy for us to know and understand the ways of the Lord. Perhaps you've reached the end of what you can do here. Perhaps you are meant to be giving more of your self to Edwin and his support and strengthening'.

She looked at him steadily.

'Is that what people say at church?'.

'Well, you know how it is. People say strange, even unkind, things though sometimes there's a kernel of truth in them too. You know, about leading and teaching other women whilst being unable to look properly after your own husband, and about him not being a Christian. Some worry about that, given our firm adherence to the scriptural principle of headship. If he exercises headship over you as a non-Christian does that not inevitably tarnish your work? That sort of thing. It's only a few who say that, but they also have a voice that the elders hear. And perhaps this is a message from the Lord about your own priorities at this time'.

'Is this what you think, Paul?'.

'I think you have done good work among us. I do sometimes worry about the key role you have been assuming. It is one thing for a woman to act as assistant to the pastor in regard to ministry among and to women, but there is a great danger that it will become more than that.

'Women cannot be in leadership positions, you know that. It isn't our decision, it's an absolute of scripture, and we both know what happens to churches that fail to follow scripture. Look what it is already doing to the Church of England. They now have loads of women vicars almost in direction proportion to the rate their churches are emptying. Our church is growing at such a pace because we follow scripture to the letter, because it is the Lord's word to us. And therefore even though this will perhaps be a bit of a disappointment to you, if it helps you do what the Lord wants for you, then, and only then, can you discover true joy'.

It was not disappointment that Sylvia was feeling; it was

devastation.

Paul said that he had to go though not before leading Sylvia in prayer'

'Lord, we praise and thank you for your guidance, that you never leave us without comfort even when things are hard and dark. We praise and thank you for all that you have been doing through Sylvia's work for your glory. And we ask that at this time your guiding light may be with her so that she may strive always to do your will with a joyful countenance. And we just ask that today your Holy Spirit will anoint and strengthen her in her life with Edwin and Megan. Lord, we really praise you for Jesus, your Son. May his redeeming love which we have seen on the cross enter even now into Edwin's heart and draw him closer to you so that he may know that healing he needs, that he may repent of his sins and come to know you as Lord and Saviour. All this we ask in his name. Amen'.

Sylvia echoed the Amen and held tightly onto Paul's hands. He leant forward and gently kissed her on the forehead.

March could disappoint. The balmy days of February hinted at an imminence of the Spring that was not always realised. The wind that was causing the clouds to move so fast was from the north-east, and even here in the south of England was raw. Edwin wandered without much thought. It had rained heavily during the night and much of the meadows was flooded. Still it meant that he largely had the town-path to himself apart, that is, from the wildfowl. It was not raining at present but it might at any time.

He stopped about half-way across the walkway and gazed over towards the cathedral. He could see the O'Connell's house, the museum and almshouses and above them and behind them the mighty west end of the cathedral with its spire towering over all. It was beautiful place. And in that beautiful setting what kind of hell had he unearthed?

He had long since given up trying to correct those who out of ignorance spoke of Pandora's "box". As every student of classical mythology knew, it was a vase out of which came all the dreadful things which have affected mankind. But whatever the source the end was the same. The same myth recurred in all the great religious traditions of the world – the innocent wonder of Eden lost for ever. And there it was before him: the tourists' paradise, the spire as symbol of the aspirations of men across the ages, stability, order and beauty in the buildings about it. But beneath and between, albeit perhaps on a smaller scale, all the hatreds and jealousies to match all the wars that could ever be. But it was odd to find himself as the enemy against whom the forces of the allies had united.

He knew of course that they could not make him leave. He was no expert in employment law but he enough to know that his tenure was secure - legally. But he also knew that he probably had little choice. They were right. He was finished. And oddly he felt relieved and at ease about it. He smiled inwardly. Libby might say that this was what he had been, albeit unconsciously, seeking to engineer all along.

So maybe the old middle eastern myth (as he preferred to think of it, given the way in which Christianity had claimed it for its own and then distorted it) of the exile from Eden was true. There was to be no way back. A solicitor with a flaming sword barred the entrance. Pleased with his image Edwin pulled his collar up. It had finally begun to rain and his hands were suddenly very cold. And as he headed home he began to be anxious about what he would find there. Adam might indeed be pleased to be out of Eden; of Eve he was not so sure.

By the time he reached home he was soaking wet. His coat had been inadequate to withstand vagaries of the wind, but when the rain came its shortcomings had become immediately and, even more obviously, apparent. And that started them off completely on the wrong foot, for in becoming immediately cross about his clothing Sylvia had rapidly moved into the mode she had hoped to be able to avoid.

'Look at you', she said, catching sight of the bedraggled figure entering the doorway. 'Why must you be so stupid? Considering how clever you're supposed to be you just have no idea. It's no wonder everything's fallen apart. For heaven's sake, go and change'.

He re-emerged a few minutes later and went into the kitchen to make himself a cup of tea. She followed him.

'Well?', she asked.

'Well what?'

An unlikely and unconvincing innocence.

'What have you got to say for yourself? Why, why, why did you ever go and see that woman. She's the one who's done this. She's the one who's poisoned your mind and our life. I have a good mind to go round and see her and tell what havoc she has wreaked in our home. It's not your mother, Edwin, it's you that's the problem. You and that... , that..., therapist. She's evil and just look what has happened'.

'Don't over-react Sylvia', replied Edwin, continuing to put a tea bag into a cup and busying himself doing anything rather than look at his wife.

'Over-react? Over-react? Oh, so I just get told we've got to go, sell-up and move where I don't want to go. Told that we've got to take Megan away from her school. Told that my husband is not wanted because he can't hack the job. Told that I am not wanted in my job. And then I'm told not to over-react. Well thank you very much'.

Edwin picked up the reference to her work and asked what she meant. She was getting somewhat agitated.

'Paul told me that because of you, because of what's happened to you the people of the church think I'm not able to do my job properly, that I should be spending more time caring for you and making you better'.

'Very Christian!'.

'But the point is that they're right. What have you done for me? I moved to Edinburgh when I didn't want to. I left there when I most definitely didn't want to. Both times it was because you wanted to, because of your career. And I did it. But what have you done to support me in my work? Why couldn't you have come to church even sometimes? Why did you have to get into all this psychological nonsense?'

'You would have preferred me to be hypocritical then, say that I believe what I can't?'

'You go into the cathedral. You go to Evensong there, so you tell me. Why is that not hypocritical but giving your wife support is?'.

'Because it is wholly non-intrusive. They let me be me. Whenever I have been to your church they are always requiring me to be something I'm not. They don't accept me as I am. They want to me to change to be acceptable. They want me to be like them in every detail, all believing the same thing. And only if I do that am I allowed to be regarded as satisfactory. Cathedral Evensong isn't like that'.

'That's because it's just a free concert of nostalgia put on for the benefit of the tourists. We believe certain very particular things. What's wrong with that?'

'Nothing. People should be free to believe what they want, or what they can. That includes me, and your church does not offer that freedom. Your church does not believe in that freedom. And it obviously doesn't even believe in it for you either. Otherwise why would they be wanting to get rid of you? Why on earth should what happens to me have anything to do with how effective you are at your work?'.

'Because we are one flesh, Edwin, and part of that deal is about giving and receiving, and I think it would not have hurt you to put your precious intellectual superiority on one side and come and support me'.

Edwin was feeling as if the clouds outside were pressing down upon his head, he needed to sit down, to defuse the tension. He picked up his cup of tea, took a deep gulp and then headed out of the kitchen into the sitting room.

'Don't you think you need to check this out with your pastor? In any case they employ you and you have rights under the law, whatever Paul might say. Just as I have. They can't get rid of me just because I've become a source of embarrassment to them. Employment law protects us both. To be honest I don't trust Paul Raven. He reminds me of Bunyan's Mr Facing-Both-Ways'.

'I think for you to be applying names to anyone is a case of the pot calling the kettle black. You are the problem, Edwin, not Paul. It's you that have made such a drama out of everything. I just can't believe that you had to go and have your performance in the doorway of Anthony Whitmore's chambers. I can't believe that you were shouting at someone at work yesterday. If anyone needs to be considering their position it's you, not Paul'.

Edwin was startled by what he was hearing. Clearly weeks of resentment had been building up ready to overflow with force. And what was this about him shouting at work? How could anyone not have heard that woman screeching at him? How come it was now he who was supposed to have been shouting? And what had that American woman said to the others? And all these things he should have been voicing, and about some of them he probably should have been shouting. But he could not. Indeed suddenly all his energy seemed to surge out of him. He felt utterly and completely overwhelmed as if he was caught in the flood of a river against which he was powerless.

There are silences and silences. Edwin had always enjoyed hearing about Geoffrey Day in Hardy's Under the Greenwood Tree of whose silence it was said: "There's so much sense in it. Every moment is brimmen over wi' sound understanding".

Libby's silences were always of concern to Edwin. Sometimes he felt he could hear her thinking. At other times he felt she was almost playing with him and using silence as her tool. But on this morning, as he told her about what had taken place on the previous day, her silence was almost electric as if she was devoting all her attention to every word whilst simultaneously suppressing the sense of shock he instinctively knew she was experiencing. And it took some time for her to speak after he had finished.

'I'm at something of a loss to know what to say in response to all that', she began. 'Perhaps it would help both us if you were able to let me have some indication of what it is you are feeling about it all. You've given me an account of the various encounters but I don't know how you are actually feeling about them all this morning'.

'I suspect that I am not at all sure what I feel, but then again, I am beginning to realise how true that has been about most things and people for a very long time'.

'There have probably been very good reasons for that. Indeed I would suggest that not feeling things too much has been your way of coping with them. But the very fact of your being in therapy is indicative of what happens when you have a whole lifetime of doing that. We might wonder what it is you are steering clear of.

'Anger, I suspect'.

'Some of the things you have described to me about yesterday would certainly have the effect of producing considerable anger in some people. Did it not make you feel angry?'

'Oh, well, yes, of course, but then I just found myself thinking: what's the point in getting angry? What would it contribute to making things better?'

'Does injustice not make you angry?'.

'Yes, of course, very angry'.

'But only when it is perpetrated against others? Not yourself?'.

'The way of dealing with injustice is to seek justice. Anger in my experience seeks only revenge. That takes none of us forward'.

Libby could feel her own levels of frustration rising rapidly.

'So your response to what happened yesterday – the assault upon you by your colleagues, and I think that is not too strong; the attack upon Sylvia's work; her own attack upon your integrity – all that, and you think a quiet, almost resigned, detachment is the appropriate response?'

'I know what you are saying but to be honest I'm more hurt than angry. I mean, I can see how they must see it. I have become an embarrassment to the practice and I am still clearly not able to function without my emotions getting the better of me. I find it hurtful but I can see why they are thinking as they are doing'.

'And the accusations made by Sylvia about what you are doing here? What about those?'.

'She doesn't know what she's saying, and in any case she was so upset by what Paul had said to her. I do feel angry about that because he had no right to say those things to her and I have urged her to go and see the pastor without delay'.

'Had he the right to say the things he did to you?'.

'Well if you mean: "Have my partners the legal right to get rid of me for having been ill?", the answer is quite simple: No. But he did not come and say that. He came to say that he thought I was finished, professionally speaking. He had the right to give that opinion, however uncomfortable it made me feel, and no doubt made him feel too'.

'And what about what Sylvia said to you about therapy? I'm sorry to ask again but for some reason you seem to be avoiding the question'.

'I refer the honourable lady to the reply given to a previous question'.

Libby was beginning to seethe.

'Edwin, please don't play games with me. Your employment and livelihood have been placed in serious jeopardy by your colleagues, your integrity has, quite unjustly, been impugned at work and at home, and you seem to regard it as you might a slight chill'.

'Perhaps I'm terrified of how I feel. Has that occurred to you?'. He turned and looked at Libby. 'Maybe, maybe, I'm just shit-scared of what might happen if I allowed myself really to feel and express my feelings. Look at what happened in October when I did that then. Perhaps it's just better to hold it all in'.

He turned away from her again. She could see his hands shaking slightly. She suddenly felt as if she were handling a volatile explosive.

'It is my belief Edwin, that what happened to you was caused not by allowing your self to feel what you did, but because for years and years you did not and suddenly did.. What happened was a kind of controlled explosion. If you had not come to this then I honestly believe you would have suffered far more serious damage than you have. I don't know how, but I do know it would have happened and the consequences would have been much more serious. That may be scant consolation for you or Sylvia, but it is my considered professional judgement'.

Edwin reflected upon these words for a while. Then, quietly and with feeling he replied: 'Thank you, Libby. I think I was beginning to have doubts myself.

She needed to press home her advantage.

'And if you are to have future that is worthwhile, it seems to me that the key lies not in resort to legal niceties about employment legislation or in giving moral arguments their appropriate and measured weight but in being in touch with the truest and best and long-lost Edwin deep inside. And if anger is the only thing that will enable a breakthrough, then so be it'.

18

In the days since Paul's visit Edwin became aware that the two
women he most often saw were becoming frustrated with him. He
knew it and felt completely impotent. Indeed, impotence best
summed up for him how he experienced depression. Part of him
knew full well that he should be feeling angry, that he should be
doing something to redress the wrongs done against him. From his
somewhat perfunctory reading of "psychology for lawyers",
Edwin knew that in certain circles it has been asserted that
depression may be caused by suppressed anger. Fury that should
be turned outwards wreaks its revenge on the inner self if denied
an outing, and in extreme cases can result in suicide. But the part
of him that could see that he ought to be feeling angry seemed
utterly powerless to act.

He had once read a book about melancholy. It had been written
in the later middle ages and sought to understand and analyse an
experience common to so many. Though it was some time since
he had read it and his powers of recall were limited, he
nevertheless felt that the basic impression the book gave was of
melancholy as essentially something creative and out of which
could emerge new perception and insight. There was too a
burgeoning of popular psychology which in too facile a way spoke

of shadows and darkness, something matched in various popular novels, especially of the fantasy genre. But what was becoming apparent to Edwin day by day was that such writers had got it completely wrong. Edwin was finding nothing creative in depression. In fact nothing could be further from the truth.

Depression was to him a loss of touch with the exterior world, mainly through the loss of his capacity to engage directly with it. He trudged along mostly without direct experience of what he was feeling. There was always a delay between event and recognition. What was it Eliot wrote? "'To have had the experience and missed the meaning"? Was that it? Mostly he felt resigned in the face of Libby and Sylvia, and kept repeating to himself "What's the point?". To this was added a mounting sense of self-blame for all that happened. And that at least was reality for he had brought all this upon himself and his family. If he felt the burden of responsibility for them that was because it was his.

He was at least trying to learn how to manage his depression. He had discussed with his GP the effect of too much exercise - the burst of energy followed by its rapid dissipation – and took shorter, slower walks. He was also taking his tablets earlier each evening to allow himself good sleep before midnight and, hopefully, a clearer mind first thing in the morning. But it was also clear that he had been somewhat precipitate in his return to work and he had agreed with the doctor that he would not attempt another return without having discussed it with him and, *a fortiori*, with Libby first.

At the back of his mind there was also the question of the letter to his mother. Two weeks had now passed since he had posted it. Each morning he watched for the arrival of the postman though he was unsure whether he was relieved or saddened by the non-appearance of a reply. That she had received it he had no doubt. Now he had to wait.

It was the week before the clocks went forward, something to which Edwin always looked forward, for he loved the light evenings however chilly they might be in late March. The daffodils in the garden were at their best. Sylvia's undoubted gardening gifts meant that they could enjoy a marvellous springtime show across the bank up the field behind their back lawn: a range of different sorts of daffodil and narcissi meant variety and change. She loved this house and garden and it would be a terrible wrench for her should his incapacity force another move.

Again the postman brought nothing from France, and once Megan had left for school and Sylvia for a women's bible study, Edwin decided to drive along the Chalke Valley on the other side of the racecourse and follow a woodland path he had noticed on the OS map. He had noticed buildings labelled Kennels on the map and assumed they were of a boarding kind. He parked about half a mile from them but could hear dogs barking as he walked towards them. When he was about 150 metres short of the buildings he noticed two men emerge from them, one of them with a large dog on a lead. They walked onto the footpath and then turned in again. Moments later Edwin's heart turned cold as he heard a gun shot. It wasn't the noise of a shot gun or even an air rifle, it sounded even to his ignorant ears like a pistol. As he reached the buildings he saw beyond them a muck heap. The two men were standing on it and at their feet lay the body of the dog. They had just shot it. He could see blood pouring from its nose, and one of the men was undoing the collar round its neck prior to lifting in onto a waiting wheelbarrow. As Edwin looked he saw the body of another dog close by. When the men saw him, one of them quickly put what was obviously the gun they had used into his pocket, and nodded a kind of acknowledgement at Edwin.

Edwin stood there aghast at what he was witnessing. Indeed what was he witnessing? The other man walked over towards him.

'I'm so sorry, sir', he began, 'we hadn't seen you. We usually make sure there's nobody around. It's not our intention to upset anyone'.

'But what on earth are you doing?'. Edwin was suddenly feeling very much in the present and was getting worked up.

'They're old hounds, foxhounds whose working life is over. We have no choice. It's very humane, sir, I can assure you'. He was not intending to continue the conversation. 'Once again please accept my apologies for any distress it may have caused you'. He turned and walked back to his colleague.

Edwin did not know what to do. He was horrified by what he had just witnessed, or at least, heard. He began to walk on slowly. Never in all his life had he ever seen or encountered such a thing. It was terrible. He suddenly found himself gushing tears. He kept thinking of the poor dog on its final walk, its eyes gazing at the master it trusted. And then... bang.

What was he to do? He felt he couldn't just turn round and walk back past the kennels yet there was no way back other than that way. He was sufficiently aware to know that he was getting into a state and should do all he could to get himself back to his car and home. But how was he to do it? He suddenly veered off the track to his left and pushed himself through the branches of the trees. One caught his face and cut it; he could feel the blood running down his cheek mingling with the salt of his tears. He felt wholly out of control, thrashing out blindly before him. Finally he came to the edge of the wood. Beyond the wire fence was a field sown with winter wheat already well advanced. He knew that he should not enter the field but felt there was no alternative and doing so, slowly made his way back along the track formed by the tractor's wheels as it had sprayed the crop, towards the road where his car was parked. At one point there was a break in the wood, now to his left, and he saw the kennels through it, horses in a field and lots of hounds running round a high fenced paddock. And when would their day come for the gun?

By the time he arrived back at his car he was sweating profusely, breathless and, had he looked down and noticed, covered in mud. He could not escape from his powerful sense of identification with the dog: it had been used to its full extent, then taken by hands it had trusted and simply shot dead. And he thought he would never forget the sound of the gun, and the incongruity of it, as it seemed, on such a nice morning in spring surrounded by all the signs of the return of life after the cold and darkness of winter. But here was death – cold and stark.

Eventually he drove home and as he entered the house Sylvia took one look at him in his bedraggled state and cried out 'I can't take any more of this', before running upstairs and slamming closed their bedroom door behind her. Edwin too was beginning to think he had run his own course and that the best thing for everyone would be for him to disappear – for good.

It was Pippa who brought the news. She was by a long way the most discrete secretary Edwin had ever known, much to the frustration of his partners who sometimes complained that she would not disclose to them even relatively trivial matters which they needed for their own work without obtaining the "explicit permission of Mr Lyons". She took the most ancient description of her office as determinative of her style: she was someone privy of necessity to secret matters, and it was not for her to disclose them to anyone. That was what a secretary is, not a typist.

She had come to see Edwin with a document requiring his signature. She had also come to see the man she admired and respected and whom she feared was having far more rough a time than he possibly deserved. The business completed she turned to news from the office. If she had heard anything from the partners' meeting she did not pass it on. She did however tell Edwin that Shelagh (one of the typists and most definitely not a secretary) had been on a train passing through the station at Bath and swears that she saw Veronica Ashby in the arms of Donald Strachan.

'What do you make of that Mr Lyons?'.

Edwin would have preferred to make nothing of it but his mind would not let it go. They were two of his partners and both married to other people! Veronica indeed was a Vicar's wife.

'Well I expect she was mistaken, or a little tipsy. Donald and Veronica!'.

They both laughed.

'And the American woman, what do you think? She was in the tea room yesterday morning. Apparently she's having counselling, something to do with the stress of living in such a small place as this – I don't understand that, most people would think this is one of the least stressful places '.

She stopped, realising what she had just said.

'Oh, I'm so sorry Mr Lyons, what a stupid thing to say. I didn't mean anything about you'.

'Don't be silly, Pippa, I know that. So go on, tell me more'.

'Well, apparently she goes to see a woman here in the city, up on St Edward's Road. Isn't that strange, needing to see someone like that? Do you think it's because Americans are into all that sort of thing or what? I wonder what happens. What do people find to talk about? I wouldn't know where to begin'.

Pippa continued for a while, but Edwin heard nothing after she mentioned the name of the street. That was where Libby lived, that was where Libby worked, that was where he went to therapy.

Libby detected at once that something was not right with Edwin. He had looked coldly at her as she had opened the front door to him and she could sense a difference in him. She waited. It was a long wait. He was angry and did not know how to express it other than by silence. Eventually he spoke.

'Why have you taken on Jayne Callard as a client?'

'I hope you know Edwin, that just as I would never mention your name to anyone – I don't even use your real name in supervision – and it was Dr Nuffield who contacted me on the day of your breakdown, with your permission if you remember, so in no circumstances whatsoever would I ever mention the name of any other client to you. I would not even confirm or deny that a particular person was my client'.

'But how can I possibly speak freely here any more, knowing, as I do, whether you deny it or not, that she is coming to see you?'.

Libby decided to answer a different question altogether.

'My commitment to our work together Edwin is, as I believe you know, considerable. I would not do anything to place that in jeopardy, anything at all'.

'But how can I speak about someone whom I know you see. That surely affects how you see that person. I just don't know how you could agree to see her when you know what she has done to me'.

'When you come here you come alone. You bring with you all sorts of names. Some of them I might know, given that this is a small city, most of them of course I do not. But I have never believed that those people actually come with you physically. What you bring is your perceptions and feelings about people. They are not my clients, you are, and we work on your inner life. Quite what the relationship is between your perception of someone and the actuality of their life matters very little'.

'Does that mean you think I lie?'

'Of course not. The thought has never occurred to me. Indeed I feel that the quality of the work we have been able to do is due primarily because of your commitment to the truth. But you would not be in therapy if there wasn't some sort of mismatch between your inner and outer worlds'.

'But how can you work with two parties involved in a dispute? Solicitors cannot'.

'Well I should hope not, but GPs do it all the time. Nurses on an orthopaedic ward can care quite successfully for two parties who have tried to beat the hell out of each other'.

Edwin was beginning to feel a little stupid and eased the tension with a small laugh at her analogy.

'It sounds like I have over-reacted'.

'Why so hard on yourself? Why call it an over-reaction. It is simply your reaction. Neither good nor bad. The important thing is to try and understand why you had it and what it betokens'.

'And that is?'.

'I'm a therapist, Edwin, not a magician, and I don't do mind-reading'.

Edwin smiled. He had wanted to give this session over to sharing his feelings about his walk and the dog-shooting incident. He had been side-tracked but at least now felt that he had the opportunity.

Libby listened intently, perhaps greatly relieved that the direction of their conversation had changed.

When Edwin finished she said, 'That's a horrible experience. But there are, I think, a number of very positive things to observe about the way in which you have dealt with it. In the first place you survived it. A lot of people might have become hysterical or even violent, and whilst you were clearly affected you managed yourself, getting back to the car with the maximum of self protection, more than adequately. The second thing is to note that despite what you sometimes say here about no longer being able to feel anything, you did feel something and directly. These are very positive signs of your well-being and inner reserves. You might not have been able to handle it some weeks ago'.

'It didn't feel like I was handling it well'.

'No, well as I say, most people would have found it no less, and possibly considerably more, distressing than you. I am however more interested in your sense of identification with the dog that was shot. In particular I think there may be an important link between your account and what we began with this morning, and also that which runs through many of our sessions, and that is the matter of the betrayal of trust'.

Edwin shifted somewhat uneasily.

'You spoke of the dog being led by hands it has trusted, once they had no more use for it, and then suffering the ultimate rejection and betrayal: the bullet in the head. I suspect that is exactly the issue you are facing. Betrayal by a mother, betrayal by a father (in the sense of not properly caring for and protecting you), betrayal by colleagues, betrayal by the natural law you have earnestly longed to believe in and, of course, your fear that I am now joining the list, betrayal by your therapist. It's little wonder that you felt that it was you being taken out to be shot'.

'When you put it like that', said Edwin after a moment's reflection, 'I suppose it makes some sense that I should have reacted as I did'.

'Yes, though don't lose sight of the fact that even without your possible predisposition what you saw, even though it wasn't the act itself, was pretty horrid. As I already said the fact that you were able to feel the horror in that moment can be taken as a good sign, betokening a sensitivity I know you feel you have lost'.

'Yes, but you'd have to be pretty numb not to have felt it'.

'Even so'.

Edwin had managed to get away from the discomfort of his first minutes there this. As if reading his mind and determined not to let him avoid his earlier discomfort, Libby brought him back to where they had begun.

'But the key issue of our time together, as I understand what we have been handling this morning, is the question of trust, and whether or not you think I also intend to shoot you when you are of no more use'.

'I think that's a bit extreme', responded Edwin.

'Yes, but it is the logical extension to what you have been

speaking of. You began, you see, with the accusation that I am just another of those who betray you, and of course mostly they have been women. I hope I have been able to reassure you of my commitment to our work together, but it raises the far more important issue of how you are going to face the future in your own strength.

'You see, we might suggest that possibly, and it is no more than a working hypothesis, what you have achieved and accomplished (and no one could seriously doubt that it has been significant) has been primarily the result of reaction, the way in which you have been striving to work out the consequences of all that life has thrown at you, and mostly in your infancy. Now we move into the proactive era. What are you going to do with the rest of your life, Edwin?'.

'What life?' murmured Edwin under his breath.

19

Sometimes in his therapy Edwin was aware that so much arose and so rapidly that he barely felt he had sufficient time to attend to it all. Some of it was unconscious material emerging from dreams – "the royal road to the unconscious", Libby described it, quoting Freud. It also sometimes took the form of new ideas he needed time to ponder. Something Libby had slipped in this morning was troubling him. At the time he had to allow it to pass under the weight of other, more obviously pressing, matters, but he had adequate space now to consider it.

He decided that he would go to the cathedral. If he arrived early enough the turnstiles might not yet be in operation and the place would be relatively still and tourist-free. He might also have time for a cup of coffee and a scone in the cafeteria attached to the cloister.

As he wandered round the inside of the building he reflected upon how ineffective it was in the glare of daylight. The Purbeck marble was light and, to his mind, best seen in the shadows of late afternoon or early evening. The cathedral seemed to lose some of its potency when exposed to the light. It seemed a pertinent symbol for his own thinking.

Libby had been speaking of the various betrayals of trust he had experienced – mother, father, therapist even. She had also mentioned the natural law to which much of his life had been given. He wondered why she had said it. Had he spoken of it? He could not recall. And yet he did concede that she might well have a point. Ever since he had returned the corrected proofs of his book he was acutely aware of an unease within himself whenever he thought of it. He was now not at all looking forward to its publication and primarily for one reason: he no longer believed in what he had written.

The book, he supposed, had been above all a statement of faith, a creed, fashioned as he was now beginning to understand, out of the raw material of the injuries he had sustained. It was a defiant claim that in spite of all he knew the world to contain, there was in and behind it all a fundamental principle of order and reason. But what if that faith (if that was the right word, perhaps hope would be better) were nothing more than whistling in the dark, a momentous exercise in wishful thinking? What then? He had a sudden sense of panic and shivered. How could he possibly allow his book to be published. He must stop it. He must do something now, today, at once.

He stood up to go, but then thought better of it. He hadn't finished his coffee and there was still half a scone to be eaten. He sat down again. He was being ridiculous. In any case the die was cast. He had signed a contract. It was too late. He took a sip of his coffee and began to butter the rest of the scone.

At an adjacent table there sat a young clergyman. Edwin had seen him occasionally at Evensong, sitting, like himself, in the congregation, rather than taking his place in the serried ranks of the vested clergy. He sat alone and was reading while he drank coffee. The book was *Dr Faustus* by Thomas Mann. The young man noticed Edwin's glance.

'Heavy stuff.'

'It is', replied Edwin, 'but worth the effort. I read it a long time ago. All about Adrian Leverkühn, if I remember aright, thinking he had sold his soul to the devil when all along it turned out to be the effects of syphilis'.

'Not a bad resumé' replied the clergyman, laughing.

The cafeteria was still empty and it was not difficult for the two men to talk quietly.

'Is it a great problem for clergy? I mean, people imagining something is of God, or the devil, and then discovering it was just indigestion?'.

'It's an interesting question'.

'Oh, don't you start'.

'What do you mean?', replied the priest.

'Oh I know someone I often speak to who's usually more interested in the question than the answer'.

'Yes, there was a bishop once who said that a psychiatrist is a man who goes to a striptease show and spends his time watching the audience'.

Again, they both laughed.

'But is it?', continued Edwin.

'Is it a problem, do you mean? I can't speak for anyone but myself. I fear that these days far too many people in the world of religion take everything at face value, without thought. You wouldn't believe some of the things that people claim have come to them direct from God. Someone once rang me up with a "message straight from the Lord" and I was left concluding that whatever else the Almighty may be, illiterate he most certainly is. Oh, I'm sorry, perhaps I'm treading on your toes, in a manner of speaking.'

'No, not at all'. Edwin smiled, and then to continue the conversation asked, 'Are you on the staff of the cathedral?'.

The young man hesitated before replying.

'No. I'm having some time-out, as the Americans call it, a sort of sabbatical. And you?'

'Likewise'.

The young man clearly felt sufficiently at ease with Edwin to allow himself to speak further.

'Actually, I'm recently widowed. I suppose I'm trying to find out whether and how I can go on, but please excuse me, I don't mean to burden you with my troubles'.

'I'm sorry to hear what you say', replied Edwin, 'it must be terrible'.

'I keep trying to say to myself that I've dealt with death a hundred times in my work, that I've sought to minister to others in my situation, that I ought to be able to experience something of the comfort I sought to give. But I don't seem able to. Odd, isn't it'.

Edwin found himself deeply moved by the young man's words.

'Not at all. When it happens to us all our theories have a habit of falling apart. They were designed for others'.

'Yes, but I feel that I have been such a hypocrite, offering simple solutions to situations I wasn't mature enough to know about because I had never been there'.

'"Zeus, whose will has marked for man the sole way where wisdom lies; ordered one eternal plan: man must suffer to be wise"'.

The priest smiled wryly. 'Who said that?' he asked.

'Aeschylus', said Edwin, 'in the Oresteia. My scriptures'.

'Well, he knew or thing or two then. Though my difficulty is that it was Helen who did the suffering – Helen is, was, my wife'.

'I suspect what you are suffering now is real enough. Had she been very ill – do you mind my asking?'.

'No, not at all. No, indeed quite the opposite. We had just discovered she was pregnant. It would have been our first child. She was 27. We were overjoyed. We went to stay with her parents at half term in October last – she was a teacher. They live in Truro, or just outside. We decided to go out onto Bodmin Moor to walk, something we'd done many times. We stopped for lunch early because she kept feeling herself getting out of breath. All of a sudden, she collapsed. It took ages for an ambulance to reach us and by the time we got to hospital, she was dead. A heart attack. The consultant said it was most rare. I think he meant it as a consolation'.

'It was double loss, wife and unborn child'.

The priest nodded, looked up and gave an ironic smile.

'You must miss her terribly'.

'Well at first it was all too unreal. I just carried on in the parish and it was as if at any moment she would just walk in the door. And then it hit me. And I began to see that everything was falling apart, and me with it. Happily the bishop said I could take as much time out as I needed. I come here sometimes because it feels quite safe – the stones, and even the scaffolding'.

'Oh, I can understand that', said Edwin. 'I come here for much the same sort of reason'.

The young priest, noticing that the cafeteria was beginning to fill, suggested they go for a walk. Edwin was glad to do so. They wandered first around the cloister and then out under the west front of the cathedral, and through the north gate out of the Close and towards the water meadows.

'I don't know how I would survive what you have had to endure', said Edwin. 'I certainly don't think I could have kept a faith intact'.

'It hasn't stayed intact, I can assure you of that. I meant what I said. I have discovered that all the things I used to say to the bereaved, the reassurances, the nice words – they mean nothing. Do you know, I always used to read at funerals a piece of what I suppose should be described as doggerel, written by a famous clergyman at the turn of the century, in which he speaks of the beloved dead not really being dead at all, but just as it were, in the next room, to be spoken to much as before. People loved it and I used to have copies to give people.'

He stopped and turned to Edwin.

'It's a lie. And it doesn't stop being a lie because people want to believe it.'

At this moment Edwin thought his heart would break for the young man and he wanted to take him in his arms, and because he was English and this was in public, he did not.

They walked on in silence. Eventually Edwin spoke.

'Does that mean you can't go back to being whatever it was you were?'.

'I don't know, to be honest. I certainly can't go back to peddling sentimental stuff now I know what it is, and I am not sure the Church and those who come to it are ready for the alternative'.

'Is there one?' asked Edwin.

'Possibly, but it's not one that allows for an easy existence, which is what I think many people are coming to church for these days'.

'And what is it?'

'Well, it's not a new idea, but it's the possibility that God actually suffers with his creation. In some ways it's quite close to what is called pantheism, the identification of God with all that is. Instead of a creator who sits outside like an architect watching and observing and who has to be worshipped like some mighty potentate, it is a God who's very being is so bound up with all that is so that every moment of suffering is a suffering to him too. In that way the cross of Christ is not the supreme moment of triumph that many Christians proclaim it to be but the moment of supreme self emptying in which God and every miserable moment of existence become one'.

The young man gave an embarrassed smile at Edwin as they walked.

'I'm sorry. Preaching's an occupational hazard. I don't mean to embarrass you or force upon you my views'.

Edwin shook his head. He could barely speak.

'No need to apologise, I can assure you', he finally forced himself to reply. 'It was brilliantly put in Helen Waddell's book on Abelard but, to be perfectly honest, I don't think it will catch on. My wife is a Christian, an evangelical one, and how. She and her friends are so triumphalist, it turns me off completely. That sort of approach to me is utterly incredible. I don't know whether what you are suggesting can mean anything to me, but it certainly isn't offering the sort of slick consolation they are after. But I guess the only thing that matters is whether it works for you. I mean, that's all that counts, isn't it?'

'Sometimes it does and sometimes it doesn't. Faith for me isn't a hundred per cent thing, if ever it was. It's much more like the occasional signpost that just reassures me I'm not totally lost even if it tells me I'm further away than I was last time I reached a signpost'.

'And do you think you'll manage it?' asked Edwin. 'Could you live that way of thinking and still carry on in an institution that sounds like it's going in a quite different direction?'

'The jury is still out, I'm afraid'.

They stopped by the weir and watched the ducks. The spring sun was catching the buds of the trees. New life. The Spring. And he thought of the dead wife and the dead baby, and their husband and father, parts of whom had died with them. One of the reasons why he could still go back to his beloved Greek writers was because they could describe these things so well, they could tell of the horrors and the hell of loss and bereavement in ways the Bible never could. In that respect there was more humanity in them than in anything Edwin had ever read in the New Testament, save perhaps in the descriptions of the crucifixion.

'And what of you? I'm sorry, I don't even know your name,' said the young man, as they walked on.

'Edwin, Edwin Lyons'.

'Edwin, I'm Angus Gledenning'.

They shook hands as only the English could do at such a stage into sharing their life histories. 'Well,' began Edwin, 'my story is nothing compared to yours, nothing at all'. He then proceeded to tell Angus something of what had happened to him.

By this time, they had crossed the park and had turned left into the main road on its further edge as if by unspoken agreement they were set on completing the circle of their walk.

'And what sustains you in all this, Edwin. I have my somewhat inadequate faith inadequately lived, but what have you?'.

Edwin paused as they walked.

'That's not a bad description of what a faith might be. I like it. As for my own inner resources. I guess I have been discovering just how totally inadequate they are too. I have never really believed in a God and still the idea seems quite impossible to me, at least in the sort of sense in which people speak of God – something personal that constantly or even occasionally intervenes in the world. I would therefore call myself a non-realist Platonist, by which I mean I have been committed to the idea of Platonic forms embodying principles of existence – justice, truth, though quite without believing that those forms exist anywhere "out there"'.

He waved his arm in the general direction of the sky.

'I used to hope that there was order implicit in nature, an order supremely embodied in the idea of law and manifest in all sorts of ways and means of existence. Now I am not only not sure, I'm beginning to think I have been radically mistaken and that there is no order. It all seems random. And you see whilst I can be moved by your account of how God might suffer with and in his creation – and I can admire the beauty of and feel the strength that might be derived from such an idea, my problem is that I think it would only serve to tie me into yet tighter knots. I prefer to cut the Gordian Knot by doing without that specific hypothesis, as a famous scientist once said when presenting his magnum opus to

Napoleon. It may be a bleak place but at least I am beginning to see that it helps me understand and appreciate how my favourite Greek writers must have seen the world and their place in it. And I love them the more for it'.

Edwin stopped again and looked at Angus.

'Now it's me that's preaching, and probably being unkind to you by what I'm saying', added Edwin.

'Not at all. I find myself deeply moved by what you say. You see, some of the time, if not much of the time I'm there as well. Perhaps it's mere cowardice that prevents me being sufficiently honest all the time'.

They had reached the south gate of the Close. They could see many more tourists than when they had left. They stopped.

'Thank you, Angus,'.

'And you, Edwin'.

Once again, they shook hands, and departed in different directions having expressed the hope that they might bump into one another again.

Edwin returned home. Sylvia was making some lunch for them and he joined her in the kitchen.

'I've been talking to a young priest this morning', said Edwin. Sylvia turned.

'Really? What about?'.

'God, life, death and meaning'.

'In one morning?'

She smiled.

'What do you and your church people think about the idea that God suffers with us, that he shares our sufferings, that in suffering on the cross God enters into the misery of existence. It was first expressed by a medieval writer called Abelard, was castrated because of a relationship with a lady called Heloise.'

'A catholic theologian'.

The tone of the last words seemed somewhat damnatory.

'Weren't they all then?', offered Edwin in mitigation.

'It sounds very nice', continued Sylvia, wielding a knife at some carrots, 'but it's devoid of content. It offers no hope. God in Christ redeems us by the cross. That's what the scriptures teach. The cross is the throne of God's triumph over the devil. If it isn't, then God would simply be as powerless as anyone of us. He isn't. Your Abelard's Christ is not the redeemer. How could he be? If no redeemer, so saviour; if no saviour, no salvation and we all die in our sins. But thanks be to God who gives us the victory – as Paul says'.

Sylvia was in full flow, spouting religious formulae, but Edwin was far-off and not hearing a word. Sometimes when he awoke in the morning the effect of his tablets kept him in a strange hinterland in which he could hear the radio on somewhere but not hear a single word. That was how it was now.

He found himself reflecting upon Odysseus and why it had taken him ten years to return home to Penelope, his wife, after the fall of Troy. The distance he had to travel was small, so why so long? Was it possible that having seen and experienced so much, it was just not possible to return to the familiar domestic hearth? He could not return because he was not the same man who had set out and the very idea of being restored to his old palace was unbearable. After all he had seen and known how he could endure being tethered for life to an ageing weaver going on and on about the price of wool?

His wonderings were interrupted by the sudden awareness of a pregnant silence.

'Mm? Sorry, I missed the last bit', he muttered.

'I said that if you are going to listen to the views of clergymen who don't believe what scripture teaches, don't you think you owe it to yourself to give a fair hearing to someone who can tell you exactly what scripture maintains? Jeremy would happily talk to you'.

'I'm sure he would', said Edwin defensively. 'I was just interested to hear what you had to say on the subject, that's all'.

As they ate their lunch Sylvia was feeling encouraged by Edwin's sudden interest. It was what she had been hoping and praying for. It would certainly enable him to get better and return to work. It might also help her keep her job. She offered a silent prayer of thanks.

Edwin, for his part, was thinking no longer about Odysseus and his homecoming from the wars, but about his friend Agamemnon, the king of Mycenae. His return was somewhat different: after surviving the wars and the terrible storm that claimed so many ships and so many lives he arrived home to be welcomed by his wife Clytemnestra with open arms and words of praise in the streets. Once inside, she murdered him by repeated stabbing.

Bored to death by Penelope or gored to death by Clytemnestra? Not prayed for but preyed upon. It seemed a somewhat stark choice and what troubled Edwin was that he knew he was no longer the same man who had been in that house a year ago, even months ago. He too had been to war and been changed.

But if Edwin was thinking in that moment that the wars were over then he had forgotten that the siege of Troy also lasted ten years. And it was the telephone, as they ate their lunch, that called him back to reality.

'Edwin', said the voice as he answered the call, 'It's Iris. I think you'd better come. It's your dad. He's taken a turn for the worse'.

20

"A tum for the worse" – it was, thought Edwin, one of those phrases that probably owed its origins to the ancient classical image of the labyrinth, such as the celebrated labyrinth devised by cunning Daedalus in Minoan Crete to keep at bay the minotaur that dwelt there and fed on the youth of the vicinity. Unlike, say, some of the medieval mazes to be found on the floors of great European cathedrals which trace a certain path from beginning to end, the labyrinth of ancient times was such that one might indeed take a tum for the worse, and for the worst. It seemed that his father's time had come.

Iris had said that he had been rushed into hospital after collapsing and that they were likely to operate on a perforation of his colon. She also warned him that he would see a change in his father's appearance when he arrived but did not specify what it was.

Logistically he either took the car, which would be a major inconvenience for Sylvia and Megan and a considerable source of exhaustion to him, or went by train. That would mean a very late arrival in Carlisle but at least he could be in hospital first thing in the morning.

The easiest route was via London, and he set about packing his bag. He also rang Libby to tell her he wouldn't be able to be at their session in the morning. He got the answering machine.

When he arrived at the railway station he found to his total dismay that there were no trains running. There had been a derailment just about a mile up the line and there would be no further trains today. The station staff were not altogether sure what to recommend and in the end Sylvia drove him to Basingstoke, where he caught a train to Birmingham and there changed to another for Crewe before finally getting a train to Carlisle. He arrived shortly after midnight. He had been unable to settle on the journey and was deeply anxious about what he would have to face on the following morning.

Edwin called Iris to say he would be delayed and was intending to get a hotel in Carlisle on his arrival and would meet her at hospital first thing in the morning.

Edwin was relieved that she was not there to meet him, and he was able to get a room at the Station Hotel.

He had taken his tablets because he knew they would help him sleep and it was after eight when he woke. He made himself a cup of tea and looked out of the window. It was snowing heavily. He groaned at the sight, but at least he was already in the city and it ought not delay his visit to the hospital. He showered and then went down for breakfast.

Even in a small city an unexpected snowstorm can create havoc. A "lambing storm" his grandma would have called it, and he imagined that a few miles to the south farmers were out on the fells anxiously seeking out the new-born. They had their lambs late this far north because winter weather could quite easily last well into April. A storm such as this could cause great losses in a flock. Hungry vixens too were more likely to kill new-born lambs in this weather.

Because of the weather he decided not to check-out. He would have preferred to be staying with Iris but if the snow persisted he would need to be in the city. In any case until he got to the hospital and could see for himself, he did not know what would be best.

He took a taxi, though in the end he would probably have been there sooner had he sought to walk. It continued to snow heavily and by the time the road had been cleared of slush it was building up again. He wondered how on earth Iris would get in but discovered when he reached his father's ward that she was there and had not been home overnight.

He knocked on the sister's door and introduced himself. 'I'm so glad you've made it', she said.

He knew.

'He's in the side ward down here', she went on, leading him. 'Iris is with him'.

Edwin entered the room.

Iris sat holding his father's hand. She turned towards the door as he entered.

Edwin was shocked. His father did not look like his father at all. He was a strange yellow colour and had clearly lost a lot of weight in the past few weeks. The skin was hanging off his neck. It seemed to Edwin that his dad was unconscious. His breathing seemed laboured and attached to his throat or chest was a kind of strange syringe that every so often worked automatically.

'Edwin's here', said Iris to his father.

His father undoubtedly twitched in response to this. His eyebrow moved as if somewhere still there was life and that life was capable of recognition.

'Hello dad. It's me, Edwin'.

But there was no more movement, no further sign.

'I should have got here earlier'.

'We didn't know where you were stopping', explained Iris. 'I rang Sylvia but she had no idea either and you must have had your phone turned off. We just had to hope you'd get here... you know, in time'.

Though Edwin had been in the room no more than a couple of minutes he could tell that there had been a change in his father's condition since his arrival.

'I kept telling him to hold on', said Iris. 'He wanted you here'.

Edwin kept looking at the figure in the bed and it was a struggle to stop himself saying out loud "But that's not my dad". It all seemed so bizarre. Here was his father, his dad, dying a ghastly death, whilst out of the window three feet to his left there was the most beautiful snow-scene imaginable.

Edwin approached and took hold of his dad's other hand. His breathing was becoming shallower and there seemed to be sighs followed by a pause in the breathing pattern that quite frightened Edwin. His nose too had gone a strange colour, indeed as if all the colour had drained out of it and the contrast with the yellow of the rest of his face made it look grotesque.

He looked at the hand he held. It was the same hand that had held his as a tiny child, as a little boy. It was the hand of a craftsman, that had created beauty out of plain wood, that had transformed the ordinary into the special. It was the hand he had shaken, that had waved to him. He lifted it and kissed it.

Without his realising it a nurse had entered and was standing at the foot of the bed. Edwin looked up from the hand to his father's face. It looked as if it were more at ease, and just for a moment he was convinced that this was all a silly joke and that now his father was surely past the worst and beginning a recovery. But it was only a passing fancy. For moments later he realised that his dad was now barely breathing at all and the colour had completely drained from his face and that he had nearly gone.

'I love you, dad, I love you. Thank you'.

The nurse had left them. Iris and Edwin each held a hand as his dad slipped away from them and was gone. Only the syringe thing continued to be alive, making its strange, automated noise.

Iris wept silently. Edwin looked out at the snow falling.

They sat silently together, each with a cup of tea, in the visitor's room. Edwin had rung Sylvia to tell her. There had been no let up in the snow and Edwin was concerned as to how Iris would get home. The sister had allowed them to stay as long as they wished in the room, and they had waited a good ten minutes before emerging. Two nurses had gone in, and the sister said that they would be able to see him again if they wanted before they left.

And Edwin could only give thanks, again and again, that he had got there in time. If only, if only, he had let Iris or Sylvia know where he had been staying; if only he had not slept so late; if only he had not taken so long over breakfast; and then the slow taxi ride. If only. But he had made it. He had been there. And he knew, he knew for certain, that his father knew, and knew for certain, that he had been there.

They looked in again before they left the hospital. It was all so different. The syringe machine and its stand had gone, and the bed was all tidied, and the pillows gone. His dad looked fast asleep. No. No. He looked what he was: dead. He looked as he never looked in life: tidy and clean and peaceful. And it occurred to Edwin in that moment that perhaps his dad had never known much in the way of inner peace in his life. And as Edwin looked at the stranger before him the tears crept down his face.

It finally stopped snowing at about noon. They had gone to Edwin's hotel for some lunch though neither could eat much. Edwin checked-out and they took a taxi back to the hospital. Iris's car took some digging out but eventually they made it and headed out of town. April snow soon turns to rain and the County Council had been able to get its fleet of snow ploughs into action. The road was remarkably clear as they drove back to Maryport in the mid-afternoon. Already the sun was out, and the fells looked simply wonderful. They would have to return to hospital on the following day to collect the death certificate but had been told that they should contact a funeral director who would come to meet with them to begin making the arrangements.

Edwin had arranged a few funerals in his capacity as a solicitor but never of anyone close to him. In any case he knew that the wishes of Iris had to take precedence. It may be that she and his dad had discussed his wishes though as it turned out they had not. Iris knew of one firm in the town and Edwin telephoned them. It was, unlike so many in the south of England, still a family firm. A visit was arranged for that evening. Edwin had no idea whether it would be a church funeral or not, a burial or cremation. He suddenly realised that he knew little or nothing about the man his father was, the man his father's friends knew him to be, the man others had worked with.

This was revealed when Edwin raised the question of his father's will.

'There is no will', said Iris. 'He wouldn't make one'.

'Really?'.

'There's a good reason too. The thing is, there's no money. I shall have to leave this house as well. You see, your dad blew it all in the last couple of years'.

'What do you mean "blew it"'. Edwin was puzzled and a little uneasy.

'Your dad gambled, Edwin'. She spoke easily, not at all embarrassed. 'The horses mostly, but even the dogs sometimes, and more recently even on cricket and football. And from time to time he won. But mostly he lost and a couple of years ago he lost everything. He was in a syndicate, and he got into big bother, out of his depth. So he took out a second mortgage on the house. It's all gone. We were fighting to the end to stay here'.

Edwin sat there dumbfounded.

'It was an addiction, I think', she continued. 'Well, it started as a bit of excitement. He always said that life with your mother was hell and I think he did it for the kicks. But then it became something he couldn't free himself from, and later, well in the past couple of years, as I say, he got involved with a more serious group. Scotsmen in the main – Glasgow. Not nice men either, some of them. They'll have this house now. They'd have had it last year had your dad not been poorly',

'What will you do?', asked Edwin numbly.

'Go and live with my sister in Workington, I should think'.

'Iris, I'm so sorry'.

'Oh, it's not your fault. I knew, and I tried to stop him. But it didn't stop me loving him'.

In the course of his work Edwin had occasionally been involved in major family scandals subsequent upon revelations emerging after a death. This was not the first, but the shock was no less great.

'Well, I'll pay for the funeral and everything, and make sure you're alright'.

'Oh, I'm not so green as I'm cabbage-looking Edwin. I've made sure there's enough here and there, places your dad knew nothing about. I'll manage. And in any case I wouldn't have wanted to stay in this house. Too many bad memories from these last two years'.

Edwin didn't know what to say, didn't know what to think. It was as if a stun grenade had exploded in front of him. Last time he was here he had had to listen to his father telling him the painful truth about his mother. Now the boot was most definitely on the other foot. And that reminded him. What was he to do about informing his mother? Should he telephone? What should he do? That she ought to know he did not doubt but how should he tell her?

Iris had made them some tea and sandwiches. Edwin smiled when he saw that they contained ham - what else at the time of a death?

'What do you want to do about the funeral, Iris?'.

'Did your dad ever mention Frank Pembiss to you?'.

'Not that I can recall'.

'Well he's a retired vicar, a canon or something, that's in Rotary with your dad. They were good friends and I think it would be nice to get him to do the service – you know, as he knew your dad and that'.

Edwin agreed. His father hadn't been a churchgoer and in all honesty he was amazed that he knew a clergyman of any sort.

'We'll just keep it simple. Straight through to the Crem I should think. Nothing special. We don't need cars or anything'.

The funeral director, when he came, was a jolly man and not at all the lugubrious person Edwin had been expecting. He carried a briefcase and produced from it a book containing pictures of every kind of coffin imaginable. In the end they went for the cheapest. It would be the following Thursday afternoon. Iris had telephoned Frank Pembiss and he was intending to call in early next morning before Edwin took the train home.

Edwin took his tablets early and hoped for a deep sleep. It was strange to think that on this day his father had died and yet as he fell into what was to prove a troubled slumber all he could think about was his father's double life and the "unpleasant" people he had fallen in with.

He awoke feeling even more tired than he had before taking to his bed. No more snow had fallen though there had been a frost. The roads were open however and Edwin assumed that the railways would be running on time. After washing and some breakfast he packed his bags and awaited the arrival of the canon.

Frank Pembiss turned out be what Edwin might have called an "amiable buffer", exactly the sort of clergyman to grace the hallowed dining tables of Rotary: not enough religion for it to be a problem but no doubt a good friend in dark times. He had unquestionably given the best of his years to the service of his fellow men and there were no doubt countless people with a great deal of affection for him. Whether he mediated anything of God, Edwin rather doubted. He was an English "character" and in some ways the epitome of the Church of England at its best.

They decided on some hymns and Canon Pembiss said he would prefer to use what he called the *old* service. It was a matter of some indifference to Iris and Edwin and they willingly agreed.

They didn't need to be especially proactive in any part of their encounter with the good canon. He could talk for all three of them! In the course of his utterances he mentioned he was heading back to Carlisle and Edwin decided to take the risk of asking him for a lift to the Railway Station. The canon was more than happy to oblige.

True to form the clergyman talked most of the way into the city and it was with some relief that Edwin took his leave in good time to catch his train. When it arrived, it was full of Scots heading south for the Easter holidays and Edwin had to stand all the way to Preston.

As the train made its way through Cumbria Edwin glanced over to the west and saw the Saddle of Blencathra covered in snow and looking astonishing in the spring light. And he remembered that he was alive and there was beauty and a whole world going on – and his father knew nothing of it, for he was no more. His dad was dead. And so also was something of his own image of his dad. That too had just died. All in just twenty-four hours.

Edwin found the idea of the survival of death something beyond his capacity to believe. He could understand why people might want to believe in it but he could not. He knew he would not be seeing his father again. And for his father, no more light, no more snow, no more anything.

And he thought of Housman's wonderful poem about the Cherry tree covered in blossom like snow for which even fifty more years would never be enough to appreciate it. Well, today all the trees were dressed in snow for Eastertide – even if it was still a week away. Easter but no resurrection.

Edwin changed in bleak Crewe and remained on the same slow stopping train all the way to Basingstoke. He did not wish to read, and his mind was mostly blank. The snow had thinned and south of Warrington had mostly disappeared.

And still he wondered and worried what to do about his mother.

Having changed at Basingstoke he eventually saw the spire as the train slowly entered the cutting. On the platform Sylvia and Megan were waiting for him, and their welcome was warm.

And he was glad of that, and glad just to be with them again. They would all have to travel north for the funeral in the week ahead but for now they were together, and that evening there was a unity they had mostly not known for a long time.

His mother did not telephone. And neither did he.

On Sunday morning Edwin and Megan went for a long walk together, and they spoke about her grandad and what it had been like to be with him as he died. Edwin was touched that she could speak of it with such ease and sensitivity. Sylvia too had spoken of it on the night before, but with less grace than her daughter. She was at church this morning. Edwin had not spoken of what he had learned about his dad and wondered whether he would do so at all. He felt ashamed of what he knew. Nor was the subject of his mother referred to by any of them. But he could not let it rest for much longer. The funeral was just a few days away.

21

'The other day – do you remember – you said to me something to the effect that what matters now is not the past but the future. At the time I thought it such a helpful and even a hopeful thing to say. But it isn't so easy, is it? My past seems to be taking on proportions I most definitely had not anticipated'.

It was the Monday morning before Easter and their penultimate session before the funeral and Libby's Easter break.

'You have had to come to a recognition that neither parent was quite as you have spent most of your life imagining them to be - that is certainly true'.

'Wonderful really. Here I am, a member of a law-abiding and respectable profession, an upholder of values that I believe to embody the highest principles of human existence. And what do I find? That my mother was a whore and my father was a gambler who in the end got into criminal company and lost everything. Something of an irony, don't you think?'.

'That sounds a little melodramatic. Most people have skeletons in the cupboard. And in any case it doesn't actually change you and your life, does it? I know it has been something of a shock to make these discoveries, but before you stands the future, not the past'.

'But doesn't the knowledge of what actually was my past, rather than how I imagined it, affect the future?'

'Inevitably. But the extent to which it does so is in your own hands. That means attending to your feelings about your parents, and of course you will still have dealings of some sort with your mother'.

'But what sort?', asked Edwin, more of himself than Libby.

'At the moment you have seem to have surrendered the option to decide that for yourself. You are waiting upon her and I suspect that was how it always was – and that still gives her power over you. It may be that she will maintain silence for a long time, at least she may if she is still the person she obviously once was. What you have to decide is whether you want to take some of that power away from her. I don't mean by just telephoning her to tell her your father has died, but by using that as an opportunity to challenge her silence. After all you are not now the little boy now over whom she once held terrible power and you do not have to put with her attempts to manipulate you'.

Edwin thought for a while. It seemed such sense and yet a lifetime of conditioning meant it also seemed so dangerous a thing to do. He also knew he had to make contact with her and had to say something, or would he hide behind the fact of his dad's death and avoid the matter altogether – returning the skeletons back to the cupboard?

'It's odd', he said eventually. 'When I think of her I still do so as huge and overwhelming, when of course she is getting older and is quite small. I thought of that in hospital on Saturday. There he was: my father. Once he seemed to tower above me and represent everything strong and powerful. And there before me lay the reality – a small, distorted figure breathing his last'.

'How much did he stand up to your mother?'.

'Not much. They argued of course but mostly he gave in and found distractions from her and me. And now I begin to learn what some of them might have been. One way or another he was mostly never there. It now appears that he lived a secret life'.

'Maybe it's called survival. You chose your way of surviving – the route of academic and professional success. He chose his way and it does at least sound as if he chose a good partner to cope with him as he did so in the second part of his adult life'.

'Yes. I have a lot of time for Iris and I admire her strength and faithfulness. I have known in my work a lot of women who have left their husbands for considerably less'.

'And might it also be that there are worse things for humans to do than gamble? I'm not trying to say it is nothing and of course it has had a considerable effect on Iris, but from what you told me she has obviously been wise enough to make her own arrangements for the future, and as she was the only one hurt by his gambling, perhaps what your dad did wasn't so bad'.

'But gambling is such... '. Edwin stopped. Gambling is what? He did not know what to say. Perhaps Libby was right. Perhaps there are no eternal verities by which to judge the things we do. Some people split their infinitives, other people gamble. And who is to say whether either is wrong, and by what standards could they judge in any case? Pedants might object to what they would regard as the misuse of language but if people communicate effectively why worry about syntax?

Gambling might be foolish but it is not per se criminal.

Libby interrupted his thought sequence.

'Yes, I think gambling is such a waste of money, and I imagine you do too. But many, many people enjoy it. There's the lottery, or go up to the racecourse in summer and see just how many people indulge. I also believe that it can become an addiction and cause great suffering in many homes and lives. The question for you, Edwin, is whether you can accept the truth about your parents and allow it to be and go on to live your own life with its choices and options – for yourself?'

'I don't understand'.

'I may be wrong, but it seems to me that what you have been discovering in this past year is that much of what you do and have given yourself to has been the effect of your past and how you have seen and experienced that past. It may be that as you learn more about it, you will want to change the future to make it more of your own work, the product of your own determination'.

'That's quite a task, if you don't mind my saying so'.

'It is', replied Libby, 'but what is the point of your coming here otherwise?'

She answered the telephone in English. It would have been asking too much of her to learn anything but the most basic French.

'It's Edwin'. Silence.

'I have some bad news'.

'Oh?'.

'Dad's died'.

'Died?'.

'Yes. On Saturday. He suddenly took a turn for the worse'.

He could hardly believe he had said it!

'You should have let me know'.

'The funeral is on Thursday. We're going up on Wednesday'.

'And I bet that she will be getting everything. It ought to go to you, but I bet she's twisted him. You'll get nothing'.

'That's right. I'm getting nothing'.

'You're a lawyer, for heaven's sake. Contest the will'.

'I thought you should know'.

Was he going to say something about his letter? The difficulty was that he became so wooden when talking to his mother, and he was wholly unused to having anything even remotely approaching a real conversation with her.

'Well, there we are', he said, for the sake of something to say, in the hope that she might make a move.

'And how are you?'.

There was cold in her voice as she asked her question.

'I have been off work for almost six months. I suffered a breakdown in October and have been being treated for depression'.

He wanted to go on to say something about it having to do with what he had written to her in his letter. He wanted to ask if she was going to reply.

'I knew you were ill', she said, and he felt certain he could hear a tone of elation in her voice. 'I knew it. I said it to Claude and to my friend Victoria. I said "He's ill". I knew it.'

He had lost.

'Yes', he replied limply. 'I must hang up now. I just wanted you to know'.

'Of course, of course. What a terrible thing to happen to you. Poor darling. No wonder everything seems so upside down. Well, I hope you're better soon. I know all about that. Your birth brought it on. We always were so alike. Anyway, remember me to Sylvia and dear Megan. Bye.'

The phone line was dead.

And he had made it alright for her. He had taken the responsibility onto himself. He was ill. She hadn't wriggled off the hook but taken hold of it, carried it to the riverbank and then attached it to the fisherman's own foot!

Edwin knew he had failed. And his failure and his lack of guts, and all his failures in life, made him feel bad. And he went on feeling bad all the hours of the evening and into the night.

Despite having taken his tablets he could not sleep and in the long hours of the night he found himself wishing that it was himself and not his dad that was dead. He would have given anything to change places with him. He wondered whether there was anything any longer worth living for. It all seemed to be rotten: his past and his present. So what point was there of thinking about some fantasy future? He would still be the same person. He would still be rotten and everything he continued to touch would turn to dust and ashes.

It was the first time that Edwin had thought he would like to be dead, the first time that the idea of suicide entered his consciousness. It was not to be the last time.

'The combination of a conversation with your mother and the fact that you are in a state of recent bereavement would be bound to have a profound effect upon how you are feeling. It would be more surprising if you were not feeling quite so bad'.

Edwin did not know how he had got through the thirty-six hours or so since his telephone conversation with his mother. After having been unable to sleep on the first night most of the subsequent day had been spent alternating between moments of despair and falling asleep, to the extent that the two ran into one another. His dreams were vivid and grim. In one he had found himself inside a mortuary, surrounded by cadavers, calling out for someone to come and open the door and find him still, albeit only just, alive. As he recounted the dream to Libby, he found himself saying that this expressed exactly how it felt to be himself at present and also that he envied those other occupants who had at least achieved the final peace of extinction. "Their torture is over", he had commented.

Libby was about to begin an Easter holiday break. Was she too abandoning him to the mortuary? Although breaks always come at a bad time in therapy, this one did seem particularly inopportune for him. He had just had a major failure in his dealings with his mother and tomorrow he was to bury his father. Now the surrogate mother was having a holiday.

She had been endeavouring in the immediate context of his father's final illness and death to focus Edwin's thoughts onto the future, but now wondered whether she had done right. He seemed to be moving into a deeper level of depression. That was not surprising given all that had happened.

But in the face of it all her training told her that the best thing was to encourage and enable the client to go with it, and here was she advocating the opposite. She knew why. A young psychiatric registrar from the city hospital had come to see her. She was younger than Edwin but like him accomplished and able. They had worked together for six months until one morning the young doctor had failed to turn up for a session. Later that morning her body was found in her flat by a cleaning lady. She had taken a massive overdose of insulin.

As Libby remembered, tears came unbidden to her eyes. And had Edwin turned at that moment and seen her he might have assumed the tears were for him. And if he had known of whom he was thinking he might have thought they were for the young doctor. And the fact is that the tears were Libby's for herself and the human suffering she so often (and perhaps too often?) encountered in this pleasant room in a pleasant road, in a pleasant city, in a green and pleasant land.

To drive from the south of England to Carlisle on the Wednesday before Easter is to enter into something akin to a medieval doom painting. Around Birmingham Edwin felt that Dante's ascription at the gate of the Inferno "Abandon hope all who enter here" would not have been inappropriate had it been scrawled across the three lanes of tarmac currently occupied by stationary traffic. He was relieved that Sylvia was behind the wheel. He had driven very little in months. At least the clocks having changed meant that their journey would be concluded in daylight, and once they were north of Preston the M6 became what motorways were probably intended to be.

Edwin had no idea how many people would be coming to the funeral, and he realised that this was so mainly because he did not really know the man whose passing they were coming to mark. He would be, with Iris, principal mourner, and yet increasingly he felt as if the man in the coffin was a stranger to him. And of course, as he discussed with Libby often enough, it was so.

The crematorium was, as most are, soulless. The music was the product of a terrible electronic organ played by a terrible organist. 'What a ghastly job', thought Edwin as he caught a brief glimpse of the somewhat appropriately cadaverous young man seated at the console. The coffin was carried in by members of the undertaker's team who left at once. The funeral director himself led Iris, Edwin and the family to the front pew, and the directed a large number of people, mostly unknown to Edwin to their places behind them. At the front Frank Pembiss was in full flow declaiming the words of the funeral office.

Edwin was glad to be hearing the familiar words of what he assumed was the Book of Common Prayer. He could not have borne to have been subjected to something trendy. He recalled attending a funeral at Sylvia's church. The principal aim of the event had seemed to Edwin to be the denial of death. Everyone worse bright colours and behaved much as they might at a wedding. The hymns ('songs' would have been a better description) gave the impression of having been deliberately chosen with one intention in mind: that if we shout something loudly and often enough we shall start to believe it. Thus the reality of someone's death was passed over because those present seemed unwilling or unable to face it and added pop music to emphasise the point.

The Prayer Book did not allow such evasion. Its sonorous tones sought to tell the truth about our human lot and as he listened Edwin found himself, to his wonder, in agreement with most of it. The words may have been penned in the sixteenth century but they spoke exactly to his condition now:

"*We brought nothing into the world and it is certain we can carry nothing out. The Lord gave and the Lord hath taken away; blessed be the name of the Lord".*

"Man that is born of a woman hath but a short time to live, and is full of misery. He cometh up, and is cut down, like a flower; he fleeth as it were a shadow, and never continueth in one stay".

Even the hymns chosen by Iris: 'Abide with me' and 'Rock of Ages' had a force because they did not seek to conceal the pain and fears of life behind a screen of false cheeriness.

Frank did not include a sermon or panegyric in the service. Perhaps he knew too much. But Edwin did not feel they had been cheated save at the end when the curtains closed around his dad's coffin. He wished that they had been burying him; that would have been final. This suggested that they had simply reached the "end of the show" with the actor removing his greasepaint behind the scenes and slipping out of a side door. It did not feel right leaving the chapel with the coffin still there in the room albeit concealed by a curtain.

Edwin shook the hands of many people who spoke warmly to him of his father. Most of them were known to Iris and for a few moments he and Sylvia felt much as they might had they wandered into the wrong funeral. And already the doors behind them had been closed and as they stood in the hallway, they could hear the tones of the next service already underway.

Rotary had laid on a funeral tea at a local hotel. Edwin was amused. There really were ham sandwiches! 'A real funeral', he found himself thinking. And a lot of people getting on with life and often laughing and then remembering they were supposed to be mourning. Most of them were on their Easter break and seem relaxed and in holiday mood. There were a few distant relatives present but they mostly made their excuses and disappeared quickly.

Edwin wondered whether they had been drawn by the lure of a possible legacy and had to withdraw disappointed. He hoped so.

Sylvia had not enjoyed the funeral. Not altogether surprisingly she had found the language and form of the service most definitely not to her liking. Megan on the other hand had never heard the Prayer Book words before and had been strangely moved by them. Edwin thought that his daughter knew things his wife did not. Words bear more than literal meaning. He had recently come across an interesting work by a former Professor of Poetry at Oxford in which the author made precisely this point. The function of poetry wholly transcends literal meaning which was why translating poetry was so difficult and usually unsuccessful.

They had a quiet evening with Iris. She had cried a little when they had returned to the empty house. She was leaving the house in a few days, much to Sylvia's consternation and confusion. Edwin had said nothing to her about his father's financial affairs and did not want to do so now. But it could not be kept from her. Whilst Iris made them some supper, he tried to explain that his father had lost the house – and with it most of his savings – as part of a failed business gamble. It was economy with the truth, but he did not mind. He might have been able (just) to accept Libby's account of the place gambling had played in his father's life but, all the same, he did not want others to know about it, even his wife.

The following day dawned sunny and warm. It was Good Friday but Sylvia he said she wanted to go and do some shopping in Keswick. It was a pretty place in the shadow of the mountains which still had snow on their tops. They had a meal in a restaurant followed by a long walk along the eastern shore of Bassenthwaite. Edwin wondered how long it would be before he returned. This part of the world, no matter how beautiful, echoed too much of the past. He not only had to let it go, he wanted to.

22

He couldn't remember Libby telling him that their next session would have to be in a different room from normal, but she must have done. The chaise was the same however though the room was small and narrow. Libby was behind him to the right as usual. He lay down and was suddenly aware that he was naked and in an aroused state. He turned to look round at her as if to apologise. She was sitting smoking and laughing at him.

He was sweating profusely as he awoke from the dream and was aware of an intense back pain. Later he took paracetamol provided by Iris but it didn't seem to help. Twere due to travel south to the Fens to stay with Sylvia's parents for the rest of the week. Edwin again awoke in considerable pain and decided that the real culprit must be the bed. Over the next few days it did not get any better, indeed if anything it worsened. Sylvia's parents were willing to make an appointment for him the see their doctor, but Edwin said he preferred to wait until they reached home, which they did on the Saturday.

Edwin rang for an appointment on Monday morning only to discover that Dr Nuffield was on holiday that week. Reluctantly he agreed to see another of the partners who could fit him at the evening surgery. Much to his surprise Dr Clark, who turned out to be a woman, said she thought it wasn't his back at all, and making him lie down on the bed began to prod his abdomen. It hurt. She listened with her stethoscope to his gut,

'Blimey, it's like the Underground down there', she commented, before washing her hands and asking Edwin to get dressed.

'You've got an irritable bowel', she said after he had taken her seat. 'I see from your notes that you had a colonoscopy some months back and that it showed nothing untoward. I think this probably accounts for the bleeding you had then. The bowel is very tender, and probably caused by the stress for which Dr Nuffield is treating you. So, I'll write you a prescription for Mebeverine. It's a drug which helps bowel tissue relax. It should help the pain settle down'.

Edwin was too late for the chemist that evening and so resigned himself to at least one more night of pain. He even wondered whether he should increase the dose of his antidepressant in the hope a better night of sleep but decided against it.

Later in the week came some difficult news. The publishers of the Law Journal wrote to tell him that they felt "in the circumstances" they had decided that the editorship of the Journal should pass into the hands of someone who could guarantee its further development. It was a lot of words, but the effect was the same: he was sacked. He could not argue because the terms of the contract had always allowed for such a change and withdrawal by either party. Academic law is a cut-throat world and this time he was the loser.

That might not have been so bad had not, in the very same week, a letter arrived from the law faculty at Bristol. They were planning their timetabling for the following year and reluctantly they were being forced to make cuts. For "obvious reasons", he was informed, these must begin with part-time staff and they could not offer him any work in the subsequent academic year and that in view of his continuing ill-health, his present supervisees were now being re allocated to "help relieve the pressure" on him.

Edwin had been thinking during their holiday that he ought to be considering a move to begin work again. He even mooted the possibility of a return to Scotland, something to which Sylvia had given an instant expression of consent. She would love to return. And Edwin knew that no matter how much he had every legal right to continue in the practice he was probably finished, much as Paul had claimed. Now these other changes in his work had become apparent making a move became both necessary and possible. He had nothing to hold him.

The tablets given him by Dr Clark were not helping at all. He even bought a book on IBS but felt that its description of symptoms was not exactly what he was experiencing. He talked over with Sylvia the need to change his diet. But his night pains increased. He was waking almost every night at about two and struggling to get comfortable and back to sleep. As a result, he was more tired than ever in the morning and later in the day.

He began to sense that he was holding on for one thing: the return to Libby. What was she going to make of what had happened? There was much to speak of: the funeral, the loss of his work at Bristol and the Journal, the pain, and of course, the dream.

From her colour Edwin assumed that Libby must have been abroad during her holiday (paid for by him? he wondered). She smiled her customary welcome at the door and then followed Edwin up to the room in silence. It was the normal room.

'I don't know where to begin', he began, 'so much has happened'.

In fact, and to his surprise, he spoke first about the pain he was in. It had worsened considerably over the weekend, and he had been taking more and more painkillers. He had made an appointment to see Dr Nuffield later this same morning.

Edwin then narrated the details of the funeral and their visit to

Edinburgh. As he had anticipated Libby was most interested in the dream.

'It was most odd. I felt I was being squeezed into a narrow place, not here. It was darker, more oppressive, and I was surprised because though I thought I could not recall your having said we would be in the new room I knew you must have done because I trust you. But then there was the terrible realisation that I had no clothes on, and I wondered why. Plus the fact that I was obviously feeling aroused by it – though I think that had everything with needing to get up and go the loo. But then I turned to see how you were reacting to this and I was shocked to see you just sitting there smoking and obviously enjoying what was happening to me'.

'What does smoking represent to you?'.

'My mother smokes; always has. To me it's a horrible habit. Those who smoke don't realise how much they smell'.

'And the fact that I was smoking?'.

'It seemed to identify you with my mother'.

'Sitting there in callous detachment enjoying your embarrassment and perhaps even receiving some pleasure from it?'

'Yes'.

'And the narrow room, the sense of being squeezed. I wonder whether that is to do with how you perceive not just what colleagues have been doing, and fathers, but also me'.

'Not until this morning', he said with a rare honesty.

Edwin turned to look at Libby.

'Do you really think all that could be expressed in a dream?'

'That you think it might be a possibility worth considering is not without significance', she said, wholly evading the question, allowing him to make his own conclusions. 'It is important to remember, for both of us to remember because we can both easily forget, that I am nothing more than a guide accompanying you on your journey. I have comments and observations to offer. Some may be of use, some not. My job as a guide is to go where you go and not to try and make you go by a predetermined route. It may be that some of your chosen journey will make me feel uncomfortable but that's my problem not yours. Of course, I'm only a human guide, not the Delphic Oracle, and I make mistakes but while you want me as a guide I go where you take us'.

'The oracle at Delphi was only human too, just divinely inspired'.

'I knew when I said it that it was mistake to say it to a classicist', she laughed in reply. 'But I would say this, as your guide: it's clear that you are moving into new territory. Perhaps your father's death has made that possible. It can and does sometimes happen like that. That may be exciting and challenging. It also seems to me vitally important to take note of the pains you are experiencing. They are a kind of warning, and they need to be heeded too'.

'I have an appointment with Dr Nuffield later this morning'.

'I'm sure that's very sensible, but don't be too surprised if he's not as much help as you might hope. He's only a doctor, albeit better than many. My own guess is that we will have to listen carefully to this pain if we are to find the way forward to the future that we've spoken about'.

23

As Libby had predicted Colin Nuffield was of little immediate help to Edwin. He had merely suggested persisting with the medication already prescribed. They did however discuss the matter of how long Edwin should be remaining on his anti-depressants and whether the time had come for him to return to work. The doctor was at pains not to apply any pressure but encouraged him to continue the anti-depressants, saying that he believed that as a minimum patients should take them for six months. Nor did he think Edwin should return to work, but he allowed Edwin to tell him that. He signed him off for a further period of eight weeks.

Edwin did confide to him the thought that he might have to move to pick up his work again, and that his colleagues seemed to be opposed to his returning.

'But they can't do that'.

'Not legally, and they know I know they can't. But there are other ways of applying pressure'.

And what Colin Nuffield also knew was that when you are depressed there are ways of applying pressure against yourself that does the work of unpleasant colleagues for them. He could only hope that whatever work Edwin was doing with Libby would enable him to realise that and fight.

By the time Wednesday morning had come Edwin was having difficulties getting out of bed. The pains unquestionably waned as the day went on but seemed to gather itself for a further attack some time after two in the morning. Most mornings now he was waking in considerable pain and then struggling to get back to sleep whilst simultaneously endeavouring to find a comfortable position in which to lie in bed. He wanted to disturb Sylvia as little as possible, but he was sometimes in so much pain that it was difficult not to. She was sympathetic. This was a pain she could understand and relate to.

When he arrived at Libby's he was in a great deal of pain and she could see what it was doing to him. He reported on his inconsequential visit to the GP.

'I'm not sure he believed me about the pain', said Edwin. 'And yet it has got lot worse even since Monday. If it goes on I'm going to have to get some help. It's proving a real struggle even to get out of bed and to bend to fasten my shoes even'.

'Have you ever heard of Michael O'Connell?' asked Libby.

'No'.

'He lives and works in Swindon. He's a medical herbalist, and a somewhat gifted one. I have known a lot of people who have found him a real healer and he does have particular diagnostic skills. He might be able to see you at quite short notice if you were to call him and tell him what is happening. It's no reflection on Dr Nuffield, I assure you. It's just that orthodox medicine doesn't always know quite what to do with the sort of symptoms you are presenting other than hand out pills'.

'This is alternative medicine, is it?', asked Edwin, a slightly disparaging note present in his voice.

'I think Michael would call it complementary rather than alternative, and what I do know for certain is that all sorts of people have found that he has been able to be of use to them when orthodox medicine has not. But it's up to you. I can give you his telephone number if you wish'.

'Oh Libby, I am so fed up. I really feel I'm getting to the end of my tether. It's just been one thing after another, and this physical pain just leaves me feeling so tired and miserable. But you know how it is, the thought of having to give an account of how I am to someone else feels like hard work'.

'Yes, I think I do know, and I fully appreciate how that must be. I don't think I would have suggested Michael had I not hoped it might prove to be very worth your while'.

'I realise that. I guess I am a little tender in the hope area'.

'That certainly brings us to that important dream again. And I think it is important, Edwin. I know that you are sceptical about dreams and their interpretation. That seems to me to be very wise, but I think this dream is important'.

'In what way?'

'Your anxiety about possibly feeling stupid in my eyes ties in exactly with the sense you described in the dream of feeling totally exposed to my almost voyeuristic regard. It suggests that you might find it impossible to make certain decisions and choices in your life if you fear that I wouldn't approve of them. That might well place considerable constraints upon you, and I think I need to let you know that such constraints will be wholly of your making. You see, one of the theories of the psychoanalytic process is that the client knows nothing or next to nothing about the therapist, and that means that when presuppositions arise, we can safely recognise that they originate in the client and we can try and understand why'.

'But no therapist, however professional and detached can wholly conceal from their clients something of themselves', said Edwin.

'But I don't represent right or wrong, and it isn't a competition, so what I think doesn't matter. If you were suddenly to tell me if and when I let you get a word in edgeways that you are thinking of undergoing a sex change then I shall feel it is my therapeutic task to ask you questions and try and help us both understand why should want to do this so that you can know it is what you really want to do, but in the end it is your decision completely'.

'But what do I want? Isn't that the real difficulty? You talk, albeit in jest, about decisions I might make to do this or that. My situation is that I do not know what to do, and indeed I don't even know what sort of decision it is that I have to make? I'm at least one and probably many more steps behind you'.

'I think I understand a little, enough anyway, of where you are Edwin, and it is not an easy place to be. I hope I can stand there with you'.

'Oh no, Edwin, please not'.

Sylvia was not delighted to receive the news that he was going to contact a medical herbalist.

'It's just one daft thing after another'.

Edwin felt strangely guilty upsetting her in this way. He would have preferred to say nothing but a trip to Swindon needed to be arranged between them. For a start he was not sure that his pain would permit him to drive.

'First you go and see this woman and now you want to go and see some sort of witch doctor'.

'Don't be silly', retorted Edwin angrily. 'What's the difference between what I'm doing and some of the really way-out wacky stuff I see in some of your church magazines with all sorts of ludicrous claims about miracles and healing?'

'I'll tell you what the difference is. You are still off work, you are doubled up in pain, you are spending a fortune on this therapist woman, and you're not only not getting better, you're getting worse day by day. Now she wants you to see some way-out herbalist who'll cost even more money. Those who you can read about in my magazines are being healed. That's the difference, and it's considerable'.

Edwin did not know what to say, but, in any case, Sylvia had not finished.

'And the simple truth of the matter is that this woman you see says something and you jump in accordance with her commands. You'll go off to Swindon or do this or that. When I suggest something, that you see one of our Christian counsellors for example, you treat it with contempt. It's not right, Edwin, and it's not fair. And it's not getting you or us anywhere'.

It was true what she said. He was prejudiced against those who belonged to her church, and he did not believe what he read in her magazines.

'I wish it was as easy as that', he said, 'I really do. Don't you think I don't realise how much easier it would be if we shared the same beliefs and presuppositions about life. But we don't. And I sometimes think you feel I do it deliberately, that I intentionally fail to believe what you believe. But I don't. It pains me, it really does, but I don't and can't. It's beyond me. I wish it were not so, I really do. But because of that I can't go and see your people because I can't accept their basic premises and couldn't make myself fit their theoretical framework. I'm sorry, really sorry, that it's like this, but it is'.

Edwin telephoned Michael O'Connell and they made an appointment for the following afternoon. Edwin decided that he would do all he could to make sure he got himself there if Sylvia was unwilling to go with him, but in the end, she relented and agreed to drive.

That night he almost cried with pain. He could not find a place or position of ease and three o'clock found him downstairs curled up taking whisky and paracetamol in a fruitless effort to win some release. "O God" he said out loud to no one, "please help me" but no gods came. It was not until five that he returned to bed. He slept fitfully until breakfast time. He was determined to get through that family ritual to ensure that Megan's life remained as normal as possible, but on this morning the cost of that was heavy. Megan could not fail to notice.

'Are you alright, dad?', she asked with a worried look on her face.

'I'm getting a form of indigestion, something to do with anxiety and stress following grandad's death I suppose, and it hurts. I'm seeing someone today who might be able to give me some medicine to help, but it'll go away soon enough. It's just not so good this morning'.

His reply might have satisfied his daughter and allowed her to go to school with a more contented mind, but Edwin was far from convinced himself. Just what was happening inside? After all, his father's cancer had been bowel cancer. Was it not just possible that he had it too?

By the time they arrived in Swindon and found Michael O'Connell's house the pain was beginning its afternoon retreat. Edwin was hugely relieved to be free of it but concerned lest the herablist did not realise just what it was like when it was there.

He had been told that an initial appointment would last at least an hour, and probably half an hour longer than that, so Sylvia went off into the town to do some shopping leaving Edwin to go to the door of the house. There was a small brass plate inscribed "Michael O'Connell MNIMH, Medical Herbalist". Edwin rang the doorbell.

The door was opened by a giant of a man with a big bushy beard through which appeared the warmest of welcoming smiles.

'Hi there, I'm Michael O'Connell, and I imagine you're Edwin. Welcome and come in'.

He spoke with a gentle southern Irish accent.

Edwin followed him into what was obviously his consulting room. The first thing to strike Edwin was the rich aromatic smell and the sight of dozens and dozens of large brown labelled bottles, all presumably holding herbal preparations. To the right, and behind the door, was a couch and a desk. Michael directed Edwin to a chair and sat down opposite him. The desk looked not unlike that of any GP, there was a stethoscope and one of those instruments for taking blood pressure.

'So now, I can see you're in a little discomfort. What we need to discover is what position is best for you. Would you prefer to lie down or are you happy as you are?'

'No', said Edwin unused to such a question from anyone medical, 'this will be fine'.

'Ok', said Michael picking up some paper and his pen, 'I shall need to make some notes as you speak, but perhaps we can begin with you telling me all about it'.

Edwin spoke about the pains he was having, their location and frequency.

Michael did not interrupt, and Edwin was aware of receiving his total attention. When he had finished describing his symptoms and recounting what his GP had said and done, Michael said to him 'Right and now tell me about the life that these symptoms manifest themselves in. Symptoms belong to a person, and I need to understand something about the person you are'.

Once again Edwin was aware of receiving Michael O'Connell's undivided attention as he sought to tell him all that happened in the previous months.

'Thank you', said Michael, when he had finally come to a halt. 'Now I need to ask you some questions to help me understand a little bit more about how your body functions', and he proceeded to take a full medical history.

This was much as he had experienced from orthodox doctors but some of the questions were unusual. Michael asked him detailed questions about the contents of the toilet bowl after he had finished emptying his bowels. When Edwin evaded the detail

Michael was most specific.

'Why do you need to know such things?'.

'Well Edwin, your GP sent you for a colonoscopy. I understand why he did it. The only trouble with that is that it takes a snapshot of your gut in a totally unnatural state. They empty it to get the camera in. As a result, what it tells is a totally atypical story. I prefer to find out the details of the place by asking its most recent visitors. They can tell me a great deal and far more than any colonoscopy. Normally I'll take your word but sometimes I may need you to provide me with samples'.

Edwin warmed to the man who had now put down the pen and paper. 'Right, I need to examine you. First of all, show me your tongue'.

Michael looked at his tongue for a long time, far longer than Edwin had ever known a doctor do so. He then took hold of his right wrist and felt his pulse, but then surprised Edwin by also taking hold of his left wrist and feeling both pulses together.

'Why do you do that?'

'Well, you see now, a pulse is often regarded by some medical practitioners as simply a guide to the speed of heart beat but it is considerably more than that. I'm not much interested in speed but quality of beat. Together the two pulses can tell me a great deal I could not otherwise know'.

Edwin then undid his shirt and had his chest listened to through the stethoscope before being asked to loosen his trousers and lie on the bed. The first thing Michael did was to look at Edwin's abdomen and he went on looking. Edwin found it somewhat unnerving. Then Michael took his stethoscope and placed it on Edwin's lower abdomen.

'Right, now we're into the painful bit, I'm afraid, though I'll try and keep it to a minimum'.

He seemed to know exactly where the places of maximum discomfort were, and his fingers found them unfailingly. Finally, he asked Edwin to roll over. Once again Edwin was aware that Michael was looking long and hard at his back.

'I'm sorry Edwin but I have to do something that is going to hurt, but it will be a brief pain'.

'Ow!', exclaimed Edwin as Michael pressed on just one place at the side of his spine. 'You weren't kidding'.

'No. But we're done. You can get dressed again. Would you like a cup of tea?'.

'Oh yes please. Milk, no sugar, or it is herbal?'.

'No, no, definitely Yorkshire Tea from Sri Lanka'.

As Edwin dressed Michael popped out of the room for a moment and within a short while the door opened and an unseen hand deposited two cups by the door, which Michael went over and brought to the desk.

'The good news is that we can completely rule out Irritable Bowel Syndrome'.

'Oh!', said Edwin.

'Ah well to be honest I had ruled that out before you arrived. You see there is no such thing. IBS, bowel pain, is simply a symptom and you can treat the symptom sometimes quite effectively with mebeverine but it doesn't deal with the thing that it's a symptom of. What we have to find out is the cause'.

'If that's the good news, what's the bad?'

'It's not the only good news. One of the things you can perhaps rejoice in is the fact that your body seems to be trustworthy. You can rely on what it tells you. Indeed, as a messenger it is functioning very well indeed. It's what it is striving to tell you that we need to consider'.

Michael stopped to take a swig of tea, and then pointed to his head.

'I think the Almighty got it wrong when he placed our brains up here, because it means we too easily identify our self with the bits of us that are most definitely only above the neck. I don't see it that way and the medicine I practice does not either. Brains have their place of course but they're very limited in so many ways. In Chinese medicine the central organ, the ruling organ if you like, is the heart, and a great deal of pre-modem thought in the west would have totally agreed with it. And what you are suffering from is heart trouble'.

Edwin gasped.

'Not in the narrow physiological sense a cardiologist would mean by the term, but in the much deeper sense of your heart knowing full well that it is not functioning as it is meant to. Your condition is really caused by your vocation – I apologise for the term, it's my catholic upbringing emerging, but then again, its very near the truth. The old priests used to speak about the need for us to discover and discern our vocation, to learn what it was that God had in mind for us. They weren't wrong about that even though they were about just everything else. Because to discover what it is we are meant to be doing with our lives, what we are here for, is the most important work any of us can do. And your heart, Edwin, is most definitely crying out to you that you're not getting it right. Your pain is so acute because I think your heart is telling you that the matter is urgent. "Learn from your father", it seems to be saying though that is not the same as threatening you with cancer, at least not yet. But if you don't attend to these matters, if you don't attend to your vocation, then you're in trouble'.

Edwin was silent. 'What sort of trouble?'.

'A serious form of dysfunction, I would say. Your body is already on that road, and you need to get off it. I can do a great deal to deal with some of the worst symptoms you are experiencing, but it is only treating the symptoms. Only you can deal with and attend to the cause'.

Edwin swallowed some tea.

'Your intense pains are easily explained in terms of body functioning, or in your case non-functioning. The nerves from your spine through to your gut are on strike and you're getting a massive build-up of half-digested food in your small gut leading to foetid gases. They can't escape in the usual way because they're so high up and basically poisoning the system, slowing the nervous functions down and leading to intense pain, muscular spasm in your back causing you to hold your whole abdomen in a state of tension'.

Edwin was both shocked and not all surprised by that he was being told. All that had been happening to him told him that this genial Irishman had eyes that saw far deeper than any X-ray machine, and that he saw truly.

24

Sylvia had sat outside waiting for Edwin. She desperately hoped that this would not prove to be another false dawn for him. It wasn't fair on him, and it wasn't fair on her. She knew full well, and perhaps better than he did, just how tenuous their position was. Her own work seemed likely to be coming to an end in the autumn and if they were going to move, sooner would be better for Megan than later. Once the GCSE syllabus was under way it would be hard for her to change. Yet how could they move with all Edwin's support structures in place here? She may have nursed violent feelings of antipathy towards his therapist, but she was not so foolish as not to recognise how important she was to Edwin's stability.

She saw the door of the house open, and Edwin emerge accompanied by a huge man with a beard who walked with Edwin towards the car. The bearded man came straight up to her side of the car and opened the door.

'And you must be the lovely Sylvia, and even lovelier in the flesh if I may say so'.

She was immediately entranced by the words and the accent.

'I was just saying to yer man here that it was so good that you were able to come with him. First appointments can be mightily exhausting, and I think he'll be hurting a bit, so I'm glad you can do the driving'.

'So drive carefully and come safely to your home'.

He said it as a kind of blessing, as Gandalf might have done.

'Thank you, Michael,', shouted Edwin through Sylvia's open door just before Michael closed it upon an entranced and stunned driver.

She finally recovered sufficiently to start the engine and drive away. Michael had gone. She nodded at the white bags Edwin was carrying.

'Potions?'

She smiled at him.

'What an amazing man', he replied, then realising she had asked a question, continued. 'Herbal medicines and a special sort of tea'. And at once he set about trying to describe Michael's consulting room and his total and undivided attention, even his questions in all their detail.

'I've never known anyone look at me like he did. Yes, he touched and felt, but only after he had looked for a very long time. When he did touch it seemed to be because he had already seen something and was simply using touch to confirm what his eyes had told him. And you should have seen him making up the medicine, pouring mixtures together. It was astonishing to watch - and smell!'

'So, tell me', she said when he had finally finished his paean of praise, 'what did he say?'.

'He told me that I had to listen to what God was saying and calling me to'.

They were on the dual carriageway by-pass to the east of the

'He said that? What did he mean?'

Edwin then tried to explain to her all that Michael had told him about the symptoms of his body manifesting deeper hurts and pains of his heart, and that it was through these that the deepest self, the truest self was to be found, and that it was here that we are addressed and called to life by God, however we might understand the word.

She could say nothing. She did not know whether to be pleased or not. The part of her married to Edwin of course desperately wanted him to become a believer; the part of her which was a converted Christian was unsure whether the language the Irishman was using even qualified as slightly Christian – it sounded so vague as to be capable of almost any possible religious slant. They were regularly warned at her church about the danger of heresy and error entering the true faith through simple and appealing religious language, but really the devil speaking. The trouble was that she hoped, and wanted to believe, that all this was a sign that her constant prayers (and not only hers) for Edwin were being answered and that he was being drawn into faith.

Edwin too was unsure about the language Michael had used. Just what did it mean to speak of his vocation, his calling? And in any case how on earth could he find out what it might be? It sounded wonderful but was it quite as good as it sounded? And yet he could not escape the knowledge that he had just spent an hour and a half in the presence of someone who really was a healer, who could, as it were, see into the soul (whatever one of them was!) or, as Michael clearly obviously would have preferred to say, the heart. And what connection was there, if any, with the sort of religion practised by Sylvia and Paul Raven? None, he suspected, or was that just prejudice? Were the roots of all these different traditions actually one and all he needed to do was discover which one could feed and nourish him? Or possibly it all meant something quite different. Perhaps all the language was being used in an entirely symbolic sort of way with no necessary religious connotation. He didn't know. But he was sufficiently intrigued to ask the questions and to wonder as to how he might find out some answers.

The medicine tasted as foul as he had expected though he was strangely impressed with the herbal tea. It was called 'Tea of Happiness' and had been put together by Michael himself, though based on a French recipe. He had been told to continue taking his anti-depressants but to stop the mebeverine and to take such analgesia as helped with the immediate pain.

The pain itself was not such as to respond to instant dismissal simply because Michael O'Connell had been involved, and it was shortly before three in the morning when it woke Edwin. If anything, it seemed even more intense that it had before and he screwed up his face as he tried to manoeuvre into a more comfortable position. He had known nothing like it and whilst it was helpful to know what he had been told by Michael about its physiological cause, the knowledge not help reduce it.

At that time of the morning, when it was still dark, he felt at his lowest. He had lost some of the energy generated on his visit to Swindon and all he could focus on was what he had lost.

Slowly and agonisingly he shifted himself to reach for two tablets by his bed. They were strong pain killers which Colin Nuffield had prescribed and Edwin decided he could manage no longer without. Unfortunately, as Michael had pointed out when Edwin had told him about his current medical regime, they also caused constipation and thus inadvertently increased the very pain they were designed to numb. Edwin took them all the same. Quite how much sleep he was getting he was not altogether sure of, but the process of waking was always one of considerable agony – no other word could describe it. Megan and Sylvia had both been shocked on the previous morning to see how difficult it was proving for Edwin to get out of bed.

He spoke warmly and with a hint of excitement in his voice as he described to Libby the visit of the previous day.

'I found his language of meaning, purpose and vocation strangely and unexpectedly alluring. It isn't new to me. Greek writing deals with it the whole time. Even speaking of God or the gods is not entirely foreign to me provided there are not the kind of shackles placed upon it by Sylvia's friends. Then it becomes simply unreasonable because too reasonable or, I should say, too rational, if you see what I mean. When clergy and for that matter anyone, speak about God, they don't tell me about God but they do tell me a great deal about themselves. No doubt that's also true even of Euripides, but to read, say, Ion, is to know full well that I'm taken to a deeper level of my humanity in reflecting upon meaning and purpose in life. He speaks of the gods in a way that genuinely communicates something of value to me'.

'Intellectually, or in your heart?'.

'Ah'.

'What on earth did that mean?', said Libby.

'I suppose I mean that up until now the answer would have been quite clear. Now I would still reply that it was an intellectual response but that I know it should be with my heart. But I don't know how to do that'.

'Well perhaps we should not make too much of a distinction. After all you have to use your brain to understand the words and I imagine that you wouldn't love the classics as you do had you not already been responding to them with that part of you used for feeling.'

'No, that's true. And I have been known to dissolve in tears at the opera'.

'Sentiment may not be quite the same thing as Michael O'Connell implies by the word "heart", however', responded Libby guardedly. 'I don't know, of course, because I have never met him but from what you and others have reported from their encounters with him, I suspect not'.

'Does it mean anything to you?'

'He also spoke about the self, did he not? That means a great deal to me. One might say that my work is helping people to make contact with and listen to their own truest and deepest self. If that is what he means by heart, then we might be said to have a similar purpose. But again, I would say it does not matter, because what matters is the extent to which you, Edwin, can get past your characteristic defence of intellectual analysis and get on with seeing if there really is a self or heart in there by which and with which to live'.

'How?'

There was a note of desperation in Edwin's question.

'I think there may be two answers to that. The first is to say that it seems to be happening, slowly and painfully. Your life is very different from what it was twelve months ago. You may not have chosen this path to knowledge, but you do seem to be on it'.

'I feel as if I'm descending into hell not climbing the mountain of enlightenment'.

'Yes. In ancient times what help would one of the mortals seek if they needed to know the secrets of the gods?'

'They would consult a priest in one of the temples or in extreme circumstances they would journey to Delphi and consult the oracle'.

'Well, perhaps the first set of circumstances – your state of "descending into hell", as you described it, doesn't just allow but possibly demands that you do the second'.

'You mean coming to see you?'.

'Me? Good God, no. I'm no oracle. That is not what I'm here for and it would be entirely wrong for me to assume that guise. No, I am nothing more than a guide – a Virgil to your Dante, if we can change eras. I ask questions about what you decide and why, but I cannot supply answers'.

'So where and what?'.

'Considering I told you less than five seconds ago that I don't supply answers you have already managed to ask me two. That must be some sort of record'.

'I'm too desperate to play games, Libby'.

'And I'm not playing games either, believe you me. This is the turning point of your life we are talking about. It is perhaps literally a matter of life and death, but I cannot do it for you'.

It was a lovely Spring morning as Edwin slowly made his way home from his session. Walking was painful and he felt utterly downcast. Life seemed to have become nothing more than series of false dawns and disappointments. Even as Libby had been speaking, he had been desperately hoping to hear something from her that pointed the way towards the future, towards life and hope and freedom from the terrors of the inferno he felt he now bore within his body.

He passed children and their parents on their way to school, he passed people on their way to work or the shops able now to cast off their winter attire and enjoy the warmth and sunshine, some of whom greeted him with smiles as they passed by. And the sun shone from a clear blue sky and Edwin felt worse and worse as each step slowly took him home.

He now knew what he had to do. She had given him the clue and he saw it clearly. "Literally a matter of life and death" she had said. It was so obvious. He had once read somewhere that suicide is the only real free act of a human life.

He decided that it would be best to leave a note downstairs for Sylvia to see and which would tell her to call for help before she came upstairs. He knew it would be her and not Megan who would be home first. She was due back for lunch with one of her colleagues so she would not be alone. He took out his pen and began to write.

My dearest Sylvia,

I now know that I cannot take any more and want no longer to inflict upon you and my darling Megan the terrible hurts that my circumstances have brought upon you. Please try and understand why and forgive. Please try and do all you can to discover new life. My will and all the insurance policies are ready in my desk drawer.

Please do not come upstairs. Telephone for the police and an ambulance.

I love you and am sorry I was never able to love you enough and as you hoped. Ed

The letter finished, he moved quickly. He went upstairs and began to run the bath. He had once attended an inquest in which the coroner had said that slitting the wrists in a hot bath must be one of the surest methods of suicide. That was what he would do.

He undressed to his underclothing. As the bath filled, he opened the bathroom cabinet and took out his razor. He caught sight of himself in the mirror as he closed the door. He knew he was doing right. He turned to face the bath and moments later he was unconscious and lying in a pool of blood.

25

Sylvia had forgotten the Bible programme for the new computer at Church which she had borrowed the previous week in order to install it on their computer at home and was due to return it today. As soon as she arrived home, she ran up the stairs shouting a greeting to Edwin wherever he was in the house. She heard water running but did not notice that it was sleeping under the bathroom door until she had collected the disks from the study. Then she saw it.

'Edwin!' she shouted, assuming he must be downstairs, and sought to push open the bathroom door. Something was blocking it and then she saw that water was running under it. She forced it further open and saw Edwin on the bathroom floor, water all around him and blood.

'Edwin!' she screamed, 'Edwin!'

From somewhere came the reserve of strength to force the door completely open. She rushed and turned Edwin over. He had an open wound on the side of his head which was still bleeding, and he seemed to be unconscious but she was sure he was alive. She lifted his head up and with her other hand turned off the tap. The water was boiling hot, and the room was steamed up and a total mess. What on earth had happened? She looked up and saw the answer. The bathroom cabinet had come off the wall. It lay behind her and had been blocking the door. It had obviously hit Edwin's head as he had been preparing to have a bath and shave and had knocked him out.

She needed help. She propped Edwin against the wall, quickly pulled the plug out of the bath and sped to the study where she called for an ambulance.

They arrived within five minutes. By this time, Edwin had regained consciousness and was wondering what on earth had happened to him. She tried to explain about the bathroom cabinet, but he couldn't understand. The ambulance men dried him and attended to the wound and then covered him with blankets and helped him downstairs and out to the waiting ambulance. Sylvia was still wearing her coat and followed them, got into her car and drove behind the ambulance as it made its way to the hospital.

Edwin's head was x-rayed and the wound stitched. As he had been unconscious (though he had no idea how long it had been for) it was decided that he should be admitted for observation. Sylvia came with him to the observation ward. She had said nothing to him about his letter though he couldn't believe she had not found it.

'My mind's a complete blank', he said in response to her question about how much he remembered of what had happened.

Eventually a nurse suggested she might like to go home for a while and give him the chance to sleep. Edwin realised that she mustn't have yet found the letter, but that of course she would when she arrived home. The next visit would be very different.

He slept throughout the afternoon but was awakened by the voice of Megan. 'Dad... Dad...it's me'.

Megan was grinning and holding some flowers. Sylvia was next to her and smiling. How could she be smiling knowing what she now knew about what he had done, or tried to do, or at least had wanted to try to do?

His head was throbbing and was given some pain-killers, but he was so pleased to see Megan and Sylvia and he listened with delight to the account of the school day and Sylvia's efforts to arrange for a man to come and fix the bathroom. Apparently, water had begun to come through the kitchen ceiling and the repairs would cost a great deal but she had already telephoned the insurance company and they were completely covered.

'It was a miracle that I found the insurance papers so easily', she said, 'but they were all together in your desk'.

No mention of the letter.

They stayed about three quarters of an hour. Sylvia disappeared for a while to talk to the sister and reported back that all being well Edwin would be home on the following morning.

Edwin slept well. He had not mentioned the fact that he was on anti-depressants but they obviously had given him some sort of sedative. He was aware of abdominal pain in the early hours, but it seemed far off, something that was just touching him, there but somehow also simultaneously distant. He drifted in and out of sleep.

Sylvia and Megan collected him shortly after ten o'clock. They fortunately remembered to bring his clothes. The nurse pulled the screens round him in order to allow him to dress while Sylvia and Megan collected some painkillers and sedatives for him from the Pharmacy.

When he was dressed Edwin felt in his inside pocket for his wallet. Tucked in the pocket was a letter. It was *the* letter. He could hardly believe it. He took it out and looked at it. There seemed no reason to think that it had been opened. He had stuck down the seal and clearly it had not been opened and then re-sealed. He was completely puzzled. He felt for his pen which he normally kept in that pocket. It was not there. He must have finished his letter and then in a state of total distraction put the letter into his pocket and (presumably?) left his pen for Sylvia to find. He tore the letter into pieces and placed them into the wastepaper bag attached to his locker. He pulled back the screens and emerged.

26

Three weeks had gone by. The cricket season was under way and Edwin went down to Southampton to watch a. Megan was well into the Summer term and Sylvia was preparing to take part at half-term at some evangelical extravaganza called Spring Harvest at a camp in Northamptonshire. To Edwin it sounded like a close approximation of hell.

His failure at suicide ("I'm not even good that", he told Libby when he met with her the first time after his non-attempt) made him decide to act. He formally resigned his job, having first forced the partners to accept a financial settlement they would undoubtedly have preferred not to have given, as it mostly came from the expected bonuses each was anticipating, but they knew the publicity of a wrongful dismissal would be harmful to the practice. As he pointed out in the words Chuck Colson, President Nixon's henchman from way back when: "When you have them by the balls, their hearts and minds tend to follow!".

He had also read in the paper about a place in Somerset, about 30 miles away where he could go for a complete rest in relative luxury with three meals a day without religion. It was there he met a young woman called Nicky.

'I had a strong sense, just from looking at her,' he told Libby on his return, ' that we could communicate. And we did. We walked and talked a great deal. She's younger than me and she has been through a great deal of pain and suffering. She was there for much the reason that I was – an excellent example of what Jung called synchronicity. We spoke from depth to depth, quite simply and naturally. We laughed a lot. She's very beautiful, though it's a beauty which is the work of an artist who uses materials sparingly. Even the pain she has known is etched upon her but with grace and light'.

'It sounds like an important encounter'.

'Oh yes. Oh yes'. Edwin spoke quietly, almost as if noise would fragment something precious.

'And?' asked Libby.

'And ... such moments are precious, because they enable us to know that we are not entirely alone. She and I shared moments of honesty with a tenderness I could hardly have dared to hope existed in this world. I could speak to her of what has happened to me, and she to me, of doubt and darkness and death, and it was safe. That's rare. And it wasn't therapy.

'You see I know it's safe to speak with you here, but it's not exactly a meeting of equals, is it? No matter how terrible your life maybe I know nothing of it. Of course not. But when Nicky and I spoke, we did so from heart to heart. We could even belly-laugh together and it's a very long time, if ever, that I have shared like that'.

Libby was unsure what to say. She felt it was not appropriate to intrude on something so obviously special, and the last thing she wanted to do was to mar what was a source of such joy for Edwin. There had not been so many in the past twelve months. But she was also anxious for him.

'She's much younger than me, so it's probably just displaced libido', he said with a hollow laugh to attempt to conceal the depth of his feeling.

'I'm not a moral policeman, Edwin. In any case sexual attraction is part and parcel of most relationships, you know. Freud said so, so it must be true'.

They laughed.

'When a relationship, as it were, clicks', she continued, 'then it is made up of all sorts of bits and pieces. We are bodies as well as minds. I'm glad you can at least recognise that she is not just another philosopher to you, but real flesh and blood'.

'Yes, she is very lovely. But I'm a married man, and she lives a long way away. And life is never quite so simple is it? But we shall see each other again – of that no doubt'.

His voice trailed away as thoughts of recent times returned.

'And so, what now, Edwin?'

'I've decided, Libby, that our time of working has come to a close. Asking me about the future, as you just have, means the past is sufficiently laid bare for me now to struggle forwards, but at least it will be my struggle and it will be forwards. I don't yet know what it can possibly hold but I want to be making my choices without endlessly looking backwards. I couldn't be saying any of this without the work I have done lying here so often, but this is the last time. I am leaving a cheque for payments to the end of the month.'

'When we began working, Edwin, the agreement was neither of us would end peremptorily.'

'Yes, but the parties were not equal in knowledge of what that meant, and it was not a written contract. I've sometimes thought of you as a surrogate mother, but I think now you have been more of a midwife, and I have now managed to leave the maternity suite. It's not easy for a new-born to survive but I must do it for myself now, Libby. I should be dead and perhaps I'll continue to fuck up my life, but that's the risk I now choose. I'm declarting my innings closed.'

When he arrived home there was an email from his publishers informing him that his book on Natural Law would be out in October. He smiled, reflecting upon the irony. A book that might well be published to acclaim and now he mostly did not believe in what he had written. It reminded him of a moment in the novel by Thomas Mann that Angus had been reading on the day they had met in the cathedral. The composer Adrian Leverkühn, the Dr Faustus of the title, was at a concert of his early music, something from which he now felt very separated and towards which he felt considerable antipathy having moved in a quite new and important different direction. At the conclusion of the concert the audience cheer and applaud him but he can hardly bear being identified with the music. The acclaim is truly terrible to him.

Edwin went into the bathroom where there was a new bathroom cabinet on the wall. He looked at it. Had the old cabinet in fact saved his life? Would he have gone through with it? He would never know. His thoughts were disturbed by the sound of the door bell. He closed the bathroom door and went down the stairs and opened the front door. Angus Glendenning stood before him.

'Hello', said Edwin with great surprise in his voice.

'Hello. I hope you don't mind me calling round to see you'.

'Not at all, come in, come in'.

Edwin closed the door behind his visitor and showed him to a chair. 'Coffee'?'

'Thank you'.

'How did you find out where I lived?', began Edwin as he sat down.

'There are not that many people who attend Evensong in winter and when I mentioned you to the Dean he told me where you worked. The rest was straightforward'.

'I am very glad you bothered'.

'I was wondering how things were with you. Last time I fear I did all the talking and I was not as attentive to you as I should have been. My own troubles seemed so heavy'.

'That's because they are'.

It's no excuse, as my wife would have been the first to point out. And besides I owe you a great deal'.

'Oh? I find that hard to believe'.

'No, I mean it.'

He looked up at Edwin, who smiled.

'I'd been suffering a double bereavement. I lost Helen and our never-to-be-born baby, but I also lost that overarching vision that held the universe together which I called God. But the thing about bereavement is that you cannot bring back the ones you've lost.

'It may seem odd but meeting you and hearing something of your story gave me the courage to begin to live without the loves I had known. One day I may meet someone else as a life partner, but I'm singularly unimpressed by the someone-else-Gods on the market, whatever their form or claims.

'When you were talking, I realised that other people also lose or at least have to come to terms with learning to live without a grand scheme. The suffering God is just a fantasy of the liberal theologians who, quite rightly, reject the saviour fantasy, but haven't the courage to be honest and live with the consequences of their recognition. So thank you.'

'I'm not sure how I did any of that,' said Edwin, 'but I echo everything you've said. I attempted suicide three weeks ago, Angus, and by means of a ludicrous accident survived to make you coffee this morning.'

Angus smiled.

Edwin told Angus about the death of his father, and then all about the circumstances of his breakdown and something of what he believed may have been the underlying cause. He ended with the news of his forthcoming great work on Natural Law which now he would be embarrassed to be identified with.

Angus was a good listener. He did not interrupt or attempt to rush Edwin. When he reached the end, Angus audibly sighed.

'But apart from that, did you enjoy the show, Mrs Lincoln?' he said, and they laughed, releasing the tension. They sat in silence for a while.

'I'm pleased you did not accomplish your intent, not because I believe it is wrong or anything like that, but because I'm glad you are still in the world, in my world and I dare say there are others who would say as much'.

'Thank you', said Edwin quietly.

'As for the rest of your story, all I would say is this. It seems to me that our besetting sin today is cynicism – wholesale reductionism, if you like, always assuming that the worst is true. It has happened in intellectual circles, in the Church, in Politics, in the Law I dare say'.

Edwin did not demur.

'In so many ways, of course, the Church across the ages has done this. We created the mighty edifices of the mind, the perfect systems, the systematic theologies, the brilliant intellectual schema. We did so of course for our own security because that way lay power and protection. The trouble is that they were all chimera, fantasies of our own devising. And when inevitably and rightly they began to collapse about our feet, men not only rejected us, they also rejected the very idea of meaning and purpose'.

'How does that affect me? I've never professed a Christian faith'.

'No. But for very good reasons, like the theologians of old, you also took refuge from the hurts and pains of your life in an intellectual system and in achievement. You've told me all about your understanding of natural law and it's obvious to see how able you are. But when a crack appeared the whole thing came tumbling down. It did, because the universe isn't like that. There are no great explanations, especially not theological ones. You ought to read them, all the efforts made by theologians to explain the death of Christ'.

'I've heard some of them, believe you me', said Edwin reflecting upon so many of his wife's words.

'But they' re totally unconvincing because they claim too much. Far better little and live it truly. But that's not your problem. What you're dealing with is a need to survive the collapse of the edifice you assumed you needed to survive. You nearly didn't and that would have been the ultimate act of reductionism – you, reduced to nothing more than a corpse. What both you and I have to do is to find the small signs of life and hope and live with them'.

'You mean forget the grand design and concentrate on the things to hand?'

'That's quite a good definition, for me that includes and indeed means what that novelist described as the God of small things – the beauty of nature, of art and the poets'.

'I don't think it stands much chance of catching on'.

'So what? It's all there is'.

'Possibly, though it isn't easy to know how to make the shift in my thinking'.

'Isn't that... ', he paused, 'please excuse if I'm speaking out of turn in saying this, but isn't that because you almost assume that there is a plan and a place for everything and that for you to live from day to day, not according to a pre-determined plan, but simply responding to what is here and now, would feel somewhat frightening?'.

Edwin was looking out of the window, weighing Angus's words.

'You perhaps just need to allow good and bad things to happen without finding a place for them in some grand design'.

Edwin's mind had returned to a walk he had taken with Nicky. She had been saying much the same thing and perhaps he had applied it in too limited a way. It wasn't just about religion in the formal sense, but about his whole life's effort to make sense of the senseless. But could he do it? Even now the fear mounted inside him at the prospect of having to live in a different sort of way. No wonder he had responded to the fear induced by childhood into the systems he had created and maintained. And his eyes filled with tears as he thought of the little boy he had been, and still in many ways still was.

The pains continued to torture his nights though they lessened a little as the summer came. He even began to quite enjoy Michael's medicine. Colin Nuffield kept him on anti-depressants. Sometimes he felt very low and could remember what it had been like on that morning when he had decided to end it all, but he also found that those times passed. He went for walks with Angus, Sylvia applied for and was appointed to a new job with an evangelical counselling organisation in Southampton, and all talk of a move back to Edinburgh gradually disappeared and he began to wonder if his marriage needed to end in practice as it already had in reality. In August the partners of his firm paid Edwin a princely sum for his partnership and the advance on his forthcoming book meant that they were financially secure for the time being.

Twice he went to see and stay with Nicky. He knew that they were in love with each other, but that neither was strong enough to be able to handle all that might mean in terms of a real relationship. But she gave him courage – not out of her cleverness, though she was no fool, nor out of her therapeutic skills – entirely intuitive and real though they were, but simply out of her woundedness.

In early September that courage enabled the former successful academic lawyer to apply for and get a job as an assistant curator at a local National Trust House.

On his first day he thought of the lines which ended Auden's libretto for "The Bassarids", an opera he had seen, based on Euripides's drama, The Bacchae, about wild women followers of

Dionysus: "His chances of escape are dim, these girls will tear him limb from limb". He felt torn apart, limb from limb. Angus and Nicky had brought some light but inside he feared that his chances of escape were dim, but he also knew he had to make a start here and now. It was, after all, the only place any of us can be.

Printed in Great Britain
by Amazon

37694284R00155